D0232487

37653002974551
Main Library: 1st floor
FIC TYRE
Strangers in the night

**CENTRAL ARKANSAS
LIBRARY SYSTEM
LITTLE ROCK PUBLIC LIBRARY
100 ROCK ST.
LITTLE ROCK, ARKANSAS**

STRANGERS IN THE NIGHT

STRANGERS IN THE NIGHT

PEG TYRE

CROWN PUBLISHERS, INC.
NEW YORK

94 C4190

2974551

Grateful acknowledgment is made for permission to reprint lyrics from the following:

IN THE WEE SMALL HOURS OF THE MORNING
Lyrics by Bob Hilliard. Music by David Mann.
Copyright © 1955 by REDD EVANS MUSIC CO.
Copyright © 1955, renewed by Better Half Music and RYTVOC, INC.
Copyright © renewed 1983 RYTVOC, INC.
All Rights Reserved. Used by permission of the Copyright owners.

"THAT'S LIFE"
Written by Dean Kay and Kelly Gordon
Copyright © 1964 PolyGram International Publishing, Inc.
Copyright Renewed.
Used by Permission. All Rights Reserved.

Copyright © 1994 by Peg Tyre

All rights reserved. No part of this book may be reproduced or transmitted in any form or by any means, electronic or mechanical, including photocopying, recording, or by any information storage and retrieval system, without permission in writing from the publisher.

Published by Crown Publishers, Inc., 201 East 50th Street, New York, New York 10022.
Member of the Crown Publishing Group.

Random House, Inc. New York, Toronto, London, Sydney, Auckland

CROWN is a trademark of Crown Publishers, Inc.

Manufactured in the United States of America

Design by Mercedes Everett

Library of Congress Cataloging-in-Publication Data
Tyre, Peg.
    Strangers in the night / Peg Tyre. — 1st ed.
      p.   cm.
    1. Women journalists—New York (N.Y.)—Fiction. I. Title.
PS3570.Y58L54   1994
813'.54—dc20   93-31165
                                          CIP

ISBN 0-517-59460-9

10 9 8 7 6 5 4 3 2 1

First Edition

CENTRAL ARKANSAS LIBRARY SYSTEM
LITTLE ROCK PUBLIC LIBRARY
700 LOUISIANA STREET
LITTLE ROCK, ARKANSAS 72201

To Peter and Mac, heart and soul

CENTRAL ARKANSAS LIBRARY SYSTEM
LITTLE ROCK PUBLIC LIBRARY
100 ROCK STREET
LITTLE ROCK, ARKANSAS 72201

Acknowledgments

First and foremost, I'd like to thank the talented and tactful Jane Meara, my editor, and my agent, Richard Pine. Their energy and intelligence guided a rough manuscript into a finished book.

Also, Charles Willeford, Chester Himes, Laura Wilder, Peter Blauner, Jim Dwyer, Dawn Powell, and Pete Dexter: who showed me how it's done.

I'd also like to thank Lori Andiman, K. Tracy Barnes, A. Kirke Bartley, Cary Bickley, McCaffrey Solomon Blauner, Virginia Byrne, John Clifford, Cynthia Crossen, Don Forst, Rich Galant, Joe Gallagher, Jane Hammerslough, Judy Hicks, Robert Johnson, David Kocieniewski, Arleen Maiorano, Richard Mayronne, C. Elizabeth McGrory, Deidre Murphy, Anne E. Murray, Vic Oboyski, Bill Oldham, Mike Race, William Rashbaum, John Ryan, Kim Royster, Suzanne Trazoff, and Christian Wright. Each one of these people gave me help or inspiration in the long process.

Special thanks to Pat, for her vision; Dan, for his cheerleading; and Tom, for being the first one to laugh at my jokes.

Most of all, I'd like to thank Peter Blauner, a tireless first reader, a caring, supportive husband, and my heart's delight.

Strangers in the Night

Prologue

It was one of those uncommonly warm winter mornings when a moist wind blew over the city's smokestacks and apartment buildings. The breeze carried a little bit of salty air to people who never see the ocean except for glimpses out grimy subway windows.

Feeling vulnerable in her half-sleep state, Kate closed her eyes again and made the window of her Park Slope apartment disappear. She wished that for just a few hours she could inhabit a different life. She'd spent most of yesterday walking through a vacant lot filled with abandoned cars and tall weeds, asking the drug addicts who lived there to describe the gang of neighborhood kids who'd set a crackhead on fire earlier that morning.

Before going to bed last night, she'd run out and bought the late edition of the *Daily Herald*. Even though the crackhead died before she'd filed, her story only made page twenty.

She looked at the clock by her bed and could still feel a small fist of fear in her stomach from her stroll through those frost-covered weeds. She tried to push the memory aside.

From far away, she heard a siren, a reedy scream, as men raced through the streets of Brooklyn to put out a fire. The sound, like the whisper of a guardian angel, made her relax.

She took a deep breath and threw off her quilt. It was another day on the crime beat in New York City.

1

It was equal parts loyalty and boredom that made Detective John Finn accompany his partner, "Fat" Tony Salazzo, to the homicide suspect's home. The suspect's name was Marvin Plank and he was just seventeen and on the run. Three days before, in a cocaine-induced rage, Plank shot his pregnant girlfriend as she crossed Myrtle Avenue to pick up their toddler from the Little Flower Day Care Center. Then, according to Plank's family and friends, he left town.

Add an equal measure of stupidity, thought Finn as the sedan pulled up in front of a row of burnt-out-looking brownstones in Bushwick. The architects had designed the buildings for better times, adding clusters of plaster grapes and flowers just below the flat roofline. But years of poverty had washed away the promise, and the coats of cheap bright paint seemed like all that was holding together the crumbling building facades. The block looked like a broken-down movie set, hollow and uninhabitable.

Plank's house was the worst. A fire had gutted the second story, decorating the third story with sooty black plumes. Broken childproof bars dangled from the windowsills.

"Fucking crack house," said Fat Tony, settling deeper into the driver's seat and sticking an unlit cigar between his teeth.

They listened to the radio for backup, debating who would walk up four flights of stairs to knock on the door of the empty apartment.

The patrol car was still five minutes away, but Finn was getting impatient. He didn't feel like spending any more time in a cold car when he could be sitting with a cup of coffee behind his desk at the precinct.

"I only agreed to go along for the ride," Finn reminded him.

Tony pretended not to hear.

Finn started again. "I just don't think we should spend a lot of time searching the building."

"I'm not doing it," grunted Tony. "Let Wochowsky and Gerleck run up the stairs. Give the uniforms something to tell their wives about."

Finn saw the police car pull onto the block.

"It'll take them all day," complained Finn.

In the rearview mirror, he watched Stan Wochowsky and Mark Gerleck amble up to the sedan.

"Fuck you, Tony. This is supposed to be your case," said Finn, peeved. But Fat Tony just shrugged.

"Yeah. And I delegate the footwork to Wochowsky and Gerleck," he said, looking like he was prepared to spend the rest of the afternoon in the car.

Grumbling, Finn slammed the car door. He nodded to Wochowsky and Gerleck, hunched his shoulders against the cold, and pushed through the front door. The three men began trudging up the dark, narrow stairway.

By the time they got to the second-floor landing, the dust in the hallway was making Finn wheeze so loudly that he didn't hear a pair of sneakers bounding lightly up the stairs.

On the fourth floor, where Plank lived, the three men each chose a door. Wochowsky leaned against the apartment door to the immediate right of the stairs and thumped his wide knuckles against the reinforced steel of 4B.

"Police, open up," said Wochowsky. He sounded so much like a corny television show that Finn and Gerleck smiled.

"Open the door," Wochowsky said again.

There was no sound from the apartment, and Finn relaxed. Almost as an afterthought, Wochowsky sheepishly tried turning the doorknob, but it was locked.

"Nobody home," he grunted.

Gerleck tried the second door on the landing, turning the handle, but it too was bolted. Finn halfheartedly leaned against his door, turning the knob. The door swung open and he stumbled into the abandoned apartment.

His shoulders had barely cleared the threshold when a half-dollar-sized piece of plaster leaped from the wall near his head.

In the dimness, he saw a lanky teenaged boy crouched in the filthy kitchen with a large black nine-millimeter machine pistol in his hands.

Another piece of plaster leaped from the wall behind Finn, this time near his left arm.

From fourteen years of training sessions at the range, Finn reached automatically for his gun. But as soon as his fingers touched the leather holster under his armpit and hefted the weight of his service revolver, he lost heart. It seemed like a useless hunk of metal—some broken-down farm machinery or a used-car part. Blindly, he squeezed off a shot.

The bullet went wild. Seeking protection, Finn dove for the ground and rolled toward the opening of the living room. As he rolled, both hands instinctively rose to protect his face and chest from the floor. In horror, he felt his fingers loosen and the gun slip from his hand.

Marvin Plank quickly unfolded himself and was upon him.

Finn lay paralyzed on the floor, his eyes never moving from the black gun Plank held. The barrel was so close he could smell the acrid gunpowder and feel the heat radiating from the barrel. Finn felt a small hand tracing the outline of the gold badge in his breast pocket.

He looked at Plank's eyes and he felt his bowels go slack. He saw that he was going to die.

He could hear Wochowsky and Gerleck shouting in the hallway. The teen lifted the barrel, touching it to Finn's face.

He saw something, a word, maybe a curse, form on the teen's lips, then die away. He felt the pressure of the barrel on his cheek.

Through the broken window he could hear a far-off siren and the sound of children laughing. Their boisterous sounds became a chant, first strange and then familiar.

"Oh my God I am heartily sorry for having offended Thee." He wondered why the children were saying the Act of Contrition, then he realized the voice he heard was his own.

He felt a burst of outrage, that thirty-five years was not enough time. He felt a profound loneliness, realizing he would die alone on the cold floor of this ruined Bushwick apartment. And that loneliness burnt out any memory of joy.

"And I detest all my sins, because I dread the loss of heaven and the pains of hell."

It flickered through his mind that hell was not an abstract concept.

"Hail Mary full of grace, the Lord is with thee."

He felt time become stretched out and thin, and he realized that even if he survived, he would be insane.

Finn saw Plank's forearm move and saw his finger squeeze the trigger and he waited for the roar. The gun bucked and rammed his cheek. Finn blinked. Nothing happened.

A look of confusion and frustration passed through the young man's face. Then, as the two uniformed men burst through the door, he bolted. Plank jumped up and leaped out the broken living-room window, falling four stories and breaking his left leg when he landed six inches from Fat Tony.

2

ominick Donatti woke up from a sickening dream and whimpered. He closed his mouth, feeling the soggy drool spot on the pillow against his cheek. He blinked his eyes as his forehead gave a painful throb.

It was a real nightmare. His dealer, Montoya, and two henchmen were laughing and gesturing at his crotch with a three-pronged garden tool, pretending to teach him how to walk like a woman. Dominick had laughed too, humiliation pressing on him like a cement roller, pleading hysterically with the three angry Latin men not to castrate him. One of Montoya's young street dealers, Graveyard Jones, stood in the shadows clutching a skateboard, watching Dominick with bulging eyes.

Their laughter got louder and louder and his begging turned to an incoherent scream, echoing through the dim apartment. The three men pranced around him, wobbling on imaginary high heels. Then a fourth man stepped forward and, with the seriousness of a paid killer, grabbed Dominick's hand and twisted his middle finger. There was a nauseating crunch and Dominick passed out.

Gingerly, he raised himself off the bed with his elbow and almost screamed from pain. At his side, his left hand hung limply from his wrist, the middle finger bent inward at an unnatural angle. It hadn't been a dream.

He whimpered again, forcing himself to look at his mangled hand, trying to remember how he had gotten home. His forehead pulsed again, the aftereffects of alcohol and Valium.

He heard his mother moving in the next room and delicately hoisted himself upright. Pain shot up his arm and brought tears to his eyes. He pulled off his T-shirt and, holding his hand to his skinny naked chest, walked to the bathroom. He forced his hand under the cold water.

"Nobody fucks with the Montoyas," the well-dressed man named Gusano had said, staring into Dominick's eyes as he'd splintered the bone in his finger.

Dominick stared at his hand, then stared into the mirror at his own glassy eyes.

From a distance, Dominick might have been handsome. He had straight light brown hair, dark eyes, and a nose that, while a little misshapen, might have given his face character. But up close, it appeared that the glue holding his features in place had dripped before it set. One flat brown eye sat slightly higher than the other and his nose twisted away from the center of his face. His features were strangely immobile—hardened by subcutaneous stupidity or some slight genetic glitch.

He tried to look resolute, but he couldn't shift his features from a grimace. He walked unevenly toward the kitchen, his hand wrapped in a towel. The sight of his mother, her eyes black from eyeliner and blue from eyeshadow, made his stomach turn over in fury and then fear.

"You left the back door open and those dogs got in again," she began wearily. "They go straight for the garbage every time." She reached over with two grunts and wiped the coffee grounds off the floor.

Dominick was dizzy and his tongue felt like AstroTurf. He said nothing.

"It's not so much to ask," she said, her voice becoming more energetic. "It's freezing outside. Lock the door so the heat stays in and the dogs stay out. Every time you leave it open, the heating bill doubles and the dogs spread the kitchen garbage all over the floor."

"I locked it when I came in," Dominick said. "Maybe someone tried to break in or something."

He spoke with a lazy inflection, slurring his words slightly as if his tongue was too large and his jaw muscles too weak to bother with pronunciation. It made "something" sound like "summp-in."

She stared at the muddy four-padded prints on the floor.

"You're ruining my house, just like your bum of a father," she began, scraping the upper registers in indignation.

Behind her, on the counter, a quart of milk sat in a white puddle where he had sloshed it last night.

"I didn't raise you to be a drug addict. Look at you, you worthless piece of shit. You can't even stay in school."

Dominick growled, but his mother was just warming up. "You can't keep a job, you don't even shut the door after you. You'll never be a man."

Dominick's eyes focused again on the kitchen counter. An empty brown prescription bottle lay where he had tossed it last night. A single Valium lay beside it. The white pill called out to him like a beacon in the darkness. His good hand flashed out like a striking snake, and he popped the Valium in his mouth and swallowed.

The sudden movement brought a high-pitched squeaking from his mother, a sound which dropped in tone and increased in volume to a torrent of curses. His head bobbed as she slapped him across the face and he vaguely felt her long nails rip at his chest.

He regarded her with the blank half-interest he usually reserved for barroom television sets until he saw her lift a barbecue fork from the counter.

He swung, then planted his fist in her broad, soft midsection. Before she could get her breath, he battered her twice on the face with an open palm, and she dropped like a bag of mortar. Dominick savored the sudden silence, then walked to the living room, turned on the television set, and for the thousandth time wondered how a woman as ugly as Oprah Winfrey had managed to get her own show.

In the second break, during a commercial for adult diapers, Dominick's mother walked quickly and unsteadily into the room with rags torn in strips and a tongue depressor. She had bright red marks below each ear, but she made sympathetic noises between her tongue and teeth as she dressed Dominick's hand.

"Keep your hand above your heart," she instructed him, bustling like a high-school nurse. "In order to reduce the swelling." When he complied, she laughed lightly as if he had made a joke. Then she curled up on the couch, resting her dry nest of hair against his chin.

"My poor baby," she was murmuring. "My poor baby boy."

He felt movement in his groin as her warm, puppy breath played over his nipples. Then he pointed the remote at Oprah and turned up the volume.

3

Kate's nervousness settled into her stomach as the dead boy's mother described the childish pranks of her son. Edison Monroe, a sixteen-year-old, had just been shot to death in an East New York schoolyard. He was killed by three seventeen-year-olds who drove by in a brand-new Toyota, laughing and blasting the paved playground with automatic weapons.

The boy's mother, whose enormous bulk was covered by a man's flannel shirt and a pair of stretch jeans, didn't seem to notice the stifling heat as the winter sun poured through two wide dirt-encrusted windows. She spoke with pride about a fight her son once had with the neighborhood bully and proudly showed off a collage Edison's twin brother Kimson had made her in school for Mother's Day, nine years ago.

A knot of youngsters crawled on the filthy floor. Not listening but not talking either over their mother's slow, sad requiem.

Kate scratched notes and tried to calm her agitation by taking deep breaths.

"I can't believe such a thing could happen to my boy," said Edison's mother. "I never had a day of trouble from him. He was walking the straight and narrow. Going to Harvard on scholarship, and that is the truth. Ask Kimson when he comes home, he'll tell you." Kate knew that Kimson, Edison's twin brother and a local drug dealer, was wanted by police for beating an old man to death with a stepladder.

"Are you expecting him home soon?" Kate asked, her lips suddenly dry and her throat tight. Her shoulders hunched and her hands snaked across her hips protectively, as if she could hide behind her thin arms.

"Soon," she said. "He's seeing about the funeral arrangements." She stood up, motioning for Kate to follow her.

"Oh, really?" asked Kate, anxiety breaking into a bloom of nausea. She tried to recover, forcing her arms to swing naturally at her sides, but her hands were gripping her elbows in fear. "Edison must have been very smart to be going to Harvard. Where did he go to school? What did he want to be when he graduated?"

"Edison and Kimson, Kimson and Edison. Always together. They're my little boys," Edison's mother replied in a strange singsong.

The two women had entered the boys' room. Two neatly made beds were almost obscured by four enormous speakers and a three-foot television complete with VCR. The closet door was open and Kate could see rows of sneakers and bright jogging suits with intricate leather patterns sewn into them.

Posters of the rap stars Public Enemy and the Geto Boys were hung carefully on the wall over a low bureau.

Edison's mother was still absently humming her little sad song. "Edison and Kimson, Kimson and Edison."

Kate swallowed hard and coughed to cover a small gagging reflex in her throat. She considered her next question for several seconds, wondering if there was a nicer way to ask it, and decided there wasn't.

"Your two sons are very different. How long has Kimson been dealing crack?" she said, keeping her eyes level with the boy's mother in a way she hoped was nonjudgmental.

"Crack? Crack?" said the woman. She looked like she had been struck, her eyes opening wider, moving rapidly around the room as if seeing it for the very first time. She leaned back on her heels as if she was about to keel over. Then she did, her full bulk hitting the floor like a building that had been detonated.

Edison's younger siblings crowded into the doorway, watching their mother with dull eyes. Kate got down on her knees and grabbed the woman's hand, but her eyes were rolling back into her head.

Kate jumped up and dodged past the children into a littered kitchen.

She was filling a smudged glass with water when she looked down and saw brackish green slime oozing between greasy week-old dishes and began to gag for real. The cool water coursed over her hand as Kate looked around wildly, choosing an empty Chinese take-out bag on the kitchen table to throw up in.

She brushed the tears from her eyes, wiped her mouth on her hand and her hand on her pants, and wobbled on unsteady knees to Edison's mother, who was lying where she landed, groaning quietly. Kate held her head and put the glass to her lips.

"Crack? My sweet Jesus. Crack. My poor baby," the woman said.

After a few moments, Kate eased the woman up and into a balding easy chair in the living room.

She murmured a few words, retrieved her notebook from Edison's floor, let herself out of the apartment, and threw up again when she hit the street.

4

The 83rd Precinct station house in Bushwick, Brooklyn, was built in a monotonous late-1960s style and from the outside it resembled an elementary school covered in grime. From the inside, fluorescent lights and poured concrete floors made it look like a prison.

Upstairs in the squad room, where the eleven detectives worked, was a constant parade of tearful complainants, sullen suspects, and nervous informants. Phones rang constantly and the pipes knocked every time the toilet was flushed.

Detective John Finn sat at his gray steel desk, flipping from the sports section of the *Herald* to the five pages of city news when he noticed a picture of a familiar-looking boy under a wide headline. HARVARD-BOUND STUDENT SLAIN.

The *Herald* seemed to be describing another victim than the Edison Monroe that Finn knew. The *New York Post* and *New York Newsday* were on target. They reported that the victim, Edison, was a grade-school dropout and a notorious crack dealer in business with his brother, Kimson.

Finn smiled to himself. The girl from the *Herald* must have gone to Edison's house and talked to his crazy mother. He looked over the *Herald* story more carefully. Yep. The reporter, Kate Murray, had even quoted the old crone. Finn remembered the woman—gentle, soft-spoken, but prone to hysterical fits when she would faint dead away or talk in tongues.

The reporters from the *Post* and *Newsday* must have talked to that hump Phillip Tierney, head of the 75th detective squad, he reasoned. Tierney would help out reporters he knew and liked.

Finn wondered if reporters, like detectives, had the journalistic equivalent to division chiefs, someone who broke their shoes when mistakes became public.

The grainy reproduction of the dead boy's face keyed into a picture in his own head and Finn focused his eyes on the soot-flecked window until the memory returned.

He had met that crazy family about four years ago, when he and his partner, Tony Salazzo, had arrested the boys' father, Herbert Monroe, for killing a Bushwick bodega owner during a robbery. Fat Tony forced Herbert Monroe to lie on his stomach in that squalid living room, rear-cuffing him while keeping a foot on his back. Twelve-year-old Edison Monroe appeared in the doorway, clutching his skinny little sister like a shield.

"What do you want to be when you grow up?" asked Finn, trying to talk to the terrified children.

The young boy, Edison, looked at his father in cuffs on the floor and the detectives with their guns pointed at his head and said, "I want to be a police officer."

At the time, both Finn and Fat Tony had laughed, but today the memory reminded Finn how alone he felt.

Since the arrest of Marvin Plank, Finn had noticed that the other detectives gave him wide berth. It was as if death had come too close. It marked him but did not carry him away, and its sickly musk still lingered. When the other detectives in the squad tried to speak to him, joking about sports or their latest case, Finn could barely concentrate on what they were saying. Even his own voice was like a faint radio signal, fading in and out and full of static.

It was like dreaming that he had shaved and dressed and driven to work. The precinct seemed regular and the routine was always the same, but once in a while, he would get the distinct impression that in some other dimension, he was lying sound asleep.

Finn sighed and rubbed his chin. He was waiting for Fat Tony to get back from the 75th Precinct, where he was picking up a case file that they both hoped would supply the last known address of a drug enforcer named Alex Tepper, whose two-day rampage left his wife and her three lovers in Kings County Hospital with gunshot wounds.

Restless, he pretended to look out the window while he checked his hairline in the reflection.

A decade ago, when he was twenty-five, Finn's wife, Sandy, had left him for another man. His hair had retreated a full inch, leaving him with a large peninsula of thick brown waves in front. Shaken, he bought a tan leather couch to replace the cloth one Sandy took and began a rigorous routine of calisthenics to tone his stomach. After she remarried, his life slipped back into a predictable pattern. Ten years later, not much had changed. He still worked for the department, having ascended to second-grade detective at an unremarkable rate, and still lived alone with his leather couch in a one-bedroom apartment in Bay Ridge. His muscle tone was good and his hair was holding fast. In fact, his slightly receded hairline drew attention to his intelligent gray eyes and his square stubborn chin, which had a dainty cleft in the middle. Though many women privately considered him handsome, the disappearance of his boyish waves had dealt a death blow to his vanity. He would never again consider himself anything more than average looking.

Nothing in his face had changed, Finn noted. But since he heard the click of Plank's nine-millimeter, nothing else looked right to him. It was as if someone had moved all the furniture four inches to the left. Nothing was different, it just wasn't where he expected it to be. It made him feel anxious and energetic, like he was late for something very important, but he had no idea what it was or where he was supposed to be.

On the street below, he noticed three firemen backing the truck into the station house after another false alarm. He noted bitterly how cheerful and underworked they looked. Then he saw three young boys looking down on the firemen from the roof of their project across the street.

Behind the sealed window, Finn watched the elaborate pantomime as the boys called down to the firemen and the firemen responded by slapping the insides of their elbows and shaking their fists. The boys disappeared, then seconds later, chunks of garbage began arcing onto the firemen below.

Finn smiled as he watched the look of dumb surprise and then fury as bottles and cans crashed to the sidewalk around the firemen and a half-eaten container of Chinese food splattered across the shiny red hood of the truck.

The firemen hastily drew the garage door shut, and Finn left the window and wandered down to talk to the patrol sergeant.

He'd hated hanging around the desk when he was on patrol. He resented the hairbags—beat cops who had lost their nerve, standing around the wooden station-house desk, bragging and telling lies.

The patrol sergeant, Michael Garvey, was a friend of Finn's ex-wife, and had given them a backyard barbecue for a wedding present even though they lived in an apartment. The one time Finn and his new bride tried to use it, a spring breeze blew smoke into the bedroom of the toothless seventy-five-year-old Italian man who lived next door. He stood in front of Finn, waving his spindly arms in the air, shouting low and vile curses in Italian.

Now Sandy had the barbecue with her new husband in Wantagh, but Garvey, whose deeply creased face and gray hair made him look younger and softer instead of older and hardbitten, was still a friend to Finn.

He chatted pleasantly with Garvey and Brian Edwards, the tallest police officer in Brooklyn, who lowered himself to eye level by spreading his massive trunklike legs into an inverted V.

He jutted his chin in the direction of the lock-up, where Finn saw a slight young man wearing a pea-green T-shirt slumped against the bars.

"Grand larceny auto. Caught him just after he stole a car," said Edwards. The boy, flattered to be the topic of conversation, straightened and smiled engagingly at the officers as if they had complimented him on some precocious accomplishment.

"But get this, he stole a 1973 Chevy. It didn't even have a muffler, and there he was driving this piece of junk down the middle of Church Avenue. *Vrrrooom.*"

Edwards, Garvey, and Finn laughed and the boy looked crestfallen, which made the receptionist and two surly drag queens being booked on prostitution start laughing as well.

5

"Why didn't you tell me Edison Monroe was a drug dealer like his brother?" said Kate, hunched over the telephone, trying to keep cold fury in her voice so Detective Tierney wouldn't hear her panic. "I see you're quoted all over the *Post* and *Newsday* stories calling him a crack dealer. Funny you didn't mention it to me." She heard men laughing in unison in the background and guessed, feeling helpless, that he was making an obscene gesture into the telephone.

"Well, you never asked me if he was a crack dealer, lass," said Tierney as the laughter died down. Somewhere in the 75th Precinct, she could hear screaming.

"I asked you if he was going to Harvard and you said it was under investigation," Kate reminded him. Technically, detectives were forbidden to speak to reporters, so when a detective broke rank and said a matter was "under investigation" he was throwing you a bone and it would appear in the paper the next day, attributed to unnamed police sources.

"Well, his mother did mention Edison was going to Harvard, but"—Tierney coughed, maybe covering a snicker—"any fool could see that she's crazy. Her son was a little piece of street vermin, not a scholar."

She felt humiliation like a thin film of soap stinging her eyes.

"The boys at the *Post* and *Newsday* got it right, though," Tierney said, as if that would explain everything. "And I won five dollars because I bet them that ye'd get the story wrong."

"So it was some kind of twisted joke among the boys," Kate said, stunned by his impersonal cruelty.

"Well, I must go," said Tierney with a false heartiness. "Sorry if I caused you any problems. But that's life."

"I'll get you, you woman-hating bastard," Kate said slowly into the telephone, but the line had gone dead. The noisy newsroom around her went silent for a moment as other reporters in their gray work cubicles looked up from their telephones and blinking word processors. Then the buzz resumed.

Kate's colleague and confidante, city hall columnist J.J. Perez, looked up from her phone call and offered Kate a raised eyebrow and a smile. But before she could react, a leggy blond intern tapped her on the shoulder.

"Wilson and Ridgeway want to see you. Ridgeway's office," she said, then flounced away.

Kate gave J.J. a panicked look. Nothing good ever happened to reporters in Ridgeway's office—known to the *Herald* staff as "the Black Hole."

She ran a lipstick over her dry bottom lip and tried to assume a breezy, efficient air, but her heart was pounding.

"You want to see me?" she said. She forced her arms, which were wrapped around her midsection, back to her sides, aware as she walked through the glass door that every reporter in the vast open plan room was watching her descent. By contrast to the bright, noisy newsroom, Ridgeway's office had dark paneled walls, a well-padded rug. Behind his large desk were framed front-page stories with screaming headlines—stories Ridgeway had broken during his days as a reporter. There was a shot of a buxom blonde and boozy Senator walking out of the old New Yorker hotel topped with the eight-inch letters CAUGHT! A supine mobster covered from cigar to spats with a bloody sheet under the headline 'BYE, 'BYE BOSS. Still another front-page picture of a famous serial killer from Staten Island under the legend HE BURIED THEM ALIVE.

Ridgeway, now the editor of the paper, was a shrunken stalk of man who loved expensive suits and any news story that touched upon highly sexed blondes or devil worship.

His protegé, Wilson, the florid, saturated-looking metro editor, insured his continued success at the paper by constantly reassuring Ridgeway that he was a genius.

" 'Bout time you got your buns in here, honey," Ridgeway said, his red-rimmed eyes, like infrared scopes, moved slowly over Kate's body. "Why don't you sit down?"

Anxious for cover, Kate bent her knees and sank into the yielding, black leather chair. Her eyes were level with a naked woman in a martini glass, which sat on top of Ridgeway's burled oak desk. The clatter of the newsroom was reduced to an energetic hum as the door shut behind her.

Ridgeway relit a stump of a cigar and focused his eyes directly below her throat.

"What we gotta know here, honey, is what happened?" Ridgeway barked, jabbing his cigar to the pages of the *Post* and *Newsday,* and her own story spread out in front of him. Kate wondered if this was the way the Inquisitors warmed up the *conversos.* "I mean, it wasn't the story of a lifetime, but it was the story of the day, and ya blew it."

"Ya blew it big time," echoed Wilson, self-consciously adopting Ridgeway's slang.

"I know," she said after a beat. She thought of the electronic equipment in Edison Monroe's room. She should have guessed. But if his mother said he was going to Harvard, what should she do? Ask to see his acceptance letter? She rubbed her brow. The whole thing was so damn confusing.

She took a breath and, summoning a professional tone, decided to shift the blame squarely on the cops. "I just finished talking to the detective who gave me the bum tip," she began, noticing that her voice was a little too loud.

"Nah, nah. We've all heard that one before. Blame the cops. I've used the same cheesy excuse myself," said Ridgeway.

It took her a few seconds to realize that Ridgeway was not letting her off the hook. This was serious. She felt her cheeks flush and her mouth tasted chalky, but she said nothing.

"The simple fact is, luv, that because of you, the *Daily Herald* ran with a story that was not true," he said. "And we aren't talking about an exorcism here. It didn't happen behind closed doors. It was a street shooting. As plain as the nose on my face."

Kate nodded, uncomfortably recrossing her legs, trying not to look at the shattered capillaries that ringed his nostrils.

But Ridgeway had turned away from her, pulled a beanbag football from a drawer and flipped it to Wilson, who caught it neatly.

"Good catch, pally," he said, lifting his hand to catch the return pass.

She rubbed her nose as the cigar smoke wafted toward her and wondered if there was some way she could slip out of the room without being noticed.

For about a minute, there was no sound except for the rhythmic crunch of the beanbag football being thrown from man to man.

She struggled to find something to say while trying to gauge just how ugly this meeting was going to get. Kate took a deep breath.

"It seems I made a mistake and I can only say I'm sorry," she said to Ridgeway's back. He didn't answer, but nodded to Wilson. It was going to get real ugly.

"It's like this, kid," said Wilson, reaching over his head to connect with the football. "You're either too naive to survive a subway ride or you piped the story."

Kate felt shot through with outrage. Did they think she sat in her cubicle and made up this story?

"Piped? I wouldn't pipe a story," Kate began indignantly, then forced herself to moderate her voice. "I asked the boys' mother about crack dealing. She didn't seem to know much about it."

Her outrage seemed to change the current in the air. Ridgeway threw the ball so wild Wilson had to stand up abruptly to make the catch. Wilson threw it back smoothly and Ridgeway caught it with a flex of the wrist.

"So, hon, this is it," said Ridgeway, suddenly swiveling around in his chair to face her. She was afraid for a minute he would toss the ball to her. "You were a fine copy girl, fine as a researcher, you were even good helping out on the society pages. But you haven't impressed anyone with your crime coverage. Harvard. Oh, God. I bet your college professors thought you were pretty smart, right? Well, let me tell you, sweetie, you don't have an ounce of street smarts and you have the intuition of a brick."

Kate kept a ladylike smile fixed on her lips. Look at the bright side, she reasoned. Maybe he had looked in her personnel file and remembered her "Kids Who Kill" story, interviews with seven preteenagers convicted of homicides. It had been nominated for a Publisher's Award. But Ridgeway didn't mention it.

"I said to Wilson, we never should send these skirts out on the street. They don't have the balls for hard news."

"Right," echoed Wilson.

"The balls?"

"The animal instinct. The stones. You know, *cajones.*"

Kate recrossed her legs. "I've been trying my best," she said, stalling, unwilling to let herself imagine where this meeting might end. Not believing that her fate lay with a man who referred to her as a skirt.

"So we came to a decision." He shifted his eyes away from her and lit another cigar.

I'm fired, Kate thought, feeling herself crumble. Oh, shit, I'm fired. Edison Monroe is dead and I'm out of a job.

But Wilson picked it up. "So as of today, you're officially on probation. Get it wrong again and you're out. Use the next six months to show us what you can do."

For a second Kate's mind went white like a movie screen when the film snaps and burns. No, I'm not fired, she thought, but she felt no relief. Edison Monroe is dead and I'm in a huge heap of trouble. Feeling humiliated, Kate wondered if Ridgeway and Wilson could see the tears pushing on the back of her eyes and hoped her rubbery legs would carry her out of the Black Hole.

"Can I go now?" she asked.

Ridgeway took a long draw on his cigar and tossed the football over his shoulder. It arced over Wilson and into the garbage can as Wilson held two arms over his head to indicate a goal.

"Ah, yes, luv," Ridgeway said. "But please remember. Don't disappoint us again."

6

Before he finished his first six-pack of the night, Dominick decided he had to kill Gusano, Montoya's dapper and brutal enforcer who had broken his finger. That wisdom came over him calmly and surely, like his decision to drop out of high school.

Dropping out of school was the best thing he ever did. When he was in school, he reasoned, he was still a boy. It wasn't until he left that he became a man. He dropped out after his mother's boyfriend, Tom Donofrio, known as Mr. Peanut because of his shrunken chest and enormous feminine haunches, changed the locks on his suburban tract house in Valley Stream, forcing Dominick and his mother to return to the old neighborhood in Gravesend and Dominick to Sheepshead Bay High School. There, on his second day of special-education class, he was made to understand that both driver's ed and shop were restricted to high-school juniors. Dominick, only a sophomore, was overcome with fury at the injustice and walked out of the school into the clear fall afternoon and never returned.

He let the screen door slam behind him, then he picked up a piece of broken brick and flung it at Mrs. Rigateli's German shepherd, attached by a leather leash to the bumper of her burgundy El Dorado.

Pushing his good hand deep into his pocket, he walked three blocks to the Cork and Barrel.

The small, smoky bar was named thirty years earlier, in a more hopeful time, when Vinnie's wife was alive and dreamed someday of opening a dining room. Instead it had become the local for firemen and cops prematurely retired from the job, young dropouts in their twenties, and old alcoholics. There hadn't been a cork inside the Cork and Barrel since Vinnie's wife died, and the beer came in industrial steel drums instead of barrels.

The bar was cool and dark and it took Dominick a while to locate a few of the regulars, faces as pale as new moons, already in their usual groups at the bar. Dominick could hear Frank Sinatra, his favorite singer, crooning on the jukebox.

"Got any money?" grunted Vinnie, the bartender, as Dominick took a seat. Vinnie, like many people in the neighborhood, made it clear he didn't want Dominick around. There were always more fights when Dominick was getting drunk in his bar.

"Yeah, I got plenty, plenty," said Dominick, hating Vinnie with all his heart.

He threw a crumpled bill on the damp bar, making an elaborate show of his well-bandaged hand.

"What you got there, Dominick?" said Pauly Maruzzi. "Whatssa wrong with your finger?"

As a child, Pauly caught more beatings from the kids in the neighborhood than anyone else because he liked boys. No matter how many times he got hit, no one could force him to express even a passing interest in a girl. After one particularly severe beating, Pauly bought a set of free weights, and while his tormentors waited impatiently for their boyish bodies to fill out, Pauly equipped himself with the arms and chest of a longshoreman.

These days Pauly had his brunette mane hennaed in Manhattan and wore undersized T-shirts so the thin fabric stuck to his rippled stomach like a skin.

Dominick squinted at Pauly to see if he was wearing eyeshadow, but the bar was too dark for him to tell.

"I was jumped by a drug dealer from 'cross the way," said Dominick loudly enough to make Vinnie look up. "Across the way" had two simultaneous meanings: not in Gravesend or even Sheepshead Bay, and in a neighborhood inhabited by blacks.

Pauly tsked. "It's the drugs," he said. "It's just not safe anywhere anymore with all these dealers."

Dominick decided not to mention that he owed this particular dealer more than fifteen hundred dollars and let the conversation lapse into silence. Pauly pulled out a small brown bottle and handed it to Dominick.

"Take some of these Vitamin E, to heal faster," he said.

Dominick nodded his thanks and choked down a few of the translucent pills with a swallow of beer.

Joe Dougherty, a dried-up Irish fossil who had spent a lifetime at the Cork and Barrel, had been listening to the exchange and he pecked two bucks off his thin roll, flipped the bills to Vinnie, and bought Dominick a drink. The gesture brought tears to Dominick's eyes.

"Thanks, Joe. Thanks a lot," he said, pushing aside his empty glass and plunging his lips into the foam.

Once the beer was finished, Dominick strolled back to the men's room, punching "Strangers in the Night" and "Only the Lonely" in the jukebox on his way. His long, comfortable piss was interrupted when Pauly pushed through the black swinging door.

"You having trouble holding on to that?" asked Pauly.

"Nah, I'm fine, no problem," Dominick almost shouted, then he realized Pauly was making a joke.

Dominick zipped his pants quickly and self-consciously, but when he raised his eyes, Pauly handed him a tiny spoon of cocaine.

"And here is some Vitamin C. It helps get rid of the pain," said Pauly.

"Vitamin C," said Dominick, grinning. "High C."

Back at the bar stool, Dominick drank beer, listened to a Waylon Jennings song Pauly had put on the jukebox, and imagined leaving Brooklyn for the west. He wasn't sure exactly where he would go— somewhere that looked like a Marlboro commercial: horses, cactus, and a big western sky with plenty of stars. He put his bandaged hand on the bar like an injured war hero on Veteran's Day. Spurred by the sight of his broken finger, Pauly, Vinnie, and Joe railed against Dominick's attacker and cautioned each other on the dangers drug addicts were bringing to the neighborhood.

They pressed Dominick for details, and with a hero's humility, Dominick described his valiant struggle right down to the sound of his finger being broken.

"Let's go back there and teach him a lesson," said Pauly, smacking his fifth empty glass on the counter and throwing a few punches in the air to show off his pumped-up forearms. "We could tell him a thing or two."

Dominick noticed his biceps, felt cocaine working in his head, and heard himself roar in agreement.

"Let's show him what it is to be a man," said Dominick.

With a six-pack to go and Vinnie's blessing, Dominick followed Pauly out to his beat-up Chevy. All the way down Pennsylvania Avenue, to Broadway to the Latino bar, El Fuego in Bushwick, where Dominick usually went to buy cocaine from Victor Montoya, Dominick struggled to keep his hand steady in order to bring the tiny spoon to his nose.

Salsa was blaring from El Fuego as Pauly parked his car across the street.

"So do you want to go in and fight him or wait until he comes outside and jump him?" asked Pauly.

Dominick stared at the red Cerveza sign in El Fuego's window until it blurred and reformed into the nasty snarl on Gusano's face. Dominick shifted his eyes to Pauly and noticed that by the streetlight Pauly appeared to be wearing both eyeshadow and mascara.

"Let's grab him when he comes out," Dominick said.

At that second, Gusano, a coal-gray cashmere jacket hiding his bull-like chest, walked out of the bar, jumped into his red Nissan, and screeched off. Dominick spilled his beer and Pauly dusted the dashboard with cocaine trying to ram the key into the ignition. They sped after Gusano as the Nissan ran through a pattern of red lights up Central Avenue.

By the time they stopped at Jefferson Street, Dominick's skin began to crawl from the cocaine and his finger was aching. The beer took the edge off his nerves, but something squeezed in the pit of his stomach when he remembered the claws of the garden tool and the Dominican's deadly rage.

Pauly, a skillful driver, flicked off his headlights and parked, undetected, a few lengths behind the red Nissan.

They waited, watching Gusano light a cigarette. "Who's he waiting for?" Dominick whispered. Then he felt silly for whispering and said loudly, "It's not me this time." Dominick was grinding his teeth so hard that he spoke through clenched jaws.

"Relax," said Pauly. "He won't know what hit him." He patted

Dominick's arm. "You should take some Vitamin B-12 to help you deal with all this stress."

Dominick was afraid and his finger was throbbing. Pauly was humming and snapping his fingers as if he was getting ready for a fight, and Dominick knew he had no idea how crazy and dangerous Gusano could be.

"Sssshhh," said Pauly, scraping the last of the tiny vial of cocaine into the spoon and snorting it. Dominick's anxiety exploded.

"Hey, you fucking fruit," Dominick squealed. "You could have saved some for me."

"Fruit?" said Pauly slowly. "Fruit? We are ready to fight and you are calling me a fruit?" He turned to face Dominick. "I thought we were friends."

Dominick felt confused. He had too much to drink and his jaws were sore and making dull popping sounds when he ground his teeth. "We're not friends, we're both from the neighborhood," said Dominick, not sure if that truism would make Pauly madder or calm him down.

It made him furious. Something broke beneath the skin of Pauly's face and spread upward to his forehead and down toward his chin. He lunged across the front seat and opened the passenger-side door.

"Get out," he said quietly.

Dominick tried to laugh and patted Pauly's arm, but the body-builder half-pushed and half-butted him out of the car.

"C'mon, Pauly. We're friends, we've always been friends." But the car door had already slammed and Pauly pulled away.

Dominick stood dumbly on the sidewalk for a second, then remembered Gusano sitting four cars away and ducked behind an oak. He began shivering in the night air, looking around him, realizing for the first time that he was white, drunk, and alone in Bushwick.

From far away, he could hear a fire truck siren blare. The block was empty and silent, the numbers joint at the corner had long since shut up. He saw the curtains move in a house halfway down the block; the face of an old black man appeared and then vanished. A moth-eaten dog trotted down the street with a peculiar sideways gait, his back feet appearing to move faster than his front feet. The dog looked at Dominick, lifted his nose in the air to catch his scent, but didn't slow down.

His hand was beginning to send bolts of pain up his arm and he felt tears spring to his eyes. He was warming up to a litany of curses when he heard the rhythmic rap of a woman's shoes on pavement.

He peered around the tree and saw a black woman in white rayon pants mounting the steps of a brownstone with her house keys in hand. Her long jacket swung open, and under the streetlight her uniform looked luminous, like a firefly that had accidentally ended up in the ghetto.

Gusano saw her, too, and lurched out of his car, moving toward her at a dead run. Dominick's curses froze in his throat. When the woman saw Gusano she looked like she wanted to run, too, but Gusano was at her side before she could take a step. He bent her arm in a hideous way and dragged her into the building.

Even from across the street, Dominick could hear her muffled screams and a thud as her body weight hit the wall. He felt his bowels tug with fear and he ducked behind the tree again. He heard the loud report of a gun, and then the building door slam. Dominick stood clutching the tree, straining to hear Gusano's footsteps moving toward him. But all he could hear were distant fire engine sirens and the dull roar of traffic from Bushwick Avenue.

7

Sunday morning, Kate sat in the office of the Police Public Information Department, flipping through the action reports on Saturday night's crimes. It had been a busy night, she noted. The clipboard that held the reports on homicides, assaults, and rapes was almost full.

Each form, scrawled in longhand by a bleary police officer, provided only the victim's name, address, age, and race, and the location of the incident. If there were any survivors, the hospital to which they were taken was noted.

Kate scanned the locations. Crime only became news, Kate had learned since her days on the society pages, when it happened in the right place. One seriously injured Manhattan banker was worth three drug-related homicides in a Brooklyn ghetto.

She thought about her humiliating conversation with Wilson and Ridgeway. Didn't have the balls for hard news, they said. Just once, she'd like to see Ridgeway on a crime scene in East New York. She thought about throwing up in Mrs. Monroe's kitchen and her face went hot.

She tried to remember what her friend J.J. had told her the day she was promoted to covering the police beat. Everyone wants to read about murder, she said. But no one wants to know the small-minded, banal, or nonsensical reasons one man kills another.

If reporting was easy, everyone would do it, J.J. added yesterday, consoling her by handing her a rough paper towel to blow her nose.

This morning, Kate was anxious to land a good one. Something big, something flashy. Something to get her noticed, off of probation, even get her a Publisher's Award and a promotion. There was still a slim chance that "Kids Who Kill" might get her the award this year, but she couldn't count on it.

She sighed and kept flipping through the blotter sheets. A bodega robbery—one shot. She scanned the sheet to see if the victim was dead. "5x in body, not likely to die. 9 mm. recovered," she read. That was one hardy grocer to absorb five bullets from a semiautomatic, but it wasn't a story.

A livery cab driver was shot dead in the South Bronx. She made a note to herself to call the precinct where it happened, but she knew as a news story, it wouldn't make three paragraphs on page fifty.

Two public information police officers, the blond, anemic Mickey Mase and swarthy, round Stephen Rissolli, slumped in their adjoining gray cubicles.

Unlike most police department offices, the public information section was well equipped. It had two fax machines, three simultaneously broadcasting televisions, eleven phone lines to take calls from reporters, and direct hot lines to two top chiefs, the police commissioner, and the mayor. It also had a temperamental Xerox machine, which this morning was hung with a large hand-lettered sign that read D.O.A.

On Sunday mornings, Mase and Rissolli were the sole conduit by which official police information was disseminated to the press. And this morning eleven phone lines were blinking with eleven reporters on hold, while Mase and Rissolli watched a *National Geographic* special about farms in Southern India.

"Look at that," said Mase, pointing to the television. "The leopard is chasing a cow." Mase's mouth hung open slightly and neither cop's eyes left the television.

Kate stared at Mase and Rissolli and the eleven blinking phone lines.

"When I was a kid, my brother found an advertisement in the back of a sports magazine and sent away for a walking stick made out of a petrified cow's dick," said Rissolli. His eyes wandered from the screen and he seemed to notice Kate for the first time. He stretched out his arms. "It was this big and hard as wood."

Mase looked at the span of Rissolli's arms, nodded solemnly, then looked back at the running cow with new respect.

Kate jotted down notes on a few homicides, a bias attack by schoolchildren, a particularly vicious robbery in Staten Island. Then a homicide in Brooklyn caught her eye, a nurse finishing a late shift at Woodhull Hospital shot to death in the foyer of her Bushwick home. Sometimes, on a slow news day, a minor homicide, particularly the death of an upstanding citizen, got big play. Kate knew she couldn't afford to miss one.

She quickly dialed the city desk, answered a few questions monosyllabically and double-checked a few addresses. Then she pulled her jacket around her shoulders and walked toward the door. Rissolli, gesturing with his arms outspread, didn't wave good-bye.

Ten police officers were standing in front of the house on Jefferson Street where Margaret Severing was killed, and not one of them, Finn pointed out to Fat Tony as he parked the car next to a large oak tree, had strung up the orange tape used to mark off a crime scene.

Tony looked surprised to hear Finn complain. "What's eating you?" he asked, but got out of the car before Finn could answer.

In fact, a pock-faced rookie, the first on the scene, had suggested cordoning off the area, but his patrol sergeant, a bullet-headed man whose arms hung from his shoulders like hams, had only hooted and continued pooling money for coffee.

"This is Bushwick," the sergeant had said, "not Beverly Hills."

It was shortly after eight A.M. when Finn tersely asked the rookie to string up the orange tape and ordered a light with no sugar from the coffee pool, then walked up the brownstone steps to examine the body.

Margaret Severing had been shot twice, once in the throat and once in the head, as she stepped into the foyer of her building. The bullet to the throat had severed a major artery. Her white nurse's uniform was maroon, and the dirty marble floor had a three-foot-long stain of thick, bright pink blood.

The other bullet had torn apart her head, and large pieces of her brain, like bluish sausage links, lay in the blood.

Her worn blue leather pocketbook was three feet away from her body, and using two pencils from his pocket, Finn pried it open. Disturbed by the carnage, he was shocked to see her wallet still contained sixty-three dollars.

"No robbery," he grunted, feeling horror rise and fall quickly in his gut.

Fat Tony, dressed in a smeared-looking gray raincoat on this warm winter morning, shuffled off to talk to neighbors while Finn continued checking the body.

"The neighbors heard shots," Fat Tony told Finn a few minutes later, "but they thought it was from the street. They were too scared to look out their windows." He paused to pull in a breath.

"Did you tell them the boogie man is not a suspect?" demanded Finn, peeved. "That any description at all could have helped us find out who killed her? Christ, the woman was bleeding to death and no one called nine-one-one until dawn?"

"She was already dead before she hit the ground," said Tony, more to himself than to Finn.

The Crime Scene Unit had arrived and Finn and Fat Tony walked up the stairs to Severing's apartment.

She had died with her house in order, Finn noted. Her living room was cool and dustless with plastic slip covers on the new-looking couch gleaming from the morning sun through lace curtains.

Finn looked at the family portraits displayed on her coffee table, pictures of a stylish black woman—Finn guessed a sister—getting married, a graduation picture of Severing beaming under her white nurse's cap.

The femininity of the apartment, which smelled like bleach and lavender, made him feel clumsy and obvious. He tripped on the upturned corner of a small area rug, then steadied himself. Fat Tony didn't seem to notice as he casually strolled over to the phone and began jotting numbers out of an address book on a small table nearby. Homicides that turned into biology lessons always affected Finn but they never seemed to bother Fat Tony.

"Let's see if we can get another team to notify next of kin," Fat Tony said.

Finn looked up quickly. He wondered if this one had gotten to him.

The consoling words died on his lips as his partner opened the dead woman's refrigerator and helped himself to a handful of grapes.

"Yeah, save us the trip," Finn answered.

Finding nothing out of order inside the apartment, Finn and Fat Tony returned to the sidewalk with the other detectives and uniforms and waited for the medical examiner. As the block woke up, Finn and Fat Tony bantered absentmindedly about NBA scores and the Giants' new quarterback. Finally, a good-looking white woman nosed her car to the curb and got out.

As she walked toward the knot of men, Finn noticed how the sun lit her dark hair and made it look red. He noticed the way her jeans, under an expensive-looking jacket, clung to the curve of her ass. He saw her hesitate. Her hand moved to her midsection, a shy gesture, but she caught herself, raising her chin before ducking under the tape.

Fat Tony was watching her, too. With him it wasn't so much looking, Finn thought, as a magnetic twitching of his dick whenever a female under seventy was within a five-block radius.

Someone else in the group saw her, too, and wondered aloud if she was from the medical examiner's office.

"If she's a medical examiner, may God make me a corpse," said Fat Tony. Then he passed gas audibly and the other detectives took an involuntary step away.

"Excuse me, I'm Kate Murray, a reporter from the *Herald*. Can you tell me what happened here?" Her voice was very low, almost a baritone, and Finn imagined that if she spoke softly, with her lips very close to his ear, it would sound extremely sexy. The men kept their faces as blank as dinner plates, and the strain was making her a little breathless.

None of the detectives said a word. The question hung in the air, the moment grew. Finn could see color come to her cheeks and felt sorry for her, but said nothing.

Finally, Fat Tony broke the silence. "Can't say nothing. That is the rules."

Kate nodded, her eyes focusing somewhere else, then she zeroed in and looked directly at Finn. "Mind if I look inside?"

He shrugged and nodded, and gave one word of assent.

"Yeah." For the first time since he was seventeen, his voice cracked a full register.

The other detectives smiled at his discomfort.

He scowled at them and then fell in line behind her as she walked up the crumbling steps of the building.

Crime Scene had not moved the body, and the reporter stopped abruptly when she saw the wide bloodstain, causing a pileup as Finn's thighs bounced off her ass, and the pimply rookie, who had quietly followed Finn, rebounded off Finn and almost fell back down the building steps.

"Why don't you go help the detectives canvass the neighborhood?" Finn snarled and the rookie, head down, trudged back toward the men on the sidewalk.

Kate didn't seem to notice. Her eyes were moving quickly, almost frantically, around the foyer, taking in the stains and entrails.

Finn noticed the color drain from her face and wondered if Crime Scene would bitch to Division if she threw up on the body.

"Robbery?"

"Can't talk to the press, ma'am," Finn said, sorry he had let her in the foyer.

She dug through her bag and began scribbling notes.

"Robbery?" she asked again, her eyes never leaving the corpse.

Finn sighed. "She had sixty-three dollars in her bag, but this isn't coming from me."

"Why don't you tell me your name so I can be sure to write that you refused to comment?" She looked him full in the face and then smiled.

Dazzled, Finn smiled back. Then he saw she was using a professional charm, and he felt his expression turn to stone.

"John Finn, Eighty-third Precinct squad," he answered stiffly.

She saw his contempt and registered fleeting surprise, like a boxer who'd missed a well-practiced combination.

"Thanks, Detective Finn." This time her voice was kind but she didn't smile.

She walked up the stairs to Severing's apartment and pushed open the door.

Like Fat Tony, she walked directly to the address book by the telephone and began jotting down numbers. Finn stood, shifting his weight from one foot to the other, straining to hear the sounds of the street from the quiet apartment.

By the time they got back down to the foyer, about forty minutes later, the examiner had already pronounced the body and was sliding the green vinyl body bag out the door.

Violence clung in a half-life to the walls and floor of the foyer, and both Finn and the reporter exhaled as they left the building.

Finn saw Fat Tony trotting toward him and wondered at the burst of activity.

"What's got you moving at the speed of light, Tony?" Finn said. Then he saw the division chief's car.

"We've got to talk," Tony snarled, sticking his heaving girth between Finn and the woman.

Kate dug a card out of the back pocket of her jeans and handed it to Finn. He watched her go and noticed that the card in his hand was still warm from her body heat.

9

The congenial racket of the *Daily Herald* newsroom had died down to a steady tapping of computer keys as the six P.M. deadline approached. Kate was typing the last graphs on Margaret Severing's murder.

> Margaret Severing knew the damage high-powered bullets can do to the human body. Until last night, she worked in the emergency room of Woodhull Hospital, where gunshot wounds are more common than a case of the sniffles.
>
> Last night, after working the midnight shift, Severing took the M-16 bus ten blocks up Broadway and was shot to death in the lobby of her Jefferson Street apartment. Even the best hospital staff could not have saved her. One of the bullets tore out her throat. The other tossed her brains from their soft nest in her skull onto the cold, tan-tiled floor of her apartment lobby.
>
> Police have not yet determined a motive for the shooting. Her purse, which was found next to her bloody corpse, contained $63 and three tokens.

"This could have been a great story, kid, a blow-your-breakfast, true-to-life tale of the mean streets," said Jim Wilson, his eyes scanning the newsroom.

When striding around the newsroom, Wilson limited every conversation with reporters to twenty seconds or less.

Kate stiffened. "Could have?"

"Where's the grief-stricken mother?" Wilson exploded, then quickly reined himself in. "You want this job? You should have pushed her mother for a quote," he said in a more moderate tone.

Kate had found Margaret Severing's mother after she left the crime scene. Ellisa Severing stood behind the screened door of her single-family home with the palms of her thickly veined hands together, mutely beseeching Kate to leave her to her private and total despair. Kate had left her card and promised to return the next day.

Kate looked at Wilson and imagined grabbing the thin gold pen from the front pocket of his Armani jacket and plunging it into his heart. She fantasized about pulling an unlicensed gun, say a Mac 10 machine pistol, out of her scuffed Coach leather bag and holding it to his head. Instead she shrugged.

"She didn't want to comment," said Kate.

"You could have pushed her," Wilson said, grumpy. "You'll lose page one and probably two and three to football or the Central American invasion. But go back on it, kid. It takes a good reporter, someone who has it right here." He placed a buffed hand on the middle of his hand-painted tie. "Someone who knows how to cut to the heart of these stories. Those are the people who have a future here at the *Herald*." He sounded like he was mouthing a company cheer.

Kate envisioned him being flattened by a shiny aluminum semi as he crossed Second Avenue. She imagined herself behind the wheel of the sixteen-wheeler. She wouldn't even pull the horn.

"I'll get the mom tomorrow," said Kate, with what she hoped sounded like conviction. But she felt deflated.

But Wilson, unaware, was already beginning to move away, his eyes scanning the newsroom like radar. "Great. Great," he murmured.

As the six o'clock deadline grew nearer, editors, who normally chatted over coffee, began screaming at each other, eyes bulging and telephones jammed between their ears and shoulders. The percussive sound of fingers hitting keyboards grew louder, like summer rain on a slate roof. The general assignment reporters, who spent the better part of their day slinking between the low gray partitions avoiding assignments, were grimly splicing sentences together. Columnists, who spent the day fulminating and puffing pipes, began flipping through old columns for inspiration. The clerks, attached to the telephone consoles by headsets, wearily deflected the daily weirdos who called to confess crimes, announce their candidacy for emperor, or complain about mind-altering radio waves from Russia.

Kate was about to press the button on her computer to file the story when Jessie Joan Perez slumped into the desk across the partition.

In the early 1970s, J.J., as her readers knew her, had filed a lawsuit against the paper for sex discrimination and led a pack of women off of the lifestyle pages and into hard news. While her contemporaries left the paper to write books, raise families, or collect big paychecks from public relations firms, J.J. began to write a column about City Hall.

But now that J.J. was fifty-seven, it seemed to Kate that the thumb-sized headshot that ran with her weekly diatribe dated from a happier era, before broken dates and unfiltered Camels dried her out and wore her down.

Lately, she had been filing columns more than an hour past the last deadline, and despite triage by a desiccated night editor everyone called Bartleby the Scrivener, her columns seemed less like insightful analysis and more like angry rants.

Today, Kate noticed, J.J. looked totaled. The whites of her eyes had turned the same nicotine-stained yellow as her forefinger, which was at this moment shielding a burning unfiltered Camel.

"You're not supposed to smoke in here," hissed Kate. "It's a no-smoking office." It was their old joke, left over from the time when J.J. responded to the no-smoking edict by disabling the office smoke detectors with a paper clip.

"What are they going to do? Fire me? Too late for that." J.J. took a melodramatic puff on her Camel and blew a Bette Davis–style smoke ring.

Kate narrowed her eyes.

"What do you mean? What's the matter?" she asked.

J.J.'s hand trembled slightly as she extended a memo from Wilson.

"I'm out to pasture. My column ripped out from under me. Assigned to work special projects." Kate could hear the hysterical tone in her voice.

"Oh God, Jessie, that's terrible. I'm sorry," she said.

J.J. leaned back in her chair and blew another smoke ring.

"Sorry yourself. They announced the Publisher's Awards this morning when you were out on that homicide." J.J. was the only person at the paper Kate had told about her probation. She knew how much an award for "Kids Who Kill" would mean.

Kate felt herself grow vague and breathless.

"So who got it? For what?"

"That little shit Rob Grant got it," exploded J.J.

"Wha?"

"For the story about the subway motorman who ran over that stray dog on the IND tracks," said J.J., blowing an exasperated smoke ring. "Vintage Ridgeway. The judges described it, and I quote, as 'a heartbreaking tale that pitted a helpless beast against a mindless machine.' "

"But that story was bullshit, a throwaway, a nothing," said Kate, incredulous. "He even wrote a poem for it, remember?"

"How could I forget? 'Ode to Sparky, the Defenseless Mutt,' " said J.J.

" 'Kids Who Kill' got beat by a dog story?" Kate wanted to run to the ladies' room in case she started to cry, but she felt too heavy to lift herself out of the chair.

J.J. saw Kate's stricken expression and gave her a lopsided smile.

"Hey, buck up," she said. "You're not over the hill. You can always get the Publisher's Award next year. And by next year, I'll be doing political commentary for Channel Two."

Kate nodded, wondering if she would have a job next year. She was aware that she should console J.J. but knew she would cry if she said more than a few words.

"I'll call you tonight," she promised, quickly, but J.J. had already turned, her frail-looking shoulders stiff with defiance.

Kate watched her walk across the newsroom past Wilson and, with a toss of her gray hair, out the double glass doors.

Kate double-checked a few quotes she had gleaned from Severing's colleagues at the hospital and two of her best friends from the Baptist church where Severing sang in the choir every Sunday.

Police officials have not yet established a motive for the killing and would only say the investigation is continuing.

" 'Ode to Sparky'?" she asked herself aloud. Then Kate pressed a button on her keyboard and filed her story, stuck her notebook in her bag, and walked into the elevator, which, in a long sigh, took her to the street.

10

Sometime after midnight, Kate, who spent the evening alone in her Brooklyn apartment, drinking beer, eating coffee ice cream, and watching a video of *Guys and Dolls,* began to cry. She decided that losing the Publisher's Award to a dog story was a sign from God that she should have gone to law school. She cried until she fell asleep, a half pint of ice cream still balanced on her chest. She awoke at five-thirty A.M. with a hangover, remembering the tail end of an anxious dream narrated by the bloody corpse of Margaret Severing. Kate gradually became aware that her hair was matted with sticky coffee-smelling cream. She staggered to the front door where the delivery man had left her morning edition of the *Daily Herald.*

Before she lapsed back into sleep, she flipped through the papers. The football game was low-scoring and uneventful and an American missionary was killed in Central America. Even so, the *Herald* ran the story of Margaret Severing on the third page, along with a strongly worded editorial about the escalating homicide rate in New York.

Kate reached over to her radio and switched on the all-news station. The Severing homicide was leading the segment. Her story was hot, hot, hot.

Satisfied, Kate sank back into bed, trying to ignore the spreading slick of melted ice cream that had seeped into her sheets.

*   *   *

The mayor, who woke every morning at six A.M. with the sinking feeling that the city was going to hell, got to the line in Kate's story about the tan-tiled floor and had trouble swallowing his bagel.

In his prepared speech at a breakfast meeting before a group of black church leaders, the mayor vowed to bring Margaret Severing's killer to justice, and to end the cycle of pointless violence that had taken her life.

His comment was relayed to the police commissioner by telephone. The mayor's call was followed by calls from the two news radio stations and three local news shows. The police commissioner called the division chief for a copy of the homicide report and a file on the investigation.

At seven-thirty, the division chief, Captain Mark Troutman, whose severely deviated septum caused him to open his wide, lipless, downturned mouth every time he exhaled, called Finn at home.

Finn, who had ended his day shortly after one A.M. by drinking a tumbler filled with Scotch, stared into the telephone as Troutmouth ordered him to interview everyone who had ever laid eyes on Margaret Severing.

Finn called Fat Tony, interrupting a long dream he was having about bobbing for apples with four prostitutes he had seen interviewed on cable TV. And so Day Two of the Margaret Severing homicide investigation began.

11

It was late Monday evening when Finn and Fat Tony parked their car in front of a housing project in Brownsville. They had spent the morning running down Severing's coworkers at Woodhull Hospital, each one dutifully reporting what they had already told the lady reporter from the *Daily Herald*.

Between interviews with night nurses and hospital attendants, Finn searched Brooklyn for working pay phones in order to call in updates to Troutmouth. If more than forty-five minutes elapsed without a call, Troutmouth would send out a system-wide message on the radio and a needle-tongued dispatcher would broadcast their plate number.

"The union is going to hear about this. He's treating us like criminals, just to humiliate us," said Fat Tony, turning down the radio when they got back into the car. "If it wasn't for that fucking article in the *Herald,* this would be just another goddamn stiff."

Sometimes he couldn't stop himself from laughing, but by and large, Finn tried not to encourage Fat Tony's tirades. Once provoked, Fat Tony would continue until the physical exhaustion or the desire for one of his cheap cigars calmed him.

Last night's Scotch was making Finn feel weak and jumpy. He was in no mood to laugh and he didn't want anyone leaning on him, particularly Troutmouth, who had already mentioned the term "task force" to Finn more than once today. Finn hated working on a homicide task force. They never solved a single murder except by dumb luck. Too many people got involved. It was like trying to catch child molesters from a helicopter. A homicide was between two people—one dead, one living—and was usually solved by two people.

"Relax, Tony, you're giving me a headache," said Finn.

"It's Johnnie Walker giving you that headache, not me," said Tony. "Or maybe that girl from the newspaper is weighing on your mind."

* * *

Margaret Severing's mother, Ellisa Severing, lived in a sagging white house on a dilapidated block. Outside, the house looked ready to give out a sigh and collapse into rubble, but inside every surface was scrubbed and dusted. Ellisa Severing, tiny and puckered with age and grief, poured tea before the two detectives could refuse. She gave them recent pictures of her daughter with her old boyfriend and the address of the man Margaret had been dating for the last six months.

"It wasn't her boyfriend that did it," Mrs. Severing said, following them down the front steps as Tony and Finn headed to their car. "Like I told the lady from the *Herald,* I believe he lacked the energy or the presence of mind for such a thing."

"I swear to Christ, I'm going to handcuff the next person that mentions the *Herald* reporter," said Fat Tony when Ellisa Severing was barely out of earshot. "I'll charge them with harassment and I'll make it stick."

Finn rubbed his neck and watched Mrs. Severing hop up the two small steps to her door. There was nothing sadder than a mother who had lost her only child. Over the years, Finn had met scores of them and was always touched by their pain. Their faces, like animated masks of tragedy, kept coming back to him, each reminding him that life is not cheap.

Finn rolled his shoulders to ease the knotted muscles. The investigation was going on too long, getting too cold. And reporters were crawling all over Troutmouth for a comment. Troutmouth, in turn, wanted the name of the person who killed Margaret Severing, not someday, but today, or tomorrow.

"I hope we get rid of this one fast," said Finn.

Fat Tony looked surprised. "Christ, what do you care? Don't let the media pressure get to you. We get paid whether we find out who killed her or not."

Although it was an attitude Finn had himself, hearing Fat Tony say it out loud annoyed him.

"I just want to know is all. Who did it, I mean. I want to find the guy. Make the arrest," said Finn. Anything to make one week stand out from the rest. Something to prove that he was still alive.

"You worried about our clearance rate? Calm down. After the double last month, I think we're still running ahead of the curve. You should relax," said Tony.

"It's not statistics, Tony. I'd just like to get this over."

They watched a television news truck pull up in front of Ellisa Severing's house.

"I didn't think you'd let the bosses get to you."

"It's not the bosses, it's the point of the thing."

"What other point is there? I work, I get paid, I pay my rent and child support and blow the rest in Atlantic City," said Tony. "That's the life."

Finn made a disgusted noise with his mouth but didn't answer. Fat Tony looked at him strangely but let the matter drop.

The light was fading fast and Finn and Fat Tony scanned the block nervously before trying to locate the project where Margaret Severing's boyfriend lived.

Fat Tony flinched when a dirty brown chickadee swooped overhead and landed on an electric wire not far away.

"Fucking bird," he muttered angrily under his breath. "This fucking neighborhood. It's the kind of place where the birds stop chirping and about one second later, two drug dealers level their nine-millimeters and try to take each other out."

Finn noticed two five- or six-year-old boys bumping and hugging each other as they staggered down the block. When they saw Finn and Fat Tony, they mouthed "Cops" at each other and looked like they were about to smile.

Finn put up his hand, slowly bent his fingers, and smiled.

"Hi there," he said.

The two boys scowled. The smaller one hawked and spit on the ground like an ancient wino as they stalked by.

"Hi there," Fat Tony mimicked. "Hi there."

Finn felt miserable and depressed. He remembered how much he used to love Bushwick. When he was first assigned here, he had felt like a hero, a real-life crime fighter. As he walked through the neighborhood on patrol, mothers smiled and children tagged along behind him, clutching their sides with delight.

After being promoted to detective, he investigated more serious crimes, like shootings and homicides, and at first he enjoyed the freedom. But over time, the thrill wore off and he began to conduct his investigations with minimal effort and less and less emotion. These days, it seemed to Finn, he never saved anyone, or stopped any crimes. He only showed up when someone was dead, like a member of an occupying army, to break down someone's door and drag some mother's son out of bed and take him downtown. Every day brought him closer to his paycheck. Every paycheck, closer to his twenty-year mark, when he could retire with a full pension. After that, there was nothing left but death.

Finally, they found the boyfriend's building. They pushed through the lobby, crunching across empty crack vials scattered on the floor. An arthritic elevator door opened and a wave of urine spread out into the lobby.

Tony stepped over the widening puddle and gasped, "Eau de Housing Project," grabbing his tie and putting it up to his nose. Finn unfurled a handkerchief, trying not to gag as the elevator chugged to the ninth floor.

Finn noticed the regularly spaced chips along the hallway made from a blast of automatic gunfire. He positioned himself to one side of the doorway with his hand on his holstered gun while Fat Tony, standing on the other side, pounded on the door with his hammy fist.

Then there was silence.

Fat Tony knocked again.

This time, Finn and Tony heard some grumbling and shuffling. A full five minutes later, the door was opened by an extremely dark-skinned black man dressed like a deacon in a somber morning suit. As the boyfriend stared at the detectives with red-rimmed eyes, Finn noticed that the buttons on his suit were missing and his shirt collar was wrinkled and spotted with blood from a hasty shave. The boyfriend's shoulders and hip bones jutted out like wire hangers, barely able to support the lightweight fabric.

At first the boyfriend seemed polite, almost formal, but when

Tony mentioned Severing's name, he walked away from the door without a word. Finn and Tony followed.

The living room was like an Ethan Allen showroom overrun by anarchists. The furniture, Finn noticed, had been chosen with care. The couch, which had been set on fire in a few places, matched a legless easy chair which rested uneasily on cinderblocks. Chintz curtains, now torn and spotted with grease, hung in the windows.

The apartment was dark and quiet except for the buzzing of what must have been a thousand flies coming from a small, dirty bathroom.

Through a dark archway, Finn caught sight of the kitchen, the walls blackened with oily soot and a rusty table buried beneath an avalanche of Burger King wrappers, newspapers, overdue utility notices, and food stamp receipts.

In the corner, sitting on a folding metal chair, looking cool and unperturbed, was Kate Murray.

* * *

"What's new on the investigation, Detective Finn?" asked Kate as soon as they stepped into the elevator.

"We could run it better if it was us doing the investigating and not you," said Tony, baring his yellow, mossy teeth. "You're getting in the way."

The lights in the steel enclosure dimmed and the outer door, which had been creaking shut, stopped dead without closing.

"Is that your on-the-record comment, Detective?" asked Kate sharply. "I wouldn't want my squad commander to read that his two top investigators were running hours behind a reporter."

Fat Tony didn't answer but began jamming his sausagelike finger into the floor buttons. The only result was that one of the three overhead lights went out completely.

"We're going to have to walk," said Finn.

"But this is the ninth fucking floor," exploded Fat Tony, the frustrations of the day finally catching up to him.

Finn thought his partner looked like a jowly, wizened infant and wondered for a second if Tony would throw himself on the floor and have a tantrum.

Instead, the three of them plodded down the stairs. Tony, whose hand was on his gun, took the lead. They slid on crack vials, came across two sullen teenagers with angry red hickies, and walked quickly by a landing that had been used as a pit bull run.

"Goddamn shit machines," Tony wheezed, his cigar, unlit, clamped between his jaws. "They should kill those fucking dogs."

Finn walked after Kate, noticing the way the curls of her hair stuck out in different directions as if each tendril was getting energy from a different source. Between the ninth and eighth floors, he realized he wanted to touch her hair, to confirm his belief that it would be soft and light. From the step above her, he could see the nape of her neck, smooth and slightly pink from exertion. She turned her head slightly to gasp, "How much further?" and Finn, feeling like a Peeping Tom, quickly looked away.

Once they got to the courtyard, Tony turned to Finn. "I'm going to talk to the housing police," he wheezed. "See if they know anything about Lover Boy upstairs. Maybe get the name of his interior designer," he said to Finn, pointedly ignoring Kate. "Don't go too far."

Finn watched him lumber off, then turned back to Kate. Up close, Finn saw that she just missed being beautiful. Her brown eyes were wide and intelligent. Her features were plain, and her nose was straight and well-cut. But her face was completely overpowered by a riot of jet hair rising up from her forehead in a welter of curly strands that bent back toward her ears. Her skin was delicate and Finn could trace a blue vein that ran by her temple. She looked wrinkled from a long day but clean and inviting, like sheets out of the dryer.

He imagined her naked, her small frame under his larger one, moving together. Her low voice, soft and windy, moving closer until her pointed tongue touched his earlobe.

"You think the boyfriend killed her?" said Kate.

Finn saw her small mouth move and heard her voice, but couldn't make sense of what she said. She repeated herself patiently, and her question immediately dampened the romantic scene unfolding in his mind.

"It's hard to say until Forensics is finished," he said. He shivered a little and calculated how long it had been since he had slept with a woman. It had been a long time since he had even done any calculations.

"Ellisa Severing doesn't think so," said Kate. "Most of the time,

I listen to the mother. They can gauge threats to their children pretty well.''

He thought of the bricklayer last year who had slashed the throat of his girlfriend's two young children while she was working. He didn't confess right away. First the bricklayer went to the morgue with his girlfriend, revived her when she swooned, and held her tenderly while she cried. It wasn't until he was being questioned by police and reversed the locations where he said he first discovered the two dead children that she figured out who killed her babies. The woman pawed around in her beat-up pocketbook before coming up with a small .25-caliber handgun. Then she shot him in the chest in front of fourteen police officers and detectives.

Finn wondered if anyone who wasn't a cop knew that story or if it was one of those events that was told and retold around cop bars and at cop dinners until the memory faded out as the eyewitnesses retired. He wondered if he would tell it to Kate.

"Maybe," he said, immediately wishing he had said something witty or intelligent. Her eyes moved across his face, searching.

He liked this woman—a college girl who clearly knew her way around housing projects. She had interviewed Severing's boyfriend over the buzz of his fly-filled bathroom like she kept flies at home as pets. He wondered if she thought he was boring. Finn found himself talking to fill the silence, like some teenage purse snatcher during his first interrogation.

"We don't have much more than was in your story, except that Margaret Severing's boyfriend isn't much of a housekeeper," he said, and wondered if he was blabbing too much.

It was hard to figure with a newspaper reporter. The brass always warned the rank and file about talking, and a lot of cases had gone sour because too many details got in the papers and the public knew too much. But every once in a while, an article would shake somebody loose. And with no more effort than it took to make a single call to a friendly reporter, the detective looked like Columbo.

Kate was looking at him, interested and slightly amused.

"He seemed like a nice guy, good husband material for a hardworking nurse," he said. "But when I saw that apartment . . . Whew!"

Kate nodded. "It wasn't until he brought out the crack pipe that it all made sense," she said.

Finn forced himself not to look surprised.

"You got to be careful," he said, hoping he didn't sound like every asshole cop in the city trying to pick up a good-looking girl. "You never know what a crackhead is going to do."

"Yeah. But it makes such a great lede: 'Margaret Severing loved a man, but he loved the crack pipe more. And I quote. "I loved her and promised her I was going to turn my life around and quit the pipe. Now she is dead and there is nothing in the world between me and beaming up." Unquote.' "

Finn looked at her curiously.

"He said all that?" The man had barely grunted when Fat Tony asked him questions.

"He's a fairly articulate guy. Went to Brooklyn College for three years," said Kate. "Now he has cravings for crack that just won't quit. Crackhead? Yes. Killer? You're the detective, you tell me."

She was smiling at him, like she wanted to hear what he had to say.

He was about to reply, when over her shoulder he saw three skinny young men in sweatsuits struggling under three wide-screened television sets.

He remembered that he was standing in a housing project after dark, and his attentions dovetailed—one eye watching the street, and the other watching the girl.

"I can't tell you much more than what you already wrote in the paper," he said, stalling. He wanted to take her hand, but he didn't dare.

"Your story was all right," Finn said, feeling stupid. "When I read it I thought, That's what it was like. You even got the color of the tiles right."

She tossed her head a little, like she was deflecting the compliment with her chin. Then, when she realized he was being genuine, she gave him a hundred-watt smile. Finn knew she wouldn't stop him if he kissed her on the lips.

"Fucking Lover Boy," Finn heard Tony's voice behind the project before he was visible.

Finn knew he didn't have much time.

"What about dinner, you and me?" he said, rushing to get the words out before Tony was within earshot.

"You mean like a date?" she asked. And Finn nodded yes as she held up her left hand and his head began to shake an emphatic no.

On her left hand was a small gold ring.

"To talk about the case," he said lamely, his face blazing like a former altar boy trying to brazen out a lie.

"I'd like to, but . . . " And then she shrugged. Finn was listening so hard for a qualifying tone that would give him a chance that he hardly heard the words. "I'm sorry."

Fat Tony was upon them.

"Fucking Housing won't give us the file on Lover Boy until they get the okay from their fucking captain," Tony said. "I told them to fucking call Troutmouth if they had any problems, let him tear them new assholes instead of us." Fat Tony stopped and chomped his cigar. "Will you look at that?"

Finn and Kate turned to where Tony was pointing.

The three men carrying the televisions had hooked them up to three ruined-looking automobiles at the curb. They sat on folding metal chairs on the sidewalk, watching the flickering screens. A small crowd had formed to watch the three different channels as they played simultaneously.

A dark-skinned man stood on the back of a covered flatbed in the middle of the street, screaming and gesturing for them to load the televisions into the van. The tarp on the truck only partially concealed about thirty other sets.

The more the man screamed, the lower the three television thieves sank in their chairs, sullen and unwilling to look up from their shows. Someone in the crowd reached over and turned up the volume first on one set and then on the other two.

"It's the poor man's Nielsen rating," said Tony, coughing to cover a laugh. "These are the first goddamn thieves I've ever seen who stole televisions so they could watch their favorite soaps."

Finn laughed too, watching the scene. He looked at Kate's face, flickering gray and blue, by the light of the stolen televisions.

"There's your story. A new motive for robbery," he said.

Kate picked up the joke, framing a mock headline. "Competitive programming," she said as if reading an article, "has driven them to a life of crime."

12

ominick kept thrusting, but he could tell from the lack of friction that his erection had faded. And for once, things seemed to have been going along smoothly. Suzy surprised him by seeming interested, almost enthusiastic about having sex with him. They even kissed for a minute while he pulled on a condom. Then, nothing.

He felt a buzzing in the back of his head and rammed his hips vainly against her soft thighs. Nothing.

"Ugh, get off," Suzy said, straight-arming him like a veteran running back. She leaned over to the night table and turned the radio from a station that played his favorite, Frank Sinatra, to one that played oldies rock and roll.

"Help, help me, Rhonda. Help me get her out of my life." Suzy sang the wrong words in a monotone, snapping her fingers, chewing a piece of gum, and dialing the phone at the same time.

Dominick stood up, feeling miserable, a condom clinging to his fast-receding penis like a long, loose stocking. He could feel his temples pounding.

"Why d'ya got to make phone calls when we're making love?" he asked peevishly, tossing the condom into the garbage and pulling on his boxers.

Suzy slammed down the receiver and turned her plucked-looking face to him, raising one pencil-thin eyebrow.

"I thought we were finished," she said. "You seemed to be anyway."

As she walked into the next room to pick up the screaming baby, Dominick strained to hear her snicker. If she laughed, Dominick thought, he would go straight to the kitchen, get a steak knife, and stab her.

A band stretched tightly across part of his head began to fray. What was it about women? Dominick thought, trying to put himself in a more reasonable frame of mind. The things they said could take your skin right off. They could flay you alive and leave red ants biting at your wounds. And they did it without raising their voices.

He walked into the bathroom on flat feet. He stared at his rounded gut and flexed his biceps. He kicked a smudged blue walker and splashed some warm water on his face. A man deserves more respect, he thought moodily, staring at himself in the mirror.

He gently eased off his splint and saw that his broken finger was still vividly bruised and swollen.

He opened Suzy's medicine cabinet and shook out one of her Percodan. He threw the orange and yellow capsule into his mouth and reached down to suck some water from the tap. When he straightened, he saw Gusano's huge head appear behind the dirty shower curtain.

"ARRGGG!" he screamed and whirled around, wielding a red toothbrush like a switchblade, but the head was gone. His unprotected finger hit the basin.

He wailed, kicking the toilet bowl in frustration. When he regained his balance, Dominick turned back to the mirror and reached for another Percodan.

It was hard to be a man, Dominick thought bitterly. It was hard to stand up to your enemies when they were so violent they menaced your manhood with a garden tool. It was hard to be macho when your enemies' friends would break your finger without breaking a sweat. It was hard to make love to a woman who thought you were a jerk.

"Lookit this," Dominick said to Suzy when she walked into the kitchen lugging their son. The infant, who had been screaming for the last half hour, was bright red and didn't look very happy to see him.

Dominick was pointing to the newspaper, at an article in the *Herald* about Margaret Severing's homicide. His brain, cleared by the bright path of pain snaking up from his hand, was working and he was biting the skin inside his cheek.

"It says here the police don't have any suspects."

"So," Suzy said dully.

"So I know who the killer is," said Dominick. "I saw it happen. It was the same guy who fucked up my finger. I was following him, see, me and . . ." He decided not to go into more detail.

"I'm sure you did, you saw the homicide as you were riding home from your brand-new job in your brand-new car, stopping once to buy your son a gift to celebrate his first birthday." He eyed the thin rectangular drawer where Suzy kept the knives. Flayed twice before noon, Dominick thought to himself. Then he concentrated on making himself relax.

He waved his good hand to shut her up.

"That's right," she said. "Your son." The baby gave Dominick a baleful look.

Dominick looked at her and wondered how a birthday for someone who couldn't even say his name could be more important than a murder. Besides, the kid didn't even look like him.

Then his mind skipped back to his plan. "I'm gonna call that reporter and tell her what I saw," he said, then added, almost to himself, "See how Montoya likes a reporter hanging around his bar asking questions."

"Montoya who? Don't use up my units, I have enough trouble keeping them from shutting off the phone with no help from you," Suzy said, lighting a cigarette, which made the baby ball his fists and rub his eyes. "Why don't you go to the corner and make the call?"

Her voice got quieter as she saw Dominick go silent and still.

"This is important, Suzy," he said with a deadly intensity. He imagined Suzy's nosy neighbor Ronald Scavillo finding her big fat pasty body in a black garbage bag. "This is not some stupid shopping trip. This is about honor. It's about being a man. It's something I gotta do."

Suddenly scared and nervous, Suzy picked up the baby and put him on the floor in the far corner of the room.

Heat was flowing through Dominick, like he was slathered in Vicks vapor rub. When he thought about Montoya and the garden tool, he no longer felt vulnerable and ashamed. He wasn't even afraid of Gusano. He had seen the Dominican man murder that nurse, and now Gusano's fate hung in his hands. He felt like the guy in the Bible who hit the giant on the head with the rock. A lucky shot, but a good one.

He reached for the telephone, dialed information, then the *Herald*.

He asked to speak to Kate Murray, reading the byline off the newspaper, and after several clicks a low, tired-sounding voice came on the line.

"Police desk, Kate Murray here."

Dominick was so shocked he had gotten through that he couldn't think of what to say.

"I want to talk to Kate Murray," he said, squinting at the story again.

"This is Kate Murray. Can I help you with something?" the voice repeated. This time a little impatient.

Dominick looked at Suzy, at his red-faced son, then stared at the phone, concentrating.

"I know who killed that lady in the paper, the nurse, Severing," he said quickly, feeling his neck go cold from sweat. "I saw the whole thing and I know who killed her."

13

As Kate huddled over her telephone, cajoling and cursing information out of Margaret Severing's colleagues, she was aware that Rob Grant was tipping back in his chair, watching her work.

At forty-two, Grant, who had the soft paunch of a college athlete gone to seed, had covered crime for the paper for more than ten years and considered himself the official NYPD scribe. He resented any newcomers poaching on his beat and made no secret of the fact that he despised Kate because she was young and female.

Kate had struggled to win his approval until one day last October when she had spent fourteen hours in a downpour covering the collapse of a crowded Harlem department store. Grant, who had spent the afternoon interviewing city Buildings Department officials from his desk, got a byline on her story. Later that night, she sat at the bar in the basement of the *Herald* building, her hair still damp with rain, eavesdropping on Grant as he entertained three sportswriters by describing how he had watched Emergency Medical Service workers pull the Harlem shoppers from the rubble.

With her interviews completed, Kate tried not to let the constant jangle of the telephone break her concentration. It wasn't easy. Everyone who got the newspaper delivered this morning seemed to have something to say about the murder and wanted to say it to her. She fielded the calls, absently murmuring "Uh-huh" into the receiver, pounding away on her nine-hundred-word biography of Margaret Severing. Already, Kate knew, she had made this particular victim more famous in death than she ever would have been in life.

An imperceptible signal, like the blast from a dog whistle, alerted Kate and the other reporters that Ridgeway, Wilson, and their young male deputies, pink and dewy after spending their lunch hour at the gym, had returned. They strode purposefully through the glass doors, paused for a moment, jostling each other, then headed to their offices. Wilson, a bright white towel hung carefully between his damp neck and his suit, moved across the newsroom. Grant, who had been listening to SportsPhone, quickly hung up and began talking with Wilson about seating arrangements for the Publisher's Awards dinner.

"I don't know how you can work above the roar of all this male bonding," said J.J. from behind Kate, gesturing to Wilson and Grant. She was cleaning out her desk.

"Just one day, I'd like to come to work and not feel like I was sneaking into a men's locker room."

Kate smiled at J.J., then pointed her finger at the telephone and computer screen and kept typing. Then her eyes slid over to Grant, who had grabbed Wilson's suspenders at the punch line of a joke. Both men laughed loudly.

"Not in my lifetime, I guess," J.J. sighed. "The glass ceiling in this place is so low, I feel like a botany specimen." She drove her long red-tipped finger directly into the center of her forehead. "All I need is a silver pin through my brain. Newspaperus Journisimus, female, endangered."

Kate saw Wilson wallop Grant on the back as she politely thanked the caller, placed the receiver back in the cradle, and turned to J.J.

But J.J. was standing next to Grant as Wilson walked away.

"So what are you working on, Grant?" asked J.J. loudly, lighting a Camel and blowing smoke in his direction. "I hear a tomcat got flattened by a bus on the East Side this morning. Maybe you can make something out of it."

Kate looked alarmed, picking up her telephone on the first ring, her eyes never leaving J.J. and Grant. It was Mo the Confessor, who called every day to admit that he alone had committed every homicide mentioned in the morning edition. Kate sighed. At least he was reading past the headlines.

Grant smiled tightly at J.J., lighting one of the three-dollar cigars he always carried, and accepted a cup of coffee from a high-breasted college intern.

J.J. nearly snarled. "Interns aren't here to get your coffee," she said sourly. "Why don't you get your own?" Disappointed to reach Kate's jaded ears, Mo had hung up, but Kate held the telephone like a prop, watching J.J. and Grant square off, their eyes glinting.

"Everyone has to start at the bottom," Grant began, speaking more to the blond intern than to J.J. or Kate. "That's how you get to be a reporter, paying your dues."

"Just because you're a woman doesn't mean your dues are measured in small white Styrofoam cups," J.J. replied, then she faced the intern. "Tell him to get his own next time."

The intern ignored J.J. entirely. "What are you working on, Mr. Grant?" the blond girl asked prettily.

Grant looked up at J.J. and tapped his cigar like W. C. Fields when the intern wobbled away on stiletto heels.

He had won round one by decision, but he wanted the knockout.

"By the way, J.J.," asked Grant, "you coming to the awards dinner? Or can't you find a date? Maybe you should go with Kate, she probably doesn't have one either."

Kate's face burned and she hated Grant with all her heart. She imagined luring him up to the roof of the *Herald* building and pushing him over the tar-paper cdge. She tapped a few numbers into the telephone, pretending she wasn't listening.

"Sorry. Can't make it," J.J. said airily. "I'm having dinner with the mayor. Or maybe that's the night I'm supposed to tape the show with ABC. But congratulations, son, I remember twenty years ago when I first won that little award. I'm sure it's the start of a great career for you."

Kate smiled into her hand.

J.J. turned her back to Grant and pointed into her palm, the signal for Kate to follow her to the ladies' room.

"Dios Mio," she exploded as soon as Kate hit the gleaming tiles. "Twenty years in the business and these guys are always the same." She slapped her forehead.

Kate, sliding her rear end onto the sink counter, was happy to see her friend so animated. J.J. dug into her expensive-looking leather bag and pulled out some red powder, which she began to brush over her sagging cheeks. She squinted at Kate in the mirror.

"Sometimes I think we changed the world, and other days it's the same old story," J.J. said, fluffing her hair. "You know, a lot rests in your hands now. I want you to promise me one thing when I'm gone."

Kate looked up at her, uneasy. She expected J.J. to deliver a tirade against Rob Grant, not her own eulogy.

"Christ, you sound like you're dying. You're only going to special projects," Kate reminded her.

"Don't be a smart mouth, girl," said J.J. sharply, then she relaxed. "I can read the writing on the wall. They're getting rid of us old dames. But before I leave, I just want you to promise me."

Kate smiled cautiously at her friend. "Sure, what?"

"Don't give up. Stay in hard news, get yourself the damn Publisher's Award, and make sure they pay you the same salary they pay a guy." She pulled a perfume atomizer out of her bag and squirted it into her wrinkled cleavage. "Do it for me. Do it for yourself. And when you get to be my age, get yourself promoted."

"Promoted? To what? Anything special?"

"Something in management so you can be Rob Grant's boss."

She stared at her own tired reflection in the mirror. "Then fire his ass."

*   *   *

At a quiet end of the vast open newsroom, Grant wondered absently what Kate was writing about and weighed whether he could look through her notes without attracting attention to himself. While he was debating it, her telephone rang and he lunged to pick it up. It was the detective who had been calling her all morning.

"She came in but she had to leave the office for a while," Grant lied, then turned on his warmest tone. "I don't think she saw your message. Is there something I can help you with?"

Finn sighed on the other end of the line. He had seen Grant once when he was working a double homicide and knew him by his reputation for dating dead cops' wives. He gritted his teeth.

"Do you know when she'll be back?"

"Sorry, no," Grant said. "I think maybe she's left on vacation."

"Well, just tell her Detective Finn called and ask her to call back." Finn left his number at the precinct and did something Grant knew went against all his training as a civil servant and as a police officer. He gave out his home phone number.

"Did you get that number? Can you tell her that for me?" Finn asked, trying not to sound sarcastic.

"Sure, absolutely, consider it done," said Grant, who had not taken down a single digit. Then he hung up the phone.

14

he adrenaline buzz from the newsroom was wearing off. After Kate finished writing a nine-hundred-word story on deadline, her neck was stiff and her hands ached. As she trudged up Fifth Avenue, she felt like she was lugging stones.

She thought about Margaret Severing and marveled at the way the story had taken on a life of its own. It was a slow news week and the other dailies were scrambling for a piece of it. Three local television stations, locked in a sweeps frenzy, had sent reporters to do stand-ups outside Severing's Bushwick brownstone. Captain Mark Troutman had called not one but two press conferences, only to admit that the police had no leads. The mayor had called for the capture and swift prosecution of Severing's killer.

The competition made her edgy, but with the hagiography of Margaret Severing filed, Kate felt certain the story was still hers. Sensing the momentum, Wilson was clamoring for another element that would keep the *Herald* out in front.

Kate wondered if Margaret Severing knew the person who shot her. Probably. But her mother, an obvious suspect, seemed above suspicion. Her boyfriend, too, was a likely candidate. Then she remembered the sixty-three dollars. If he killed her, he would have taken her money for crack.

She tried to re-create the call she had received from the mysterious eyewitness, feeling certain the guy was a crank. She smiled grimly, trying to mask the anxiety creeping up her spine. If she could figure out who shot the nurse, she could get off probation.

It was strange, she knew, to think about violence like a race that could be won or lost. But it was business. Homicides, train wrecks, and fires became so much fodder. Reporters and editors rarely acknowledged the lives forever scarred by tragedy. They were always calculating who was leading, who was holding their own, which news organization had missed the story altogether. It gave her a closed-off feeling, like some part of her was tightly sealed in plastic. Kate remembered reading somewhere that disassociation was the first sign of mental illness, and she wondered if she was going insane.

She looked down Fifty-third Street and saw the day's best contender for Loon of the Week. A man encrusted in dirt and wearing only a burlap sack was screaming unintelligibly at the passing cars. No. *Insane* was too strong a term, she corrected herself.

It wasn't working around violence that would finally push her over the edge, she thought, suddenly bitter. It was failure. She recalled her years as a copy girl, as a researcher, and the fifteen long months rewriting press releases for an inebriated society gadfly, Arne Russelson, before finally getting a chance at hard news. It seemed unfair that one nasty detective named Tierney and a crazy mom could derail her career track so efficiently.

"Maybe I don't have the balls," she said aloud, swallowing hard against the rising tears.

She took a deep breath, catching sight of her tired face in the black glass of a tall, unyielding skyscraper. Her arms absently crossed in front of her. It was a self-conscious, protective gesture left over from a time when she was overweight and her clothes bunched around her waistline.

Two years ago, she shed what friends referred to as her "baby fat" and her mother called "that hideous blubber" and moved in with the best-looking man she had ever met. Three months ago, James moved out. In shock, Kate asked him why he was leaving.

"You're too good for me," he had answered, emptying one of his drawers into a suitcase. "I just need some space."

She thought of the square-jawed detective who had asked her out, and for the first time all afternoon she almost smiled. She twisted the ring James had given her one month before he left. During the day, she used it like a crucifix and wolfsbane to repel macho cops. The rest of the time, it was a small gold reminder of love and marriage, a whispered promise that James might come back.

She walked on, looking into a boutique window, eyeing the willowy mannequin and the reflection of a Japanese businessman in a gray fedora with the same detachment.

She remembered her promise to J.J. It was her generation that had stormed the ramparts; now Kate was supposed to shatter the invisible barriers that still held women back. She wished she could be strong and full of political fury like J.J. But she had been seven years old in 1969. She had watched the Age of Reagan chip away at the renegade, Watergate-era spirit that had lingered around the newsroom like a dusty unused typewriter. She doubted that anyone at the *Daily Herald* now would take her feminist indignation seriously. She thought of the girl in the martini glass on Ridgeway's desk and felt a rush of anger.

"Balls? Ha!" she said out loud, then walked on quickly, feeling embarrassed.

It was true, she thought. She didn't have balls. All she had was an unkempt one-bedroom apartment in Park Slope and a stack of yellowing newspaper clippings that didn't measure up to Grant's "Ode to Sparky." She couldn't even land a decent date since James had walked out.

Her feet were moving again, taking her farther away from her empty apartment. She paused in front of another window, staring blankly at the Cartier baubles. She thought of J.J., bitchy and unbowed, lecturing her, badgering her, pushing tissues under the stall door when Kate barricaded herself in the ladies' room. J.J. was never at a loss for words. And even now, stripped of her column, J.J. was not afraid to fail. Thinking of her friend, Kate felt energized.

"They think I can't top a dead dog story?" she asked no one in particular.

A skinny woman about Kate's age with a stiff helmet of frosted hair and an armful of shopping bags gave her an odd look.

Kate put on the fierce face she used when talking to muggers in the projects and the woman looked away.

Kate took the advantage to size the woman up. Something about her irked Kate immediately. Long legs and a short resumé, she thought. Probably the trophy wife of some late-eighties tycoon. Her outfit was this year's Chanel and her nose job dated from the late seventies. A living, breathing example of how little times had changed. Kate scowled at her again, then, surprising even herself, she smiled. Maybe she should use that line, "Long legs and a short resumé," in her next murdered model story. It had a nice tabloidy ring to it.

Out of the corner of her eye, she saw a dark-haired boy move sideways through the crowd. He closed in on the blonde, who staggered slightly under the weight of her shopping bags.

Kate felt a wave of concern and tried to move forward, but the crowd seemed to block her path. The boy looked young, not more than fourteen. He had five or six wild unshaven hairs on his chin, but his cheeks were still smooth. The sun glinted off a tarnished silver chain around his neck. As she watched, his hand reached out and closed just above the collar of the woman's tailored wool jacket.

The force of the boy's grasp propelled the blonde backward and her hands began to windmill out. Her packages rained down on the pavement. The boy yanked her thick gold necklace, but its clasp held fast.

As the lady began to fall, her hand struck the side of the boy's head, and her fingers, finding a solid surface, grabbed his neck. As she righted herself, the boy looked startled, then he twisted away and was gone.

A second after he vanished, the woman seemed to thaw. Then crumble. Kate was at her side.

"I've been *robbbbbbed,*" she wailed. Her left hand touched the thick gold links at her throat as strangers bent to recover her bags. "He tried to steal my necklace."

Kate stared. Then pointed to the woman's right hand. At first the blonde didn't understand, then slowly, like a butterfly opening its wings, the woman opened her fist. They both peered inside. Wrapped around her white tapered fingers was a length of silver links and a tin St. Jude's medal. Kate began to laugh. The lady had snatched her mugger's chain.

15

Gusano had been sitting in his living room, staring down the barrel of a nine-millimeter all morning, carefully filing the lands and grooves of his two newest weapons and breathing in the sweet winter air. The rhythmic grating sound blended with the noises from the street below that filtered through the open window.

A regular barrel, with its spiral pattern inside, left a mark on a bullet as distinctive as a fingerprint. Gusano wanted all the bullets he fired to be untraceable. During his two years in Attica, he had listened to too many sad stories about cops linking shootings in completely different boroughs all because of some tiny scratch marks on the bullets.

That, Gusano thought, as he shifted the black gun between his powerful knees, would not be good.

He wasn't in any hurry to go back to prison. Gusano had only been out of jail for five months and he had to admit, life was good.

Forty-eight hours after he got off the bus from upstate, a friend from Mercuri, the town in the Dominican Republic where he had grown up, introduced him to Montoya, a Colombian citizen who had taken over the crack operations for seven prime blocks in Bushwick.

Montoya had hired Gusano, whose reputation for violence remained undiminished even while he was in jail, as a kind of one-man collection agency. The rules were simple, Montoya explained to Gusano. They were fashioned on an ancient code devised back when the Colombians had ruled the western world. A debtor must be warned, then an impression must be made, usually by killing the debtor's wife or child. Parents and elder relations were to be left untouched—unless they were hiding money. Then the disrespect they committed was greater than the respect they were due.

Like last week, when one of Montoya's part-time couriers smoked ten jumbo bundles of crack instead of dropping them off at a distribution point. He had no family but the impression had to be made. His girlfriend, a nurse, had to die in order to encourage the courier to pay back the money. This week, a young skateboard fanatic named Graveyard Jones would meet a sudden death. Less than a week after he left Montoya to join a rival drug organization he would be mysteriously shot. The newspapers would call it senseless violence. But it was business. Cause and effect.

It was true, Gusano reflected, thinking about the woman's white uniform turning red, what his wise grandmother used to say. Your life can be shaped by the company you keep.

So Gusano tried to keep himself clean. He bought some good-looking clothes, took over an apartment recently abandoned by crack-heads, threw out the rotten clothing and burnt mattresses, changed the locks, and set up house. When he wasn't working or looking for girls, he went to church or drank espresso at El Fuego.

The winter sun was getting warmer, causing sweat to drip from Gusano's forehead onto his open gun. He stopped filing for a moment, aware of an ugly grinding in his stomach. He stood up and flexed his prison-tone muscles in the mirror, carefully inspecting a thin layer of fat around the middle of his powerful frame.

He puffed out his cheeks, made oinking sounds at the mirror, then strolled to the kitchen. He could smell garlic and onions from another apartment but he tried to ignore it. Instead, he opened a packet of Dick Gregory Bahamanian diet formula and mixed the pink chalky powder with cold water.

He pulled in his stomach and imagined himself dancing in a white suit while girls with sparkling ebony eyes watched from every corner.

He imagined himself fighting, nude, like a picture of two ancient Greeks he once saw in a book in the prison library, a white scarf slung between his legs, while every man watched his bulky frame and shuddered. Gusano paused. Forget that *maricon* scarf, he corrected himself sternly, imagining himself in gym shorts instead.

He tipped the glass back and tried to swallow the strawberry-flavored mixture without gagging, and then belched.

Directly across the wide oily street, Francisco Sanchez had opened the windows of his sister's apartment and was padding through her four rooms, unable to relax but trying not to wake his sister, who worked the night shift as a hospital technician. Seven hours ago, Francisco was released from the Bronx Criminal Court lock-up where he had sat for four days trying to explain to the stone-faced guards that they had the wrong man.

It seemed like every time he turned around, Francisco, a part-time garage mechanic who had served time two years ago for dismantling stolen cars, was getting arrested for something he didn't do. Two days before Easter, the warrant squad had burst into his apartment and arrested him for failing to show up in court on a grand larceny charge. The day before Thanksgiving, Brooklyn homicide detectives had cuffed him as he was on his way to a movie. Last week, he was getting out of bed when three armed probation officers pushed past his sister and put a gun to his head.

Every time, it took the court at least four days to figure out that Franco Sanchez, a deranged crackhead who lived two doors down and bore a striking resemblance to Francisco, was the man they really wanted.

Somehow, last year, a computer in Albany had started spitting out Francisco's prison identification number, called a NYSID, and his current address instead of Franco's, although the two men were not related. So far, the mistake had cost Francisco two jobs, and his sister, fed up with cops breaking her door, had asked him to look for another apartment.

Francisco looked out his bedroom window at the bleak panorama of rooftops, complaining inwardly about his lousy luck and thinking bitterly that very little in life was fair.

Gusano, trying to ignore his grumbling stomach, decided to make sure the altered barrel didn't affect his aim.

He loaded a clip with seven round-nosed lead bullets. Their copper jackets would insure that they flew through the chamber without leaving slivers to jam the gun. Many careers had been ruined, Gusano knew, by tiny lead slivers. He eyed the blank-looking building across the street, aimed at the worn finial on the faded limestone facade, and, squinting, squeezed off three rounds.

Two bullets struck the target, cracking the finial in two places; the third, Gusano assumed, went over the roof. He unloaded the clip and began filing the second gun.

In fact, the trajectory of the third bullet had dropped lower than the first two and the bullet had struck Francisco to the right of his forehead, blowing a funnel-shaped hole in the side of his head.

His sister, who had been listening to him pace through the apartment, jumped out of bed when she heard his body hit the floor.

Gusano looked up when he heard the screaming and wondered, with a touch of indignation, who could think of doing crime on such a nice winter morning.

A few minutes after the screaming stopped, Gusano understood from the babble of Spanish dialects coming from the street below where his third bullet had ended up.

Without hurrying, he carefully packed his clothing into a leather garment bag and pulled his razor and toothbrush from the medicine cabinet. Listening for the sound of sirens, he began wiping down the apartment for prints, a precaution he took more from watching television than from any sincere belief that police could trace the bullet.

He picked up the three shells from the living-room floor, stuck them firmly down the kitchen drain with his middle finger, and lovingly placed his two guns in a gym bag. He left the apartment and double-locked the door, bouncing down the stairs and past the ambulance pulling up to the sidewalk. When he had walked a few blocks, he turned back to watch more police cars pull up. He began walking again, stooping imperceptibly to drop the apartment keys in the sewer.

16

I don't like it, Tony. It's just no good," said Finn quietly to Fat Tony, who pretended to ignore him as they stood at attention behind Captain Mark Troutman and Chief of Brooklyn Detectives Thomas O'Reilly.

Behind them was a table loaded down with bricks of cocaine. In front of them stood a small crowd of surly-looking print and radio reporters and television cameramen.

As the top-ranking officer at the press conference, O'Reilly stood behind the podium giving his best Jack Webb imitation.

"At approximately ten thirty-five this morning, our detectives, working with several uniformed members of the Eighty-third Precinct, acted on information from a confidential informant and entered the premises of 175 Starr Street, where they discovered several kilos of cocaine."

The television cameramen, who had turned on the klieg lights when O'Reilly started talking, turned them off in disgust, knowing such stiff cop talk would end up on the editing room floor. Finn saw the *Herald* reporter, Kate Murray, shift impatiently and whisper to another reporter who smiled. Finn was still hoping she'd call him back, but today he couldn't even meet her eye. He wouldn't risk talking to her in plain view of the brass.

"The detectives then placed three suspects, the occupants of that location, under arrest for possession of a controlled substance,'' droned O'Reilly.

Finn tried not to look at Brian Edwards, the tall uniformed cop who was standing on the other side of Fat Tony, grinning like a moron.

It was Edwards's fault that they were there at all. This morning, the three of them had been sitting in the back of a bodega filling out Lotto cards, drinking coffee, and talking about the Severing homicide when Edwards decided to visit a woman he had picked up three weeks ago on a prostitution charge.

"The patrol guide strictly states that no uniformed officer shall frequent a house of prostitution," Fat Tony had razzed Edwards as he headed out of the store.

"It's not a house of prostitution. Miss Consuela is a freelancer. An independent businesswoman," Edwards had called as he pushed open the cracked Plexiglas door. "She doesn't run a whorehouse. She runs a whore home."

As Finn worked out a schedule of the day's interviews on the Severing homicide, Fat Tony put together combinations of his badge number and his license plate for the Pick Five.

Ten minutes later, Edwards came running back into the bodega, holding up the pants of his blue uniform with one hand. His service revolver was in the other.

"You gotta help me, you gotta help me. Consuela's apartment is full of drugs," he practically shouted.

While Edwards called for backup, Fat Tony and Finn walked over to Consuela's whore home and arrested her. Consuela, a bright-eyed woman in her forties, immediately rolled over on her two cousins. The cocaine, she insisted, belonged to them.

"Now what are we gonna do?" Finn asked, looking over the plastic-wrapped bricks of cocaine stacked under Consuela's bed.

"Fuckin' Edwards," Fat Tony grunted.

It was too much cocaine to flush down the toilet. Even loading it into the car and dumping it into a vacant lot would be too time-consuming and risky. Aware that they had violated large sections of the patrol guide and the U.S. Constitution on legal search and seizure, Edwards, Fat Tony, and Finn cooked up a story about a confidential informant for Brooklyn Narcotics, and the assistant district attorney surprised them all by validating the arrest.

With the paperwork under way, Edwards, the stupid rookie, bragged about the arrest to his union delegate, who immediately alerted the press.

"How did the detectives know the cocaine was inside the apartment?" called out a sour-faced reporter from the *Post*. The television cameramen, hoping for a usable sound bite, again flooded O'Reilly with kliegs.

O'Reilly, flustered, slipped back into his "Dragnet" style.

"The uniformed officers and detectives developed the information in what we think was a fine example of community-based policing." The cameramen flicked off the klieg lights in disgust again. "The fruits of the commissioner's new community policing policy." Even the print reporters stopped taking notes. They had heard the commissioner's community policing anthem a thousand times. "It keeps both patrol and investigative forces in close touch with the neighborhood in which they work. Keeping their ears to the street."

"And their dicks in the whore homes," Fat Tony mumbled out of the corner of his mouth.

Finn waited for the dirty linoleum to split open and swallow him whole.

The reporters had traveled all the way out to Bushwick and they were growing increasingly restless for a usable quote.

"Tell us, Officer, uh, Edwards," said one of the over-made-up talking heads from Channel 11, her painted lips pursed as she leaned forward to read Edwards's nametag. "Is this your first big arrest?"

The cameramen, hoping for a few seconds of spontaneity, turned on the klieg lights again.

"Yes, ma'am." Edwards guffawed. "And it was a proud moment for me and for my family." Finn felt embarrassment creep to the roots of his hair. But the television reporter seemed animated by Edwards's stupid cornpone response.

"What about you, Detective? How does it feel to be a hero cop?"

Finn felt the air go dead as he realized the reporter was speaking to him.

"Excuse me?" he asked, hesitating, as if by speaking he would be forced to acknowledge that he was actually standing there.

The cameramen turned on their heels so that the blank eyes of their equipment could take in the television talent and Finn in the same frame.

He felt the heat of the lights and an impatient rustle from the reporters as he tried to think of something to say.

"Twenty bricks of cocaine is quite a bit. How does it feel to be a hero cop?" prompted the television reporter again, stepping into the frame to put her long microphone under his chin.

"A hero cop?" repeated Finn. He stared at the television reporter, wishing lightning would strike the 83rd Precinct. But nothing happened. Out of the corner of his eye, Finn saw that even O'Reilly was looking at him expectantly.

"A hero cop?" he said, taking a deep breath. "It feels fine. Just fine."

17

He couldn't take his eyes off her mouth as she walked into the room. She was wearing the same jeans she had on earlier in the week at the crime scene, but her dark areolas were visible through her thin white shirt. She looked down at her own breasts, then at his face, and her lips widened into a smile.

"I've been waiting for you," he said to her.

"I know," she said. Her voice, a low whisper, sent ripples through his thighs.

"How did you know where I lived?" he asked. His question seemed so blunt, he feared she would be offended.

But she wasn't.

"I know where you live," she said, placing the cool tips of her fingers on his temple. "I've always known where you lived."

He leaned closer and tilted his face toward hers so he could kiss her. She was just what he had been waiting for. Someone different to love. Someone who could change him. He reached up and felt the generous curve of her breast and a clap of thunder startled them both.

"Don't be afraid," he said. "It's just thunder."

But her lips were quivering and to Finn's amazement she began to retreat.

Another rumble of thunder and Finn opened his eyes. The rain was slashing against the window and lightning illuminated the room.

He looked at the clock and figured he had only been asleep for two hours. He sighed. He never had the same dream twice in one night.

He pulled the sheet over his shoulder, punched his pillow twice, and settled into the bed again.

This time, he was in a squad car and Fat Tony was driving down Myrtle Avenue. As they passed, everyone on the street stopped walking and talking and stared solemnly at the car. An old hunchbacked lady struggled to straighten out her gnarled spine as the car sped by. An infant stood up stiff-legged in his carriage and watched Finn without blinking. Three brothers Finn had arrested and sent to Elmira for robbing jewelry stores turned their heads slowly in his direction. The car crept past a double bed diagonal to the road, blocking the sidewalk. He was just about to point it out to Fat Tony when a woman, her arms outstretched like the Bride of Frankenstein, sat up in the bed and stared at the car. Finn realized the woman in the bed was his ex-wife.

"Why is everyone looking at the car?" Finn asked Tony. But Tony just grunted.

Then Finn looked up and he was standing next to Wochowsky on the landing of Plank's house. He had just witnessed his own funeral procession. Now it was time to die.

Finn began to scream, "The kid is in the apartment, he has a gun!" but the roof of his mouth was dry and no sound came out. "He has a gun!" Finn screamed again, but he only made strangled sounds.

Wochowsky looked at him. "What's wrong, Finn?" he asked in the dumb, painstaking way he talked. Just then a bullet ripped into Wochowsky's chest and he fell, lifeless, at Finn's feet. Then Marvin Plank was on him. Plank raised the gun and opened his mouth so wide that Finn could see his molars filled with black metal and the tiny pink speed bag that hung down the back of his throat. Then the teenager opened his mouth wider, blocking out the daylight filtering into the building.

Plank roared.

Finn was already sitting straight up in bed when he opened his eyes, the harsh cries still springing from his throat.

He grabbed his revolver out of a small wooden night table and quickly stuck two loose bullets in the chamber.

"Got to get him out," he muttered, rushing into the bathroom.

He flipped on the light and tore at the shower curtain. "Get out," he mumbled again.

He stared at himself in the mirror. His face was gray and his eyes were wild like the horses in an old Western, locked in their stalls while the barn was burning. He exhaled slowly and walked back to his bedroom.

His knees were rubbery and shaking slightly and his breath was still coming in bursts.

His bed looked as inviting as the jaws of an alligator.

He sat gingerly on the edge, laying his gun beside him. Another bolt of lightning flashed in the window, and Finn quickly picked it up again.

He couldn't shake the feeling that he wasn't alone. That kid Plank was here. He pulled an old pair of sneakers from under his bed and stuck his feet in them. With the gun leading the way, he searched his own living room.

Everything looked exactly the way he had left it. Newspapers on the floor. A bottle of Johnnie Walker on the sticky table. When Finn swung open the closet door, his breath caught again in his throat. But as his finger tightened on the trigger, he recognized his shearling coat, which had fallen from its flimsy wire hanger and lay in a bulky heap on the floor.

The rain was coming in a gentle rhythm. He walked to the kitchen and opened the refrigerator door. Holding the gun in one hand, he removed the ice tray with the other and put it on the counter. Then he opened a cabinet and got out a glass. Gripping the gun, he tried to crack the ice out of the ice tray but only succeeded in knocking the glass off the counter.

His feet crunched across the shards as he reached for another glass. This time he was more careful, and using the butt of the gun, he managed to get four cubes into the tumbler.

He sat on the couch and poured three thick fingers of Scotch. He kept seeing quick darting shadows in the corners, but when he turned his head, the room was empty.

He sipped the Scotch and felt the panic grow warmer and more friendly.

He took another sip.

He put down his glass to pick up the telephone and punched in a few numbers. Then he hung up.

He dialed another number, and hung up again. Resolutely, he dialed yet another set.

"Hi . . . ah . . . Tina," he said. "I'll pay by Visa. Yes . . . No. No." He sipped his Scotch. "Let's not talk about that. No. No sex stuff."

There was a long pause.

"I'm paying, so I decide what we talk about."

Another long pause.

"I just want to talk. Not about fantasies. About anything. About the weather."

He had tightened his grip on the gun during one of the last faint flashes of lightning. The storm was blowing out to sea.

18

Kate sat in a brown-paneled bar with Rick Marcell, a fat, reptilian-looking man, who wore his shirt open to his navel and enough diamond-encrusted jewelry on his neck and wrists to open a stall on Forty-seventh Street. Rick also happened to be one of the top federal undercover agents in the country. For more than an hour, she had listened to him describe his most dangerous and successful operation—breaking up a violent Central American drug gang—and she still didn't have any idea what he was talking about. Before the Severing homicide, she had spent a week persuading him to be interviewed for a feature story in the *Herald*. Now she could barely contain her impatience, praying that those two detectives, Finn and Salazzo, wouldn't arrest Severing's killer while she sat in this bar.

"So, Rick, when you went to Bogotá, was José Carabera there or not?" she asked, holding tight to a thread of the conversation.

Rick looked surprised.

"No. No. Not José Carabera. I was supposed to meet Phillipo Carabera, José's cousin," said Rick. He stressed the word *Phillipo,* as if the very mention of his name would explain everything. Kate scribbled, *José and Phillipo C.—cousins* into her notebook, then noticed she had already written the name José four times.

He is a master con man, Kate mused, forcing her thoughts from Margaret Severing, a sleight-of-hand artist who's locked up some of the bloodiest drug lords in history. But after twenty years as an undercover, Kate realized, trying to suppress a smile, he spoke in an incoherent elliptical way, a sophisticated code that only he understood.

Glancing at her notebook, Kate was struck by the tangle of *Josés* interconnected with her wildly drawn arrows. She found it incredibly funny, though she doubted Rick would enjoy the joke. Her hand flew up to her mouth and she forced herself to listen carefully. "So then I says to José Figuroa Hernandez, who is," he added generously, "not to be confused with José Figuroa Hernandez Piñero, who everyone called La Monstra. So I says to José—"

"Which José," she asked, barely trusting her voice not to betray her. "Carabera? Or Hernandez or Hernandez Piñero?"

He allowed a pedagogic pause. "José Carabera," he said patiently.

She felt another convulsion of laughter about to take over. Trying to be discreet, Kate signaled for the waitress to bring another round of soda, then let her hand rest on her forehead.

When her breathing returned to normal, she looked at Rick between her fingers. "How many Josés were in this particular drug ring?" she asked, trying to keep her voice level.

He just shrugged and flashed his used-car-dealer smile. Just then, Kate's beeper began to screech and she excused herself, then walked, almost sobbing with smothered laughter, to the telephone by the men's room. She sobered up immediately when, by the dim light, she recognized the call-back number as Wilson's. She quickly ran through the last two days' stories. Could she have made another mistake? She was almost sick with anticipation by the time Wilson answered her call.

"Got anything for page one?" Wilson asked her, dispensing with any pleasantries.

Kate was so relieved that for a second her mind went blank and she couldn't think of an answer.

"What do you have to advance the Severing story?" he asked.

She had agreed to meet the man, Dominick, who claimed to be an eyewitness, but she decided to check him out before she mentioned it to Wilson. "Nothing for today. Maybe later in the week."

But Wilson only heard her negative response and he drifted off. She could hear him, like horse hooves on some distant cobblestone street, composing another memo on his keyboard while he talked.

"No problem there," he said. For a second, he seemed to have forgotten who he was speaking to. Then he remembered.

"Listen, get up to East Ninety-first Street as fast as you can," he said. "A mental patient on leave from Bellevue psychiatric just macheteed a Park Avenue socialite."

"Wounded or dead?" Kate asked, suddenly serious, jotting down the address.

"Wounded, stabbed in the right arm with a knife."

"Knife or machete?" Kate asked, glancing back at Rick as he picked at his gold Rolex.

"Hmm. Maybe switchblade, maybe dinner knife. Just get going," said Wilson. Then he hung up.

It was after six when she filed her punctured-socialite story and drove toward Sheepshead Bay to meet her Mystery Caller.

19

It wasn't one of her best days, Kate thought, punching a Patsy Cline tape into the cassette deck and turning up the volume. On the Upper East Side, rafts of ranking police officers had officiously bustled around, acting like former model and billionaire wife Alexandra Kruply had been the target of a political assassination rather than an idle rich woman grazed on the arm by a confused and apologetic old man who had wandered out of a state hospital with a penknife.

Just a beat behind Patsy, Kate let her voice swoop up a full octave, and she sang about another love affair gone wrong.

Kate looked at a copy of today's *Herald* that lay open on the passenger seat beside her. She didn't get page one, but her third-day Margaret Severing story looked good—an inch-high headline on page four and pictures from the dead woman's high-school and nursing school graduation. Her story practically glowed compared to the Severing stories the other papers carried. The *Post* and *Newsday* had simply rehashed the details of the homicide and the mayor's reaction. The television stations were crediting the *Herald* on their news broadcasts. She was still out in front.

Nosing onto the Belt Parkway, Kate gripped the steering wheel with one hand and pretended to hold a microphone with the other. She swayed back and forth while she and Patsy keened about heartbreak. She remembered Rick Marcell's half-dozen Josés and began to laugh, tapping the steering wheel in time to the music as she drove.

For the first time since her meeting with Ridgeway and Wilson, she felt almost hopeful.

She thought about the Mystery Caller and tried not to get her hopes up. It was a symptom of her job anxiety that she'd agreed to meet with him at all. The Caller mumbled when he spoke, like he was partially drugged or terribly afraid. Most likely he was a garden variety lunatic, but if he could I.D. the killer, Kate knew she'd have the front page.

Detectives never care about the mental stability of a homicide witness. Why should she? As far as the detectives were concerned, a homicide witness had to come down from Mars long enough to sign a sworn statement. After that, the case was cleared and it became a problem for the district attorney.

Maybe she could use a tough-guy kind of lede to hide any obvious mental deficiency.

When he heard the sound of the bullet, he knew she was dead. He shrugged and continued walking. It was another murder on Jefferson Street.

She had used this approach to write about members of a neighborhood gang, the Park Street Boys, from a middle-class section of Queens. The Park Street Boys had killed a Pakistani newsstand owner for kicks. The gang members were disconnected from reality, stone-cold psychotic, but the cool detached way they talked about death made them seem streetsy instead of nuts.

Maybe the Mystery Caller would be a gang member. She quickly framed another headline: "The Gang That Rules Brooklyn: Nurse an Innocent Victim of Gang Violence?"

Nothing sells papers like a good gang story.

Or how about "The Downfall of Brooklyn's Bloodiest Gang: Conscience Turns Gang Leader into Canary After Brutal Murder of Innocent Nurse"?

It could be a series.

Maybe he'd be a straight arrow. A citizen. That would still be a great story. "Good Samaritan Helps Bring Killer to Justice." She weighed it, then sighed. Good Samaritans made great copy, too, she thought as she pushed open the double-glass door of the restaurant, but every one she had ever met had the personality of a hemorrhoid. She decided to look him over before introducing herself.

Against the backdrop of empty nets and rubber lobsters, she explained to the Greek host at the Captain's Table what she wanted him to do, and took up her position at the bar.

Before long, the Greek host reappeared and a pale man wearing a hooded sweatshirt jacket with a bandaged hand sidled up to the empty table.

*　　*　　*

Dominick hadn't been in this place since the owners had converted it from a heavy-metal strip club called Dreams to a nautical-themed fern bar. Before his eyes even adjusted to the dim interior, he decided he hated it. The sneering host handed him a greasy clip-on tie before consenting to show him a table. Feeling foolish, Dominick stuck the tie in his pocket, wishing he had thought to wear a jacket instead of his old sweatshirt. The splint on his hand looked raggedy and he knew his hair wasn't helping matters either. He liked his hair in a single, slicked-back wave, like a youthful Frank Sinatra. But for some reason this evening, instead of forming the usual well-trained curl, it was at weird angles, like boomerangs stuck into his skull. He was using his mother's hairspray to tame it when the canister gave a little aerosol gasp and stopped working. He stuck a few of his mother's hairclips, like robotic alligators, into the sticky clump, but the effect was too feminine. Panicked, he clamped his Walkman headphones on his head to hold the wave in place until the hairspray dried.

But by then it was getting late, so he threw down a few black and yellow hits of speed and grabbed the bus to the Captain's Table. Now the amphetamines were threatening to overtake him, putting little rainbow halos around the lights. Dominick sat, his teeth almost chattering from the drugs, waiting for Kate. This could be the most important conversation he had ever had. It was, without exaggeration, a matter of life and death. He didn't want anything to go wrong.

He thought he recognized his waitress as one of the strippers from Dreams. Even in her dowdy waitress's uniform, those breasts looked familiar. Where was that reporter, anyway? he thought impatiently. If he had known he was going to be so nervous, he would have taken a quarter of a Quaalude. He looked around for other waitresses to see if they were retired strippers also, but they were wearing too much clothing to tell. For a moment, he thought the girl at the bar might be another one of the strippers. She had pale clear skin and her face was framed by a mass of black frizzy curls. The skin on his cheeks itched as he imagined sticking his face in that hair. On closer inspection, he decided she couldn't have been a stripper at the old place. She was too plain in that expensive Manhattan way. Where was that reporter? By the time his drink arrived, he was so antsy, he could barely keep his voice below a shout. The busty waitress handed him his double Scotch like he had a communicable disease. Dominick decided to settle the question once and for all.

"D'ya ever dance naked here?" he asked, reaching out and giving her breast a little squeeze for old times' sake.

Suddenly, the host rematerialized and there were angry hands on his sweatshirt and the chair he was sitting on clattered to the floor. He started to complain, explaining that he was waiting for a reporter, trying to make them see that lives could be at stake. But then he was being dragged and well-dressed diners were watching him, forks poised above their plates. When he opened his eyes again, he was lying in the parking lot, staring at shooting stars in a lake of mercury. Raindrops, he thought dully, but by then he was soaked to the skin.

✻   ✻   ✻

As soon as she saw Dominick, her Good Samaritan headline shattered like glass. Almost everything about him, from his jerky gait, to his bloodshot eyes, to the thin film of sweat on his pale skin, suggested that he was no stranger to cocaine or amphetamines. His thick neck and forearms suggested a recent prison stint and made him look like a half-step on the evolutionary scale. One of his middle fingers was taped between two tongue depressors in a homemade splint. As she watched Dominick twitching and mumbling to himself, she assumed he was singing along with his Walkman. Then she realized that his headphones were not attached to a radio but hung loose at his waist. He kept checking his wrist, like he was watching the time, but from her perch on the bar stool, she could see his wrist was bare. When his drink arrived, he tried to touch the waitress, who immediately signaled for the host, who also doubled as the bouncer. The host hustled over, consoling the woman and giving Dominick menacing looks. Dominick bared his teeth like an animal and snarled. The host lunged for him and began dragging him toward the door. With an outraged howl, Dominick began to scream her name, babbling about life and death. Kate rested her forehead on her hand, hoping no one could connect her to this madman. She had a winner for the Loon of the Week contest. By a landslide.

20

Finn sat behind his desk, watching the evening news flicker on the television behind Detective Bart Genovese's broad back. Genovese was interviewing Nathaniel Howe, a sixteen-year-old who had shot a nineteen-year-old neighbor, Abdul Supreme, on the street in front of his house. When the Emergency Medical Service attendants tried to stick a clear plastic oxygen tube down Supreme's throat, Supreme, lying in about a quart of his own blood, reached into his red sweatpants and pulled out a nine-millimeter semiautomatic handgun, and waved it at the terrified EMS workers before lapsing into unconsciousness. Supreme, now near death at Woodhull Hospital, was himself wanted for robbing the grocery store nearest his home.

Howe assumed he would be charged as a juvenile, which meant one and a half years in a state home with other crazy young men. He was not facing what his older brother, convicted on a homicide in 1981, would have called "serious time."

He was hungry and he was tired of talking to this stupid cop who, Nathaniel suspected, was at least partially deaf.

"I wanted his teef," Nathaniel explained again.

"His TEEF? WHAT THE FUCK ARE TEEF?" said Genovese, who had just been transferred from a precinct in Forest Hills, Queens.

Garvey walked by and leaned toward Genovese's ear.

"Caps. Gold caps," Garvey told Genovese, his white forelock

almost touching Genovese's slicked-back black strands. "He is talking about gold teeth."

Then Garvey dropped a double cheeseburger on Nathaniel's lap, and handed another, plus a schooner of fries, to Genovese.

"So you shot him to get the gold caps? Is that it?"

"Right," said Howe, nodding, his mouth full of burger. "I wan'ned them, so I got them."

Genovese reached under a stack of papers on his desk and pulled out a plastic evidence envelope. Inside were six interconnecting gold teeth. He glanced incredulously at Finn, whose expression didn't change.

"Okay. Let me write down your statement and you can sign it and I can go home," said Genovese. "You understand your rights or should I read them to you again?"

"I got the right to remain silent," said Howe, sounding like a television voice-over. Small bits of bun sputtered from his mouth as he spoke. "I got the right to my attorney, or one will be appointed by the court."

Genovese phoned an assistant district attorney and tried for the second time to reach Nathaniel's mother where she worked.

After the paperwork was done, he walked his young charge to the lock-up, which was empty except for a foul-smelling toilet without a seat, a limp blanket, and a rough board bench.

"It ain't exactly the Hilton," said Genovese. The room had a chilling effect on Nathaniel. He slipped out of his jaunty singsong voice and his boy-on-the-street bop, opened his mouth, which already had molars paved with gold, and began to wail.

"I want my mommy, I want my lawyer. I want my mommy," he cried.

Genovese stared back at Finn, but Finn couldn't meet his gaze. Finn wanted to laugh hysterically or bury his head in his arms. Instead, he stared at a picture from the *Post* that Fat Tony had taped over his desk. It was a shot of a grinning Edwards, looking like a giant in a blue uniform alongside Tony and Finn in plainclothes. To their left were the wrapped bricks of cocaine. The caption identified them by name and the headline read: JUST ANOTHER DAY ON THE JOB FOR THREE HERO COPS.

Garvey also heard Nathaniel's howls. He walked over to Finn and watched as Genovese locked Howe in the cell.

"I think it may be too late for that boy," Garvey said, looking like the weight of Howe's wailing was dragging his features downward.

"Shit. I spent the best years of my life for this," said Genovese bitterly, trying to loosen a bit of burger stuck between his teeth. "I worked my ass off to get a gold shield. Now I work in a place where a victim is determined by who has the smaller caliber of gun."

Garvey, whose snowy hair set off his pink skin, nodded. Finn picked up the telephone. It was a sleepy-sounding woman asking for Genovese. Finn handed him the phone.

"Maybe in another hour, sweetums," Genovese cooed, his close-set eyes crinkling with effort. "Dinner? Sure. Why not? Nothing's too good for you, baby. No. No. Yes. And you, too."

He hung up and looked sheepishly for a second at Garvey and Finn.

"Nathaniel here was an abused child," said Garvey mildly, running his fingers through his hair. "He stood in this very spot ten years ago covered with cigarette burns."

Genovese looked up. "Forget that social work crap. He was born a skell. He'll die a skell. You can tell by the look of him. He's just another filthy animal."

Garvey stared at him, surprised, until Genovese began to blush.

"He's just evil?" said Garvey, smiling, trying to take the edge from Genovese.

"Nah, evil doesn't have anything to do with it," Finn said, thinking of Plank. Garvey looked up, surprised. "If Howe had waited a day, he could just as easily have been shot by Supreme."

Genovese piped in again. "And Supreme would be howling in the holding pen and Howe would be in the hospital."

"Or the morgue," Finn said.

The phone rang again. When Finn picked it up, he could hear children screaming in the background. He handed the phone to Genovese.

"No, honey, this case is going overnight," Genovese said. "Maybe a break in the homicide I was telling you about. Yeah. Probably. I'll just sleep here. Tell little Bobby his daddy loves him. You, too."

Genovese made a few kissing noises into the phone and hung it up. The call from his wife seemed to energize him.

"We spend our lives running down perps for what? To restore order. Order. Ha," he said. "You remember the first week I got transferred to this shithole precinct? Second case I catch, a concrete block falls off a building and lands on a God-fearing grandmother. How about that case Fat Tony and you worked last year? An eight-month-old baby with a bullet in his head. Where's the law and order when a baby asleep in his mother's arms gets shot in the head with a stray bullet?"

"You're looking at this all wrong," started Garvey.

But Genovese cut him off. "All we end up doing is chasing the animals back into their holes."

"Everyone in this precinct does good out there," Garvey said mildly, looking away. "Maybe you don't see it, but it's true."

"He's not talking about us, he's talking about what's out there," said Finn, suddenly agitated, talking too loud, too fast. "Maybe next week a drug dealer gets killed by a concrete block instead of the grandmother, but shit, it's like getting a bottle of Coke with a rat in it. A random thing. One day the drug dealer gets shot, next day God says, 'Fuck you,' and it's the baby that stops the bullet." Finn wanted to continue but Genovese interrupted him.

"Yeah. It's the chaos that kills you," Genovese said.

Finn could see Plank's body unfold from the shadowy corner and hear the boy's sneakers bound over the rough floor of the abandoned apartment. "You can't save anyone else. You can't even save yourself. Anytime, it could get you. Right out of nowhere. It's *bang!* Then nothing at all."

There was a long silence as Garvey watched them both but spoke to Finn. "If you think like that, how do you come to work every morning? What are you doing on this job?"

"I wake up. I get dressed. I come to work. That's how I do it. I used to think I knew why I did it," said Finn. "Now I'm not so sure."

Genovese seemed to have lost interest in the conversation.

"Is the ADA going to believe that Nathaniel shot his neighbor for his gold teeth?" asked Genovese.

Finn smiled. "Nah. Nobody is going to believe it."

Genovese shrugged. "I can hardly believe it myself except I heard it right from his mouth."

About twenty minutes later, Finn was still sitting at his desk. He pawed through a stack of papers and reread a note from the firearms board. There would be a hearing on the bullet he shot at Plank. The kid tries to kill me and I have to go to a hearing.

He found his notebook and reviewed the remarks Severing's friends had made, wondering if he had missed something. The case was getting on his nerves. Remembering the lessons of his last partner, Joe Flaherty, a twenty-year veteran detective, he tried to organize what he knew so far.

The biggest question was still Severing's boyfriend. Brooklyn College graduate turned crack fiend. But had he turned killer? He felt sorry for Margaret, nursing the sick all night at the hospital and her boyfriend all day. And on Sunday she got up early to sing in the choir.

Finn sighed. He wasn't looking forward to his early-morning phone call with Troutmouth.

He stuck his elbow above his head and massaged his own neck. He felt bones where the muscles should have been.

He looked at the television across the room and watched a blowsy-looking woman reporter wearing too much makeup stand in front of a luxurious apartment building in Manhattan. The camera panned over the wide sidewalk and the dark green awning, past the borough commander, who looked as if he was trying hard not to wave. The angle changed, catching Kate Murray talking to the doorman. The guy wore a dumb green hat with a broad, yellow plume in it.

Finn realized with some surprise that he had been waiting three hours for Kate Murray to return his call.

He shook his head and grabbed the phone, dialing her work number, where he got a gruff clerk who advised him to call back in the morning. Determined, he dialed information and was surprised to find she had a listed telephone number under her own name. He phoned her home. While the phone rang, he looked at his watch and noticed that it was after eleven. He wasn't sure what he was going to say when she picked up.

On the third ring, he got her answering machine. "I'm not home right now," said the canned message, "but I'd be happy to call you back if you leave a number."

Finn hung up, dialed, and listened to the tape again. Why would a married woman, he wondered, refer to only a single person living at that number? It seemed like something a husband might do, but not a wife. He hung up and, just to make sure he hadn't dialed the wrong number, called again. It was the same voice. Where would she be at eleven P.M. even if she was separated?

He stared at the mouthpiece until the dial tone changed to a loud squawking. Fuck it, he thought to himself. Fuck the Hero Cops. Fuck Troutmouth. Fuck Genovese and his two wives. Fuck Severing's boyfriend. Fuck the Firearms Board. He yanked the knot of his tie and pulled on his jacket.

21

The next morning, at ten A.M., Dominick awoke to the intro jingle of "The Price Is Right." He made sure that his mother was lying on the couch, upwind and out of earshot, then he pulled out two wrinkled joints. One of them, he knew, was sprinkled with PCP. The other was just home-grown weed. He pointed to each one, mouthing eenie-meanie, then lit one and called the reporter again.

He had waited for her in a freezing drizzle for two hours. At first, sitting on the curb outside of the restaurant, he felt sorry for himself. It was humiliating getting thrown out of a fern bar in front of all those people. Then he worried. Maybe the reporter was lost. Maybe she had a car accident and at this very minute was pinned under the wheels of a semi. But as the hours crawled by, he started to feel annoyed. She was standing him up. It was another sign of disrespect.

"I'm sorry," droned the clerk at the *Herald* as Dominick took in a lungful of smoke, "Kate Murray isn't in yet. I'll leave her another message."

"Hey! You didn't even put me on hold to check if she was there," Dominick coughed, but the clerk had already hung up. A flaming marijuana seed jumped from the joint, hit his shirt, and burnt a small round hole in it.

Cursing, Dominick drew in another puff of smoke and called back. To his surprise, he heard a series of clicks as his call went through.

"Murray here."

"Kate!" he shouted, thrilled by how intimate it sounded to use her first name. He was so happy to have finally got her that he almost kissed the receiver. The next second, he was very angry that she was still alive. "I waited for you," he said accusingly. "I waited for hours."

Kate was instantly sorry she had picked up the telephone. It was early, the ten-thirty editors' meeting had not yet begun, but electric currents were already flowing through the newsroom. Joe Barrister, the mayor's only declared opponent, had called a press conference on the steps of City Hall to express outrage over the Severing homicide and attack the mayor's record on crime. It was a transparent gesture on the part of the plumbing tycoon to identify himself with ordinary people, but on a slow day, it counted as news. Wilson was charging around the city desk, trying to find someone to cover the press conference.

Kate was staring at him, trying not to look imploring. The Severing story was hers, she reasoned. And covering the political fallout of the homicide edged her away from police reporting toward the prized City Hall beat. If she was sent to City Hall, it would be a sign that faith had been restored, that her period of disgrace was over. She was concentrating so hard on sending Wilson telepathic suggestions that she could barely keep up her end of the conversation.

"I must have missed you," she said. The last person she wanted to hear from was the Loon of the Week. Kate suppressed a sigh of irritation.

"Car trouble," she lied, still watching Wilson. Of course, Dominick wanted to set up another meeting. "I can't meet you right now," she stalled. "I'm on to something big." Dominick persisted. Woodward and Bernstein probably had to deflect a lot of weirdos, too. "Really big," she added firmly.

Without pausing, Dominick started talking about the supposed killer by the name of Gusano. It was the Spanish man, Dominick kept insisting, who he saw kill the nurse.

"It was horrible, like something out of *Friday the Thirteenth*." Dominick was surprised to hear himself say the words. His jaw felt unhinged and his forehead was stretching toward the ceiling. Must be the PCP. "He shot her and cut open her stomach. Like, all her guts were spread out all over. And her throat was cut from ear to ear. I mean, I'm a man, I can take it, but I tell you, it's not something I want to see again."

Kate tuned out his voice to eavesdrop on Wilson, who was slowly making his way toward her. She had a flash of self-awareness, feeling frightened by how intensely she wanted the assignment. It was almost childish, this urgent longing to prove herself, to win, to beat everyone.

Silence on the telephone drew Kate back. She could hear Dominick exhale and guessed he was smoking pot. She could hear squeals from "The Price Is Right" in the background.

"Uh-huh. Well, that's quite a story," she riffed, aware that she had stopped listening to him ramble several minutes before.

"You're not even listening!" he accused her. "I'm gonna call my friend at the *Post*."

Kate felt annoyed, then queasy. Dominick was a wacko and seemed to have most of the details about the Severing homicide wrong. But he claimed to know the killer's name. With every television, radio, and print reporter in New York chasing her stories in the *Herald,* the *Post* might end up putting him on the front page. Never mind that he was a card-carrying member of the Kook Squad.

She closed her eyes and feigned her warmest tone. "You're right. I am sorry. I was distracted by this other thing I'm working on. But let me focus on our problem for a second." *Our problem,* she thought cynically.

She gave a dramatic pause, listening to the bells dinging on the game show. She had to come up with a way to get rid of him fast so she could lobby for the Barrister assignment.

"Maybe you could act as my deputy. Yeah, that's it. A deputy reporter for the *Daily Herald.*" The idea was so absurd that Kate almost started laughing right then. "You can track Gusano"—she hoped she had the name right—"then call me when you get something, and I'll talk to my editors and decide how it should run in the paper."

There was another long pause, then Dominick grabbed the bait. "Wow. A deputy reporter."

He sounded so breathless and excited that Kate felt cruel. But Dominick prattled on. "You know, I figured I'd be a reporter eventually, ever since Career Day in junior high school. I took a test—ya know, multiple choice, stopwatch, number-two pencil, the works. The test said I would be a reporter someday. A reporter, that's right. A reporter.'' Dominick seemed to wind down, then get a second wind. ''Or a priest. Guess I filled in some of the wrong answers on that test.''

Career Day, Kate repeated silently, rolling her eyes. At least it would give him something to do besides smoke pot and watch game shows, she reasoned.

Wilson, only a few desks away, veered to the left and clapped Grant on the shoulder. Kate's fury rose. Wilson was sending Grant to cover Barrister. The assignment that should have been hers.

''I'll track him down. I may even know a bar where he hangs out. You'll see. I'll do a great job for the paper,'' Dominick vowed earnestly, like a deranged Boy Scout. ''I'll make you proud.''

22

Dominick drove the station wagon carefully, humming a Frank Sinatra tune, not wanting to get stopped while the car was packed with twenty-seven brand-new Bang & Olufsen turntables.

He turned off the Belt Parkway at the Canarsie exit and nosed into a broken-down warehouse that looked abandoned except for a double-reinforced steel door with three shining newly installed deadbolt locks.

He waited until the doors swung open, then drove the car into the dim warehouse and got out. A short middle-aged man with a dark tan and a basketball-sized gut waddled out from the back.

"*Paisano*," Birdie called out, slapping Dominick on the shoulder as he turned his attention to the station wagon.

Two teenagers with long hair, bad skin, and identical black T-shirts emblazoned with the word *Megadeth* emerged from behind the meat trucks and began unloading the turntables onto handcarts.

"What's up, Birdie, how's business?" said Dominick.

"Always the same," he said, cupping his hands against the window to count the cargo. "Whahappan to your finger?"

Dominick felt his face burn. Bullshitting Birdie meant bullshitting Big Mike, and Dominick didn't dare try it.

"Nothin'. I hurt it, that's all," he said.

The turntables were quickly unloaded and Big Mike walked over to join Dominick and Birdie in the late-morning sun.

"So you made it, at long last," Big Mike said. Big Mike, a meat wholesaler, had had an operation for throat cancer and he always seemed on the verge of choking on his own phlegm.

"How ya doing, Mike? How's business in the meat business?"

"Just great, Dommy." Big Mike was wearing a bright green polyester shirt. It was short-sleeved because he was fiercely proud of a multicolored tattoo that extended from his left wrist across the top of his back to his right shoulder. If you looked at it one way, it was a tattoo of a woman riding a dolphin. Look at it another way and she was having sex with the big fish. Big Mike reached into his baggy trousers, pulled out a wad of twenties, and peeled off six for Dominick.

"How's your mother?" rumbled Big Mike. Dominick's mother and Big Mike had dated fifteen years ago, after Big Mike's wife had a nervous breakdown and moved to Tucson to live with one of her sisters. The relationship lasted six months, until Big Mike's wife got wind of it and stormed back to Sheepshead Bay. The relationship, though temporary, was enough to guarantee Dominick an occasional job moving swag, usually stolen fur coats, televisions, portable computers, telephones, and stereo components, to the warehouse where Big Mike stored the meat.

"She's good, great," said Dominick. "How's Mary doing?" Mary was Big Mike's oldest daughter, a lightly bearded math teacher.

Big Mike looked at him sharply. "Why you wanna know? She's got a nice boyfriend, that's how she's doing." His voice sounded like a lawn mower whose motor wouldn't turn over.

"I was just being friendly," sniffed Dominick, genuinely hurt. "I didn't mean anything by it."

"Of course you didn't," said Big Mike, suddenly friendly again. "Of course."

Dominick followed Big Mike inside, past the giant refrigerated trucks to a cluttered office. He sat on a tiny bench next to Birdie, who tended a steaming stainless-steel espresso machine. Mike's warehouse was one of the few places where Dominick felt content. Mike was always here, grumbling and spewing, someone was always making coffee. This was the way a man was supposed to live. Nothing scared him here.

For the last year or so, Dominick had been living with the uneasy sensation that his life was out of control. The night Montoya threatened to castrate him with a garden tool was the bottom of a long slide toward total humiliation. He touched his bandaged hand unconsciously. But since he saw the nurse get whacked, his luck had changed. He could scarcely believe it himself, but here he was, a deputy news reporter. And that woman, Kate Murray, was going to help him more than she even knew. He grinned to himself. Soon there would be no Gusano, no Montoya. Only friends and business partners.

The Megadeth boys had finished unloading the turntables and were busy trying to punch each other in the nuts as they stared at three years' worth of Pet of the Month centerfolds pinned up over the espresso machine.

All he had to do was keep his focus. And that wasn't too easy, especially with some of the things that had been happening to him lately. Sometimes, thoughts would come into his head like someone was whispering in his ear and he'd try to answer before he realized that no one was talking. Other times, he was so freaked about Gusano, he'd see him walking right down the street in Gravesend. Dominick shook himself involuntarily. He'd have to start living better. Like Big Mike. He never took shit from nobody.

In the warmth of the room, he began to unwrap the bandage on his hand. The swelling had gone down and the bruises were fading to green. He wrapped it again.

He realized that Big Mike had been rumbling and was now holding up one finger. Dominick struggled to focus on what he was saying.

"There's money out there for a young man like you," he said. "But it's not in meat and it's not in swag."

"Whaddaya talking about?" Dominick asked.

"It took me a long time to discover it myself, but I'll tell you now. It's in garbage," Mike said, then gave two dry coughs that sounded like a shovel hitting fresh dirt.

"Garbage," said Birdie solemnly. "There's money in garbage."

"Whaddaya mean?" asked Dominick, slapping his knee broadly. "Take it out of the garbage?"

Birdie and Big Mike slapped their hands on their knees, too, and Big Mike made a strangling sound that might have been laughter.

"Not *the* garbage. Garbage. Like hauling, except with more expertise," said Big Mike.

"What kind of expertise?" asked Dominick.

Big Mike looked at Dominick and narrowed his eyes. "Selective garbage."

"Like from hospitals," said Birdie.

Big Mike nodded.

"Hospitals pay you a lot of money to take care of their special garbage—medical stuff, syringes, the plumbing they cut out of old ladies, Kleenexes used by fags who have AIDS. And we take care of it," said Big Mike.

"What do you do with it?" asked Dominick, unnerved.

Big Mike hefted his bulk onto his legs and beckoned for Dominick to follow. They left the office and walked out to the parking area, where four meat trucks hummed quietly. Big Mike approached one of the behemoths, reached up for the lever bolt, and swung open the insulated door. Underneath the rigid red sides of beef were four bright orange plastic bags marked INFECTIOUS WASTE.

Dominick thought of the deep freezer at home, filled with meat from Big Mike's warehouse. He felt his stomach turn. "Jesus, Mike. Don't you think the meat'll go bad?"

Mike swung the door closed. "Nah. It's too cold," he said. "Germs can't live when it's cold. It kind of, like, stuns 'em, I mean, sterilizes, yeah, sterilizes it." Big Mike hawked, then clapped his hands for the Megadeth boys.

"Time for the Rockaway run," Big Mike rumbled to Birdie and lumbered away. Dominick waited until he was out of earshot.

"What are you doing with that stuff?" Dominick hissed.

"The meat gets regular delivery. The special garbage we take care of while we're out there." Birdie slowly mounted the steps of the truck.

"What do you do with it, bury it?" Dominick asked.

Birdie burst out laughing. "Bury it? Shit. We drive out to the Belt Parkway, park on the shoulder by the bay, and throw it in the ocean. Let God sort it out."

23

The baby shower had barely begun when Kate decided she needed to be alone. She had spent the day in the South Bronx interviewing parents of toddlers sexually abused at their city-run day-care center. Now she was supposed to smile and clap while one of her best friends from college, Mary Gaskell, unwrapped a pile of pastel gifts. She didn't know if it was the Bronx or Mary's mother's ten-room Upper West Side apartment, with its view of the Ramble in Central Park, that was making her hyperventilate.

"Where are you going?" whispered Nina, one of Kate's oldest friends. Nina, a former college radical, was holding tenaciously to a middle-rung job at a Wall Street investment firm.

"Bathroom. Don't feel well," Kate hissed over a row of well-coiffed heads as Mary held up a shirt that could fit in the palm of her hand.

Kate wandered down a long maroon hallway crowded with pictures of Mary and her brother Bob in various stages of childhood. School plays at Brearley, on the beach at Amagansett, Mary and Bob squinting into the sun on the slopes at Vermont or Vail. Then graduation from Syracuse University, and Mary in an antique white veil with Larry, looking prosperous and satisfied, in a tuxedo. It was a towheaded, blue-eyed tableau of the life Kate's mother had always wanted her daughter to live, she thought, as her throat got tight.

Her mother's only child, Kate was born with a tornado of unruly black hair, and grew from a plump, shy girl into a fat, awkward teenager with excellent grades but no date for the prom. She studied the wedding picture again, imagining herself in it, wearing the white dress, marrying James. Then she imagined she was marrying that square-chinned detective, John Finn from the Severing case, and the fantasy dissolved.

She finally found the bathroom and was unnerved to find that she couldn't quite catch her breath as the door clicked shut behind her. It was one of the most splendid bathrooms she had ever been in. The walls were covered in chintz wallpaper, which ran to a highly polished walnut floor; an oil painting of a still life hung above the toilet tank and antique silver-backed hairbrushes and combs crowded the counter space. Facing the toilet was a full-length gilded Louis XIV mirror. She carefully wet a white Turkish handtowel with cold water and draped it over her forehead.

She started when she heard someone trying the handle.

"Sorry, I'm in here," she called out, her voice croaking.

Breathing deeply for control, she eyed a pair of sterling filigree manicure scissors near the sink and wondered why all the homicides she covered were committed with such mundane weapons: hammers, bread knives, and that old standby, the nine-millimeter. She decided she wasn't coming out of the bathroom until the baby shower was over.

She thought about the last mother she had interviewed in the South Bronx. Ellen Sanders, a twenty-two-year-old computer programmer whose two-year-old, Amanda, had both learned to count and contracted gonorrhea at the day-care center where Ellen struggled to send her. The bony, alcoholic *Herald* photographer named Reed, who smoked impatiently through Kate's interview, badgered the woman into letting him take pictures of the child.

"We'll keep her face in shadows. Your relatives won't even know it's her," he had said as he quickly pulled his camera out of his jacket and set off the flash. The child grabbed at the pink bows in her pigtails and began to scream.

Kate felt a thick band pulling tighter and tighter around her chest, unwilling to even guess which picture of the child the paper would run. She unwound her arms from her midsection and wondered if she could stay in this bathroom until tomorrow's *Herald* was off the newsstands. It would be awkward, but Mary, always the diplomat, could make her mother understand that her old college chum was having a nervous breakdown in the bathroom.

She heard a faint knock on the door, then a louder one.

"Go away. Goddammit. Go away!" she shouted, pulling the towel off her forehead. She sat down heavily on the commode, pressed her hands to her temples, and tried counting breaths. One in, one out. Two in, two out.

The voices outside the door had died away and the band around her chest had loosened by the time Kate opened her eyes again. She had no idea how long she had been in there. Almost mechanically, she composed herself to face the party. She opened the medicine cabinet like a cat burglar, selected a large amber bottle, and spritzed a little of Mrs. Gaskell's Joy under her chin and into her bosom. She flushed the toilet and tucked her shirt into her jeans. Checking her appearance in the mirror, she noted a tiny blob of blue ink on her collar. She wished she had worn nicer clothes this morning, but then remembered she had dressed with Bronx muggers in mind, not the terrifying cadre of shower guests waiting outside. She swept her hair off her forehead, inspected the reddened area around her eyes for tears and then for wrinkles, took a deep breath, and unlocked the door.

She found Nina standing on the glassed-in porch taking gulps of the icy December air that blasted through the open window.

"I've been looking for you," said Nina, blowing her bangs as she exhaled and linking her arm through Kate's. "I bet you feel like the last single career woman in New York."

"Something like that," Kate said, wondering why her friend was hitting her sore spot so hard.

"Too bad all these young fashionable women didn't invite their young, fashionable, and eligible brothers to the shower," Nina said lightly.

"You could just go back in there and introduce me as your friend the spinster, the social pariah," Kate snapped. "Maybe someone's homosexual uncle is looking for a beard."

Nina gave her a long look.

"Lighten up if you can, I was just trying to make a joke about it."

Kate looked at her friend, thinking of Nina at twenty-one, a tan, stout student radical just back from two years of farming on a kibbutz. Ten years later, she was sitting in Kate's living room, bashfully showing off a two-carat engagement ring. Kate realized, with a pang, that their friendship would never be the same again.

Embarrassed, Kate turned to stare out over the brown and frozen park. It was just dusk and the stately East Side buildings seemed like so many soldiers suddenly coming into view along the edge of a battlefield.

"Why did you lock yourself in the bathroom?" Nina asked carefully.

Behind Nina, Kate could see Mary awkwardly holding a bald baby someone had thrust into her arms.

"My job, the party, my social life, it's just . . . you know . . . stressful," Kate said.

Nina nodded, not comprehending.

Kate tried again. "I'm sitting on the commode, surrounded by chintz, and I realize that time is flying by but I'm standing still."

"What do you mean?"

"I mean, Mary is having a baby, and you're just back from your honeymoon. I'm just waiting. Waiting for James to come back. Waiting to get fired from the only job I ever wanted."

"What do you mean, waiting for James?" asked Nina.

"Well, there has to be some kind of silver lining. He said he needed space but he didn't say how long he needed it. These difficulties at work are a little more tolerable if I can still hope that my personal life will sort itself out."

"Oh my God. You really don't know." Nina looked stricken.

"Know what?"

"Someone should have told you."

"Told me what?"

"I'm sorry, Kate. I wanted to call you when I saw the announcement in the paper."

Kate just looked at her.

"James's wedding announcement."

"What are you talking about? James just moved out on me."

"In *The New York Times*. On Sunday. James got married over the weekend. To a clothing designer for Karl Lagerfeld. Kate, I'm sorry. I thought you knew."

Kate turned toward the reflective planes of the Metropolitan Museum of Art.

"Well, he said he needed more space. I guess he needed more space to plan his wedding."

Her voice was flat and a little strangled, as if she was trying to deliver a straight line as jagged shards of glass were sinking into her heart. She took a deep breath. "Oh God."

24

I thought you said this hearing would never happen,'' Finn hissed to his well-fed union rep, Doug Johnson, who flipped through the business section of the *Herald*. Finn fidgeted in the metal chair just outside the double oak doors of the hearing room on the twelfth floor of Police Headquarters.

"Relax. Relax,'' said Johnson, inspecting his cuticles in a broad, bored gesture. "They're calling the shooting questionable, but it's a formality. You're not going to open your mouth in the hearing. Your lawyer will question the legality of this unfortunate and ill-directed internal review, and *boom,* rubber stamp, you're back in beautiful Bushwick.''

"You keep saying 'Relax,' but here I am sitting two feet away from the fucking hearing room and I've never even seen my lawyer,'' Finn whispered.

Johnson stared at Finn steadily.

"Does the union take care of its men? Yes or no?'' he asked solemnly. "Didn't we hire the very best lawyer in New York for you?''

Finn knew that the flamboyant Bruce Hoffman was the best-known mob lawyer in the city. "I thought he was on personal retainer with the Lucchese crime family.''

"Somebody knows somebody, we got him cheap," said Johnson. "God, will you look at that?"

Johnson pointed to a large picture in the newspaper of a pouty little girl in pigtails. "Says here she is a sex abuse victim. Two years old and this goddamn newspaper runs her picture. Any decent newspaper would fire the reporter who did that."

Finn stared over his shoulder at the picture and Kate Murray's byline.

"It's probably not the reporter. It's probably the photographer who was behind that," Finn said mildly.

"Who are you? Tom fucking Brokaw?" asked Johnson. Just then the elevator doors glided open. For a second, it didn't seem as if anyone was getting off. Then Finn heard a thump and a quick dragging sound. Before the doors could close, a liver-spotted hand reached out and prevented them from sliding shut.

It took the old man a good sixty seconds to get off the elevator. Leaning heavily on his cane, he composed himself in front of Johnson, turned up his hearing aid, and stuck out a wavering hand.

"You must be the young hero, John Finn," he said to Johnson. "Bruce Hoffman Senior here. Forty years' experience at the New York Bar. At your service."

As Johnson and Finn began to react, the door to the hearing room opened and a sharply dressed lieutenant beckoned to the three of them.

"Your hearing will begin now," he said, his voice booming as if he were announcing Finn at the gates of heaven.

"You got the wrong fucking Bruce Hoffman," Finn said, his voice stuck somewhere between a scream and a whisper. Johnson stood frozen with a sick smile on his face. "You didn't get the mob lawyer, you got his father."

The trial room, with its oak paneling and prominently displayed flags, looked like a miniature version of the People's Court. But instead of Judge Wapner, a ferret-faced Internal Affairs inspector and a florid assistant chief were seated in tall chairs behind the bench.

As if in a trance, Finn recited his name, rank, and badge number. Then Johnson did the same.

"Uh, sir, Detective Finn would like a word with his attorney before the hearing begins," stuttered Johnson.

Johnson and Finn both turned hopeful faces to the ancient lawyer.

Johnson's voice was low and urgent. "Uh, Mr. Hoffman. We need you to stop this hearing, raise some objection, challenge its legality, so it will not go forward."

Hoffman screwed his forefinger into his hearing aid.

Finn shot the assistant chief an embarrassed look.

"This is a Firearms Review Board. They are reviewing the circumstances under which our hero, John Finn, fired his gun," coached Johnson. "They say the circumstances were questionable. Not proper."

"Or legal," Finn added hopefully.

"Firearms board, you say?" asked the elder Hoffman. Then he smiled cheerfully. "I don't believe I've attended one of these before."

Finn felt himself sag.

"We want you to stop this hearing. Put up a legal challenge." Finn was rooting through cobwebbed memories from a night class he took called "Enforcement and the Law."

"Get an injunction!" He recalled the word with triumph, but it had no effect on Hoffman. "At least make an argument. I didn't do anything wrong," Finn said desperately. "But if they think I did, they could take away my shield and my gun. I could lose my pension."

The old man stared at Finn with runny eyes.

"Well, son, tell them what they need to know," he said portentously.

Finn glanced at Johnson, who looked seasick, and decided he was going to offer him a ride home and then run him over in the parking lot.

The assistant chief was clearing his throat, and before Finn could protest, the stenographer was recording the proceedings. The hearing had begun.

As the natty lieutenant read Finn his Miranda rights, sweat began dripping from under Finn's holster. Beads formed under his hairline and dark, damp half-moons grew under his armpits.

Before he raised his right hand, he shot a pleading look at his lawyer, who shrugged.

The lieutenant began reading the crime scene report into the record, noting the address and condition of the apartment. He put a diagram into evidence marking where Finn's .38 slug was found in the wall. He confirmed that Marvin Plank's fingerprints had been found on Finn's gun.

"The suspect, Mr. Plank, was found in possession of the service revolver registered to Detective Finn," the lieutenant finished.

"Now, then," began the florid assistant chief. "Tell us, Detective. How did Mr. Plank come to possess your gun?"

Finn stared at them, confused. He'd never even noticed that Plank had reached for his gun after it fell from his hand. And so what if he had? What kind of question was that?

The hearing room was silent. Sweat continued to drip down under Finn's belt. Why was this happening? His first partner, Joe Flaherty, had always told him that success in the police department meant not standing out. You were safe as long as you swam with the school, anonymous in the sea of blue. Just be one of the guys.

Finn's mouth was so dry that he could barely speak. "Should I tell you what happened from the beginning?" he asked.

"That won't be necessary," said the feral-looking inspector. "Just answer the question."

Finn lived by Flaherty's advice. Until Marvin Plank, it had worked just fine. He had never been a cowboy or a hero. He didn't shirk or hang back. He did his part. Just his part. Nothing more. He wanted to work, get paid, eat dinner, get laid. That's the life he had signed up for. He never wanted it to end up like this.

"May I remind you that you are under oath," said the inspector. Finn nodded.

"What was the question?"

"Did you give Marvin Plank your gun?"

His confusion was wiped away, leaving a brittle clarity. There it was. The reason he was here. "Give it to him?"

He remembered the helpless feeling as the gun slipped from his grasp. It hit him again, cauterizing something in his brain. But this time it burnt hotter because he wasn't standing in an empty apartment with the enemy. He was standing among his own.

"Our investigators have heard allegations that you were selling the suspect your gun," said the assistant chief.

"My gun? To Plank?" Finn echoed, almost choking with indignation and fury. He was no longer standing among his own. He felt his breath whistle through him like wind across a desert. He was empty.

"Plank told you I was selling him my gun?" Finn's mouth tasted acrid and he pulled his dry lips tightly over his tongue in a grimace. "You believed him? That's why I'm here?"

The inspector cleared his throat impatiently. "I ask you again, how did Plank get your gun? Remember, you are under oath."

So this is the way it ends, Finn thought. Fourteen years on the job and it all amounts to nothing.

His trust in the department, which had accumulated like barnacles on a ship, exploded into a thousand needle-sharp fragments.

"I dropped my gun. I dropped it as I rushed for cover," said Finn, his voice flat.

"Plank said he fired the gun into the wall to test if it was worth the money he was paying you," said the inspector, watching Finn closely.

"I fired it," Finn said, feeling no emotion. "I drew it when I saw he had a gun, I shot wild, then dove. My hand went up"—he raised his palms to show them—"and then I dropped it."

"Dropped it?"

"It was an accident. I was scared. It fell out of my hand," said Finn, hating the police department and the faceless cogs who pretended to defend what it stood for. "Plank was firing a nine-millimeter at me. I'm not surprised I dropped it. I'm only surprised I didn't shit myself in the process."

The stenographer paused, then resumed typing. Finn wondered if they had a little symbol that represented the word *shit*.

Finn's story seemed to rouse Bruce Hoffman Sr.

"Not the most graceful ending to the story, but he did get out alive," he said, chuckling heartily like Burl Ives.

The inspector and the assistant chief did not appear to enjoy the joke.

"I suppose that concludes this hearing. Gentlemen, do you have any more questions for my client?"

The assistant chief shook his head no. The inspector, narrowing his eyes at Finn, waved his hand.

"This proceeding is at an end."

*　　*　　*

The elevator door was already closing when Johnson stopped it with his foot and forced his body into the car.

"Great news. They passed you. I saw them take the rubber stamp. No suspicion of wrongdoing." Johnson brought his fist into his outstretched hand with a flourish.

Finn looked at him with loathing and said nothing.

"They ruled that you didn't do anything wrong. It's good news. Good news," said Johnson.

"I didn't do anything wrong," said Finn. "I shouldn't have been in there in the first place. You or Clarence Darrow over there should have stopped it. It was an abuse of the working man."

Johnson's eyes were pleading. "We're sorry. The union will make it up to you. But don't you see? You're in the clear."

The elevator door had opened.

"Jesus, Finn, what do you want? You're in the clear."

"I'm gone," Finn said quietly. "Gone."

25

The apartments above the stores along Halsey Street were dark and quiet, as though everyone who lived there double-locked their thick doors and pulled down the shades at sundown. All of the merchants had fortified the storefronts with enough steel to repel an army of marauding Goths. Even the store with a bright yellow sign marked 100 PERCENT HUMAN HAIR was barricaded with a thick metal gate. Dominick wiped the sweat from his neck as Gusano disappeared into the shadowy brick tenement next door.

He had acquired this car, a sporty-looking Hyundai, three blocks from the Cork and Barrel using the usual screwdriver-in-the-steering-column method. But his weak hand slowed him down and he had to jam the screwdriver in three times before he sparked the ignition. It wasn't until he was parked in front of El Fuego that he realized the car's heater was jammed at full throttle. He opened all the windows, but then decided it looked funny on a freezing December night, so he closed all but the driver's side window. Better to roast, he reasoned, than attract attention on a stakeout.

He wouldn't have to put up with inferior, foreign-made cars if he was a cop. Something goes wrong with a cruiser, the cop gets a desk job until it gets fixed. He imagined that reporters like Barbara Walters and Regis Philbin got driven around in limousines. He wondered what kind of car the *Herald* gave to Kate. Probably an I-Roc.

Dominick reached into his jacket pocket and pulled out a can of Genesee Cream Ale. He cracked the top with his good hand, sending a fine spray over the dashboard. He hoped the beer would settle his gut, which had been nagging at him since Big Mike showed him the garbage in the meat trucks. He hoped he hadn't already poisoned himself eating Mike's skirt steaks. He belched and wondered whether infectious waste was making his stomach roil.

So far, being a reporter was fun. And he was good at it. He had been frightened when he saw Gusano leave El Fuego, but following him all the way to the intersection of Halsey and Wilson without being detected made him feel strong, like a superhero using his special powers to help humanity.

It wasn't too hard either, he thought, settling into the seat, his eyes straying from the building Gusano had entered to the fancy stereo system on the dashboard. He pulled a cassette out of his jacket pocket. You could say one thing for the foreign cars, thought Dominick as Frank Sinatra's voice filled the front seat: good tape players.

26

Three times, Finn and Fat Tony circled the block of decrepit brownstones in Bushwick where Margaret Severing was murdered, listening to lookouts and the steerers make their high-pitched whistles to alert the dealers on the stoops. Finn and Tony wanted to make sure the whole neighborhood knew they were detectives before they selected their prey. Tonight it would be a nineteen-year-old steerer named Darcy Farrell, who worked for Anthony Birdsong, an albino drug dealer who ran a drug market out of an abandoned building on Starr Street.

Fat Tony stopped the car.

"Hey, Darcy. We gotta talk," Finn shouted out the car window, beckoning to a skinny young man almost hidden by an enormous shearling coat. At first Darcy tried to ignore them, but Finn continued calling his name, enunciating clearly, doing his very best imitation of a white guy from Nassau County. Trapped, Darcy backed up. He appealed to seven or eight associates who stood around him like marionettes with slackened strings, hoping they might hide him. But they merely elbowed him forward, curious to see what would happen.

Finn began to yodel and even Fat Tony laughed. Usually, Fat Tony acted as the main irritant when they leaned on an informant, but tonight Finn surprised him, taking the lead, transforming himself into

Darcy's worst nightmare. Each day since Severing got killed, Finn seemed more anxious to close out the case.

Finn sucked in, then yodeled again. "Yoo-hoo. Darcy. Yoo-hoo."

Anthony Birdsong stuck his fuzzy white head out of the doorway like a groundhog in March, squinted his pink eyes at the detectives, and darted back inside.

Darcy threw his hat on the ground in disgust and trudged toward the cops. He stopped three feet away from their car.

"What?" he said, giving his friends behind him an anxious look.

"Get in," Fat Tony snarled.

Darcy looked at him with disbelief.

"Whassup? What you want?" he asked.

"I said GET IN!" Fat Tony shouted, and Darcy, making disgusted clicking noises, climbed slowly into the back and sank down low in the seat.

Finn waved to the other steerers as they drove Darcy away.

"How are you, Darcy?" Fat Tony said pleasantly. "You seem to have lost weight since we last talked. I hope you haven't been sick."

Darcy looked angrily out the window. "Fuck you, DTs. Why you gotta give me trouble?"

"Now, don't give us a hard time, Darcy," Finn began, gently scolding him. "We have a problem and we think you might be of some assistance."

Fat Tony nodded broadly, playing along.

"Just cut the shit, Mr. Detective-White-Man-John-You-the-Devil-Finn," said Darcy. But Finn continued to talk to Darcy as if he were a Midwestern cousin at a family reunion.

"A very nice lady got killed near your street several days ago and we need to know who did it," said Finn.

"Don't ask me. I don't know, I was out of town," said Darcy.

"Oh, really?" Fat Tony asked innocently. "What was it this time, Club Med? Or were you skiing in Aspen?" Then he exploded into laughter.

Darcy stuck out his chin. "I was upstate seeing my girlfriend and my son. So I don't know nothing. So why don't you let me out of here?"

Fat Tony feigned a shocked look. "No. No. We wouldn't think of it. You have been so cooperative, we'll bring you back where we found you."

Darcy was suddenly agitated. "Why you want to get me hurt? I didn't do nothing to you."

"Find out who killed Margaret Severing," said Fat Tony, "or your life won't be worth shit."

"Give us the word on the street or you'll be begging us to take you in," Finn said. "You'll be safer on Rikers than in your own neighborhood."

Darcy sat back in his seat and turned up the collar of his coat until he was nearly invisible. Fat Tony pulled the car around and stopped in front of the crowded Starr Street crack house. Darcy was out of the car almost before it stopped.

Finn rolled down the window. "Hey, Darcy," he shouted, "thanks for the help. We really appreciate what you told us."

The words fell on Darcy like bricks, causing him to stagger slightly as he walked to his usual spot. His associates, who had watched him get out of the police car, drew back from him like he had become a contagious disease.

Fat Tony and Finn both waved as they drove away.

27

The morning sun lit up the stained-glass angels in the church windows. Mornings, particularly sunny mornings, were the best time to pray. With a grunt, Gusano genuflected in front of the large cross on the altar, veered to the left, and stood before the impassive statue of the Virgin.

He dropped four quarters into the wrought-iron offering box, secured with a Kryptonite bike lock since the church was robbed last Easter. He felt prosperous and satisfied as the clink of coins echoed solemnly through the pews. Then he stuffed a twenty-dollar bill through the worn slot and began to light the small white candles.

While his grandmother was alive, the Madonna had been her protector. Now that his grandmother was dead, Gusano offered up prayers to the Virgin Mother twice a week so She would look after her soul.

He lit the wicks until the taper burned close to his fingers. With the feet of the Madonna bathed in light, and her cold plaster face warmed by the morning sun, Gusano felt the spirit of God overtake him.

He lowered himself heavily to his knees, rested his lower lip on his crossed thumbs, and began to pray. In less than a minute, his grandmother appeared before him, dressed in the black everyday dress she wore on their small farm outside of Mercuri, her shoulders hunched with age and hard work. She looked at him with her face full of love and his heart was swollen with longing for his Abuelita.

"Take care, little one," she said, caressing his boyish cheek with her creased hand. "God watches over you, but you must pray to the Virgin for His forgiveness."

Then she was gone, and when Gusano opened his eyes, his face was wet with tears.

Other parishioners had come into the church and Gusano could hear the murmur of voices from the confessionals. Crossing himself broadly, he lumbered to the pew directly behind a youngish-looking woman in an expensive fur coat.

Stirred by the memory of his grandmother, he mentally rehearsed the sins he would confess to the priest. There were the usual swearing and coveting, misdemeanors wiped clean with a brace of Hail Marys. He could mention shooting his neighbor, but God already knew that was an accident. Or maybe that young crack dealer, Graveyard Jones, Gusano mused, then rejected the idea. That was business, and besides, Jones was a fool. He had stood, one foot on a skateboard, on Montoya's streetcorners selling bundles of crack he had gotten from that albino dealer, Anthony Birdsong. The boy didn't even know enough about respect to hide when Montoya drove by. Colombians, Gusano had learned, could be very sensitive about these questions of honor.

As he cataloged his transgressions, his gaze fixed on the woman's fur coat. His mind roamed from his sins and he began imagining the woman, naked under her coat except for tiny black panties covering the hair between her legs. He reached out, and softly, so as not to be detected, stroked the back of the woman's coat. It was softer than human hair, made of some sleek, warm-blooded animal. He imagined having sex with a woman who was covered from head to toe with fur like a mink, and shivered, dropping his hand back to his side.

Then an altar boy was nudging him and Gusano walked quickly into the confessional. When the panel slid back, he solemnly confessed to profanity and lust. He felt a weight lift from his chest as the priest absolved him of his sins.

28

"o. You should ha' been there, it was *great,*" Dominick said, leaning over a Teflon frying pan, the telephone clamped between his shoulder and his ear. He was talking fast and loud. "I followed him, yes. Yes. I did. All the way from that bar where he hangs out to Wilson and Halsey Street." The frozen white and pink shingle of contaminated beef sent tendrils of smoke into the air as it cooked.

"No. Go ahead." He sounded disappointed. "I'll hold."

His thoughts drifted to the four days he had worked as a short-order cook for the New Square Diner. He liked the chopping sounds that filled the kitchen and the three gentle busboys who had been raised together in a small town in Ecuador.

Dominick put his hand over the receiver.

"Just a few more minutes, guys. Hang on," Dominick said to the three neighborhood dogs panting hungrily on the kitchen floor.

"Yo, yeah," he spoke back into the telephone. "Wilson and Halsey. An apartment building, brick. What a dump. I'm telling you, I'm probably the first white guy on that block in a year. And I'm tracking a killer. A bad-ass son of a bitch. It's dangerous, but was I scared? Nah. Hey, I'm from the streets, you know. I take care of myself. But anyways, during the stakeout, I was thinking about our next step. I was thinking— Yeah, I'll hold."

He poked again at the meat, then shifted the telephone into his hand, cursing quietly when he heard the dial tone. He was just getting to the good part, explaining to her how they were going to be partners in the story.

He started to call her back, but then replaced the receiver in its cradle. Even though he was calling her almost every hour, it was harder and harder to get Kate on the line. It was time they met, sat down together like real partners.

But first he wanted to get rid of some of this meat. He had worried about it since leaving Big Mike's warehouse. Even when he tried not to think of it, the steaks and roasts, wrapped like cancerous mummies in his freezer, kept pushing their way into the front of Dominick's mind. He thought about the meat when he woke up and he thought about it on the way to the corner store to get some cigarettes and a lottery ticket. He couldn't stop.

Coming back from the store, he realized that he had dreamed about the meat. In his dream, Gravesend had a blackout and all the appliances had gone off. Dominick remembered the part where he walked back from the Cork and Barrel in the pitch dark, feeling his way with his hands because it was too dark to see. When he turned onto his block, he saw Mrs. Rigateli, his next-door neighbor, bloated and lifeless on her step. In his bedroom, his mother lay blue-lipped and stone-cold. In fact, the whole block was dead. The meat had thawed and the infectious-waste germs had begun to reproduce and multiply. They burst out of the freezer compartment and settled in a giant poisonous cloud over the entire neighborhood. Dominick had woken up screaming.

The first steak looked a little rare, Dominick thought as he swung it onto the counter and began cutting it into pieces. Nothing personal, he thought, staring at the dogs without emotion, but he was tired of catching shit for them knocking over the garbage. It was time for them to go.

Even before it cooled, he dangled a chunk in front of the Labrador mutt. The dog snapped at the meat, his pearly eyetooth grazing Dominick's thumb.

Dominick drew his hand back in horror. He was glad the dog would soon be dead. He dropped a few more pieces of meat on the floor and the dogs lunged, snorting and chortling as they ate. He regarded them with satisfaction and they waved their tails lovingly back at him.

After the third steak, the dogs began eating at a more leisurely pace and Dominick decided to teach them some tricks. All three were happy to roll over or offer a paw for the steak, but only the one that looked like a wolf would do any real stunts.

Keeping his head perfectly still, the wolf dog let Dominick place a hunk of steak on his nose. His shiny black eyes never left Dominick's mouth as he waited for Dominick to give the signal. Then the wolf dog would throw the chunk of beef in the air like a furry circus seal, catch it, and gobble it down.

The first time the wolf dog did the trick, Dominick was so happy he threw his arms around the animal's neck and pressed his face into its mangy coat.

Dominick was so engrossed in cooking and dog training that he didn't hear his mother until her key was in the door.

He quickly herded the dogs out the back door.

"Dommy, what have you done?" she trilled. "Have you gone and cooked dinner for your mommy? You've never done that before."

He started to mumble about the meat but averted his head and closed his mouth to avoid being kissed on the lips. She smelled, he noticed, like unwashed flesh and old booze. Something about her odor and the way she tried to kiss him made Dominick angry.

From the time he was a little boy, she had always been touching him. Not in the nice way he had seen mothers on the street touch their kids, smoothing back hair, or pressing a Band-Aid on a knee. No, she always touched him in a way that made him feel powerless and confused. Like a big, dirty baby with a hard-on. The worst was when she was drunk and came home lonely and smelling like wine.

She reached for a paper towel, wiping some meat juices off the floor, looking at him strangely.

"I would have brought home some dessert if I knew we were going to have a romantic dinner together," she cooed. "But tell me, what can I do?"

A few minutes later, Dominick sat, watching his mother's face, her heavy makeup made dramatic by the light of candles she had placed on the dining-room table. She sawed into a thick slab of well-done steak. He was never going to introduce his mother to Kate. By the time he brought Kate home, he would have gotten rid of her for good.

"Why aren't you having any? Aren't you hungry anymore?" she asked, smiling too broadly.

"Nah. I don't want any," he said. "But you go ahead."

She launched into a long story about her bridge game, which Dominick could tell was a lie. He had seen her in McGurtie's Pub when he went to get cigarettes.

Dominick nodded his head slightly as she chewed, willing the steak from her plate to her mouth.

"You want more?" he said, interrupting her. "There's plenty."

"No, not me. I'm stuffed," she answered, but Dominick pretended not to hear and returned from the kitchen with another slab.

"Oh, I might as well. I'll start that diet tomorrow." She laughed and gave her stomach a little slap.

Dominick saw that the ten o'clock news was coming on and he turned up the volume. He wondered how long before the infectious diseases took over. He wondered if she would die quickly enough so he could take fifteen dollars from her wallet and get to the Cork and Barrel before last call.

As his mother prattled on, the news anchorwoman, who had a wall-eye and a pile of blond hair, began talking about children with AIDS. Near the end of the segment, which showed a timid, pale child walking into an elementary school in Queens, the anchorwoman mentioned that people who were infected sometimes didn't know it for years.

Dominick couldn't believe his ears. He couldn't wait years. Maybe Kate would want to come back home with him right away. He wanted his mother dead now.

"Dominick, what's the matter, honey?"

"Years," he mumbled.

"What is it, darling? What fears? Tell Mama."

"Never mind," Dominick said firmly, returning to the table.

"You always were a nervous child," she said in a confidential tone. "It's not surprising you turned out to be a nervous adult. I like to think of you as special."

"Special," he said dully.

After dinner he settled into the couch in front of the television with a bottle of cheap Scotch, occasionally wandering out to the kitchen to watch mournfully while his mother energetically scrubbed the dishes.

He woke up in his mother's bed, his head pounding from the Scotch. He raised himself on one arm. She was beside him, sleeping soundly with her eyes sunk back in the shadowy and wrinkled parchment that filled her sockets. Her mouth turned downward like an old man's without false teeth. The top of her breasts had rivulets of white stretch marks and blue-green veins.

A scratching noise made him bound out of bed. He heard it again. He pulled on his underwear and headed for the kitchen. For a few seconds, he imagined that the infectious germs were scratching on the refrigerator door to get out, and he felt a rising panic.

Then he realized the sound was coming from the back door. He opened it just a crack. The door flew open wide, almost knocking him down, as the three frisky dogs leaped in circles around the kitchen.

29

Three suspects in a string of house burglaries, all of them female and none over fourteen years old, sat on the hard bench in the precinct, slowly turning up the volume on their large portable radio.

Every time the musical refrain hit the part where the blaring horns give way to a booming heartbeat percussion and the sound of a scratching record, Finn felt his temples throb.

"Turn that fucking thing off!" screamed Fat Tony. The girls, each of whom wore her hair teased in a conical pile, leaned together and giggled.

Fat Tony swiveled around in his chair and gave them a death-ray stare. The tallest girl reached over and turned the volume low enough so the irregular squawks of the frequency scanner, monitoring radio runs in the precinct, became audible again. The other seven detectives paused briefly to appreciate the silence and then resumed their conversations.

It was a busy night. Three people had been shot in a drive-by outside a nightclub, a woman was stabbed to death in her home, and another was beaten with a tire iron near Hollywood Fried Chicken, three blocks from the station house.

Troutmouth was driving over from Division headquarters to check on the Severing case, so Finn and Fat Tony were busy filling out all the right investigation forms.

"What is an R-46? I don't think I ever filled out an R-46 before," Finn said, scrawling information onto the blank form. "Are you sure this one is for real?"

"I filled one out, back when that investment banker got whacked in the Nineteenth Precinct," said Fat Tony, gumming his cigar. He shifted the pen, which looked like a toy in his hand. "It took me four hours to fill it out in triplicate, but the case went sour. The papers knew too much. They make a big deal about us picking up the wrong guy. And when we finally nailed the guy who clipped the banker, the mutt tells reporters he was home with his mom the night the banker ate lead. And they ran his feeble alibi on the front page. If I had my way, these dirtbags would be tried in secret. Keep the reporters from making too much out of a homicide." He sighed heavily. "Instead, we got the First Amendment, and Margaret Severing has become Bushwick's Mother Teresa."

Three hours earlier, Bart Genovese had been shot in the face with a BB gun fired from a moving van. When an officer is shot, police procedure requires that the next of kin, usually a man's wife or mother, be picked up in a marked car and rushed to the hospital or the precinct. Immediately after the shooting, Garvey, not knowing Genovese's injury was only minor, dispatched an officer to bring in his wife.

Unfortunately, Genovese's partner called the other wife.

Now Genovese was being treated for a puncture wound at Woodhull and was about to be released, and his two wives, one busty with rough features and the other fine-boned but overweight, were sitting together in one of the precinct interrogation rooms.

Finn picked up the telephone. It was Darcy Farrell, the steerer from Jefferson Street, calling from the emergency room of Kings County Hospital.

"Fuck you, you cocksucking DTs, you got me shot," Darcy shouted at him through the phone. Finn could hear ambulance sirens and a woman screaming in the background. He nodded to Fat Tony, who leaned back, cocked his cigar toward the ceiling, and exhaled triumphantly.

"You're not dead yet, are you? What did you find out about the homicide?"

"I might as well be dead. I got shot right in the but-tocks." He said it in two distinct syllables, like it was a word he had just learned. "And you motherfuckers are responsible."

"Too bad you didn't get shot in the mouth—the world would be a cleaner place."

Darcy was silent.

"So?" prompted Finn. "Do we need to pay you another visit?"

"I heard that it was Spanish that did it," said Darcy. "Somebody's muscle man. Big guy. Strong. Not from around here."

Finn felt triumphant and bitter at the same time. Finally, they were getting closer to clearing the case. "Who hired him?" he asked. "Why the nurse? Something to do with her boyfriend?"

"I don't know and I don't want to know. Now, you two leave me alone." Then Darcy hung up.

Finn heard a small shout and looked up from his stack of blank forms. Joe Flaherty, Finn's first partner, now retired, walked through the door.

The detectives rose, gave him warm handshakes, and slapped him on the back.

Finn was surprised to see how worn and tired he looked.

"Joe, how're you doing? How's Mary and little Joe?" said Finn, pressing both hands on Flaherty's bony shoulders.

For five years, Flaherty had taught Finn everything he knew about police work, from identifying crack salesmen to extracting full confessions without the use of the Brooklyn Yellow Pages. They were the closest of friends, and right after Finn's divorce, it was Flaherty, solid and strong, who'd helped him through.

"My house is painted, my lawn is mowed, I play golf every day, so my handicap is improving," said Flaherty. "What more can a man ask for?" Even his voice sounded worn out.

Finn nodded and smiled, holding up a single finger as Fat Tony handed him a telephone.

He watched Flaherty's back and wondered how long he had been sick. Then realized with a flush of guilt that he hadn't talked to his old teacher and friend in over a year.

"Hello," he said into the receiver.

"Is Detective Finn there, please?" said the husky woman's voice.

"Who's calling?" he asked, as he always did, but he already knew.

He felt his face turn red and he moved his mouth closer to the phone. Fat Tony suddenly squinted at Finn and pointed to the newspaper on his desk. Finn nodded and Fat Tony drew a line across his neck with his finger.

"Kate Murray."

"This is Finn."

"I thought I recognized your voice," she said pleasantly.

"Yeah, I recognized yours, too." He stared at the desk, trying to duck Fat Tony's glare. Flaherty was standing near his desk, shifting his weight from one foot to the other.

"Listen, if you're not too busy, I'd like to ask you something about the Severing homicide," she said.

Finn motioned for Flaherty to take his seat, the seat he had occupied during his fifteen years at the precinct, but Flaherty only smiled. Finn stretched the phone cord away from the desk.

His eyes followed Genovese's fat wife as she walked unsteadily to the ladies' room, a small handkerchief pressed to her mouth. Finn noticed that she had thin ankles and well-sculpted legs.

"Uh, no problem. Just let me . . . " He motioned to Fat Tony to get Flaherty a cup of coffee. But Flaherty shook his head and his smile began to look strained.

"What's on your mind?" he said, trying to keep his voice neutral.

"I was wondering if you're looking at a big Spanish guy named Gusano on the Severing homicide."

"Well, that depends," he said slowly.

"On what?" she asked.

He didn't want to let the conversation die.

"That description has come up," he said, aware that he'd just told a reporter before he'd even told his partner what Darcy Farrell had said.

"It has?" she said brightly. "That's amazing."

"I've been trying to reach you," he blurted out.

"You have?"

"Yes, I . . . wanted to ask you a few things."

"A few things?" she said doubtfully.

"In person."

"In person," she repeated.

But he was rushing now, not wanting her to talk back. "So why don't I meet you after work?" He gave her the name of a renovated coffee shop in Brooklyn Heights.

He hung up, smiling to himself. Then he remembered where he was. The place where Flaherty had been standing was empty and Fat

Tony was sitting at his desk, his elbow on the stack of blank forms, his fat thumb on his brow shielding his eyes.

"Don't give me that look," he said to Fat Tony. "You take prostitutes from the holding cell out for dates. Don't you give me shit for trying to date a reporter."

Fat Tony didn't look up.

"Don't pretend to play dumb on me," said Finn again. "I saw you out with Red Bomb last month at the Linwood Diner."

Still no reaction.

"And I'm sure you've done a lot worse than her," Finn continued to bait him.

Fat Tony began shaking his head.

Finn heard a sniff and a slight gasp. He whirled around to face Captain Mark Troutman.

30

Kate dressed carefully for dinner, selecting a conservative white silk blouse from Lord & Taylor and a skirt that fit her like a second skin. She hung the outfit on the doorknob and walked into the shower. Sheets of water ran down her neck, chest, and thighs, loosening her soles from the slick tub bottom. She closed her eyes and remembered leaping around under a shower at summer camp, her young legs thin and springy. She bent her knees a little and lifted her weight to her toes, realizing she felt the same way as she did that summer. Except older. It was funny, being thin again. It was as if part of her old fat person's body was stowed away with last season's clothes. She didn't miss it, she just wondered where it all went.

She reached down and turned off the faucet, peering from the steaming shower like she was bushwacking through a primordial jungle.

Wrapped like a sultan, she stood in front of the small, steamed mirror.

She shook some lotion from a pink bottle and moved her palms in circles over her face. Her fingers paused around her large brown eyes, pulling the skin gently upward. Then she patted the soft spot under her chin.

She studied her face seriously. Good cheekbones. Thanks, Mom. Quick smile. Thanks, Dad. Most women looked better at thirty-one, she thought. A few looked worse. Most, she thought critically, had better haircuts and a more convincing makeup technique.

These are not looks that make men lose their senses, Kate said to herself. But, in truth, she came a lot closer these days than she had before. One year ago, in a loud, bright, crowded restaurant called Lox Around the Clock, James had leaned over a small Japanese couple and shouted in her ear that he couldn't live without her. Which was, in retrospect, a lie. But at the time, she didn't know it, and her heart had literally stood still.

She lowered her lashes, turned her shoulder to her chin, and gave herself a smoldering stare, tossing a damp towel over her shoulder like a feather boa. She stared at her reflection, letting memories of James run through her mind, to see if the seams where her heart was supposed to be mending would hold. Then she drew herself up with a little shrug and relaxed.

Letting the damp towels drop in a heap, she ran lipstick over her lower lip and dabbed it on the top one. She lifted her brows and pulled her upper lip toward her chin as she applied mascara. Then she padded to her dresser, selected panties, pulled out a bra, then another, then another, until she found one made of wire and fine-looking white lace. She pulled on the blouse and put on her favorite set of earrings.

She stopped and looked at herself in the mirror with amazement. She realized she was dressing for a date.

*   *   *

Kate's hands were icy cold and shaking slightly. Not even a loud sing-along with Patsy Cline in the car had calmed her down. And the idea that she should be jittery about eating dinner with a detective was making her crabby. She pressed one hand on the Formica table and flipped through her notebook, idly tracing Dominick Donatti's name over and over with a bright red pen. She wished she had a tape recorder so she could fidget with it. She looked around. It was one of those expensive restaurants that was made to look like a diner. It was mostly lit with neon, which gave the patrons a slightly embalmed hue.

Her jaws were starting to hurt from mechanically chomping on a fossilized piece of gum she had found in her glove compartment, but there was nowhere to throw it out.

She was debating whether to sneak it out of her mouth and stick it on the underside of the table when John Finn walked in. He looked slightly pink from the large red neon sign by the door. His square jaw and Sy Syms suit made him stand out in the sea of Armani-clad men.

She watched as he surveyed the room full of bankers and invest-ment sharks with a hard, dead-eyed expression. Let's play Pick the Detective, she thought to herself coolly, deciding at that moment that the evening would be strictly professional.

When he saw Kate, something alive and young pushed the blank expression aside.

Kate gave him a measured smile and watched the taut men in dark suits and suspenders draw away from Finn slightly as he pushed past them.

He had just about reached the table when the wad of gum in her mouth jumped to the back of her throat and settled in her windpipe.

Finn's smile faded as Kate, eyes streaming, made a small stran-gling noise and brushed past him quickly.

A few minutes later, Kate reappeared, hand at her throat, her eyes bright and her face burning.

"My gum," she said, her voice still slightly raspy. "I swallowed it."

While she was gone, he had been studying the doodles in her notebook. He looked up at her, startled, then searching, like a doctor making a difficult diagnosis.

"You're okay now?" he asked. "Would you like some water?"

Kate shook her head, sat down quickly, and tried to smile.

The waitress, who was all hair and cleavage, bent from the waist to offer them menus. Ignoring the show, Finn's eyes met Kate's over the waitress's head. "Are you sure you're okay?"

She nodded and tried to compose herself.

"So what's going on with the Severing homicide?" she asked. She reached into her black Coach bag for another pen so she could take notes.

Finn looked disoriented, as if he had asked her a question in one language and she'd answered in another.

"You know it takes five years," he said, pouring her a full glass of wine from a carafe he had ordered while she was gone.

"What?"

"To digest gum. I mean five years for it to leave your system."

Kate smiled uncertainly. Finn noticed she was wearing large diamond solitaires in each ear. She didn't wear those in Bushwick.

"So what is it that you wanted to tell me?" asked Kate, struggling to regain control. "About Margaret Severing."

"Is this on or off the record?" he asked, trying to make a joke. They both knew a detective could get fired for talking to a reporter.

"We can set the terms as we go," said Kate.

"We'll have a new mayor and you'll still have that gum somewhere in your intestines," he said.

Kate sighed. "I think that's just something schoolchildren say to each other, I don't think it's true."

They ordered chicken sandwiches, which, Finn noticed, cost thirteen dollars each.

"What about the Severing homicide?" she asked again.

"Kids know the truth about these things. Like wishing on sneakers," he said. "Make the wish, throw them up in the air, and if they catch on the wires on the first try, your wish will come true,"

"Is that why all the electric wires in Brooklyn have Nikes hanging off them? I could never figure that out," Kate said. She left pink moons of lipstick on the wineglass as she lowered it to the table.

"Every time I see them I think of my mother screaming, 'What the hell did you do with your shoes?' or I think of a little boy on a street corner, his eyes scrunched tight with wishing, throwing his sneakers up to the sky," Finn said. Then he added seriously, "It makes me think of God."

Kate briefly raised a skeptical eyebrow. She waited.

"I read the story you wrote this morning and I saw you on television last night," he said after a moment.

"On the Upper East Side. Yeah, I was there."

"I knew it was you because you did this." Finn wound his arms around his hips. "Like that. A nervous habit?"

Kate couldn't figure out how this interview was careening so quickly out of control.

"Umm, Detective, I agreed to meet you to talk about the Severing homicide," Kate began, but it sounded feeble even to her. Finn could hear the brush-off and it stung him.

"Oh, really . . . " His eyes moved over her earrings again and took in her makeup and her blouse still crisp from the cleaner's.

"I mean you did tell me that. . . . "

"Right. And that's why you came. All business. Sure. Sure," he said. He was smiling, but nothing was happy about his face.

"Of course, what did you think I—" But he didn't let her finish.

"What did I think? I think you know what I think. Don't you?" His voice was light, but there was a catch to it.

Kate didn't know which way to nod her head, so she kept it still.

She started to reply but Finn interrupted her. "I mean, what is it? Don't give me that married line again. I don't believe it. Boyfriend?" He was straining to keep his voice playful.

Kate shook her head.

"What, then?"

She could see something working to the surface of his face. She tried to smile at him, but he was looking around as if he had just arrived in this restaurant from Mars. "Maybe you don't like me because I'm not like him?" Finn angled back his head to indicate a man with a small ponytail standing at the bar. "Not a pretty boy?"

He gave a little laugh, but even under the neon lights, Kate could see his eyes were dark with hurt.

"You don't have to—" But Finn continued.

"Not as pretty as him?" He stared at another man, who frowned and moved off.

Finn tipped back in his seat, catching the eye of another man with New York Athletic Club muscle tone and a Bermuda tan. He turned back to Kate. "I don't get a chance because I don't make enough money?" He wasn't smiling anymore.

The waitress had reappeared with the sandwiches, but sensing the tension of the moment, stood by the table to see what would happen.

But Finn didn't even notice. He sat forward again so the front legs of the chair connected with the floor. "Don't work on Wall Street." Something in his voice implied that a job in the Financial District might involve smearing feces on walls. "Maybe you don't want to date a cop. You want someone who fits into your life better," he said. "An architect? A lawyer? Maybe someone who trades bonds?"

Kate started to interrupt, but Finn leaned across the table, his voice dropping to a leathery whisper.

"Baby, what do you want with someone who trades bonds?"

31

They left the restaurant together. Their shoulders were touching and they were stepping lightly, like they were dancing, instead of simply walking to the promenade. Across the Hudson River, lower Manhattan looked too large and too electric, like a garish department store window ready for the Christmas season. Clouds of white breath dissolved into the damp cold night.

"... So I'm sitting in class after doing a midnight-to-eight shift and my professor is telling me with a straight face that most men who commit homicides weren't breast-fed as infants. And the guy sitting in the front row—you know the type, tortoiseshell glasses and a turtleneck—is writing it all down and nodding."

It occurred to him that Kate would be friends with that guy, and he flushed, but she didn't notice.

"*Folie à deux,*" she said, half-sardonic, then she looked at his puzzled expression. "Two fools. I guess it wasn't easy, working and going to school."

Finn dug deep into his altar boy training, reciting a few lines of perfect-sounding Latin with a flourish.

"*A deum que laetificat juventutem meum.*"

Now she looked puzzled. "It means 'I can bear any labor for the attentions of a beautiful woman,' " he said, and Kate laughed, surprised.

Finn laughed, too, thinking that this was probably the first time in history anyone had used the opening invocation from a Mass to pick up a girl. He steered her toward a park bench and they both sat down.

"But you like what you do, right?" Kate asked. "I mean, you're the hero cop and all."

Finn felt himself blush as he remembered Kate standing among the reporters at the press conference.

"I used to like it. But lately, I think I'm about getting ready to try something new. Maybe even leave the department."

"After making a bust with twenty kilos of cocaine?" She let a beat pass. "I thought you'd be on top of the world."

"Well, the fun has been out of it for a while."

Kate waited for him to say more but he turned back to her. "What about you?"

"Well, two weeks ago I was so nervous I'd be killed by a homicide victim's twin brother that I threw up in somebody's kitchen. Then a cop gave me a bad tip and I ended up missing the story, not by an inch, but by a mile. Which caused me to come very close to losing my job. So, trying to redeem myself, I go crazy on the Margaret Severing story. And I end up meeting a very sweet and very intense detective and Severing's boyfriend, who smokes crack during an interview. And while all this is happening, a guy, Dominick Donatti, keeps calling me, claiming he saw a Spanish guy kill Margaret Severing. So I go to meet him and he's nothing but a garden-variety nut with a broken finger. You know the type: His microwave oven is telling him what to do."

She told him about watching Dominick get forcibly ejected from the Captain's Table.

"Maybe he knows something. Maybe I should talk to him."

"He says the shooter's first name is Gusano, like worm in Spanish. That's why I called you. I don't think he ever mentioned his last name. If my Loon of the Week calls again, I'll get a last name for you. But honestly, I don't think Dominick can come down from Pluto long enough to help you out. Anyway, last week he kept calling me and calling me, so I finally told him to go track Gusano himself."

"That's cold, very cold," said Finn, smiling.

"True, but I had to tell him something. I'm not a social worker. I got to get things done. Anyway, the poor bastard calls me this morning and says he tracked Gusano all over Brooklyn. He says he spent half the night at the corner of Halsey and Wilson waiting for him to come out of a building. He said he was the first white guy on the corner in over a year.'' She shook her head. ''Man, what a nut.''

Finn let a moment pass.

''How did you ever end up covering crime?'' he asked.

''You mean what's a nice girl like me doing in a—''

''I mean what do your parents think?'' Finn asked.

''My mother probably tells her friends, that small but bitter band of surgically reconstructed doctors' wives and divorcées, that I write a gardening column,'' she said.

''What about your father? I wouldn't let my daughter do her interviews in housing projects,'' said Finn, hating himself for sounding like Fat Tony, but meaning it just the same.

''My father is dead,'' she said.

Far off, through the noise of the BQE, a dog began to bark.

''But you like it?'' asked Finn.

She looked at him for a long moment. ''Like it? I worked as a copy girl, researcher, and ghostwriter for a society column to get here. I worked the lobster shift. I fetched coffee for drunken civics columnists. I gave up trying to have a love life so I could work longer hours. I told myself that a career at the *Herald* was worth any sacrifice as long as I eventually got to hard news.'' Finn saw her jaw stiffen. ''Now I'm on the verge of getting fired from the only job I ever wanted.''

''There are other jobs . . . '' Finn said, aware that Kate's voice had become tremulous.

''Not jobs where I will be taken seriously. Big-boy jobs. Reporting jobs where I can break news. I mean, when was the last time a society columnist got a Pulitzer?''

She looked out over the river, unwilling to go on.

''So why is the hero cop leaving the department?'' she asked, steering the conversation back to Finn.

He was caught unaware for a second and wished she had never attended the cocaine press conference.

''Well, I joined the department at twenty-one, and fourteen years have gone by without me wondering once what I'm doing.'' He was watching her closely, barely breathing. ''These last few weeks, I had some trouble with the department.'' He gestured. ''Things happened, things that made me realize that I'm thirty-five years old, and suddenly I'm scared about how my life is turning out.''

She didn't laugh. She didn't even smile. Finn turned away quickly, afraid that he might cry for the first time since his mother died. He decided to change the subject before she could press for details.

"You like working around cops?" he asked. "They always give reporters a hard time. And with women . . . Forget about it.''

"Only when they go out of their way to be cruel," she said, then told him about Tierney betting she'd get the story wrong.

"Cops can be humps," Finn said when she finished her story.

Kate raised an eyebrow.

"Discouraging words about the department from a hero cop?''

Finn was dismayed to find that she was talking about the cocaine bust again. "Look it, will you stop with that hero cops stuff? It was a phony press conference. A bullshit story. I got set up. I'm no hero.''

"What do you mean?" she said slowly.

"I don't want to talk about it," Finn fumbled.

"Tell me what happened," she said.

Finn said nothing.

"Give it up.''

"Put it this way, there was no confidential informant." He was swimming against years of conditioning, telling cop secrets to outsiders. But he pressed on. "A hooker was watching the cocaine. Edwards went to visit the hooker.''

Kate exhaled in a little whistle.

"Does anyone else know?" she asked. "Because if this comes out, I'm fired for sure.''

"Edwards. Fat Tony. Me. Probably one of the bosses has figured it out, but since the ADA validated the arrest, they don't care.''

Kate was silent for a moment.

"I can't believe you would deceive me," she said, anger flashing through her voice.

Finn held up his palm. "Hey, it wasn't a personal thing. I didn't want to be there. I certainly didn't want you to be there.''

She looked at him. "Well, from now on, you got to be straight. Don't lie.''

"Okay. No lies. So tell me, why did you say you were married?" Finn asked.

Snared, Kate twisted the ring on her finger.

"I almost was married," she said. "Or maybe that was part of the deception." She paused. Finn waited. "We were living together. He gave me a ring. Then he said he needed more space, so he moved out." Kate felt more melancholy than she had in a long while. "That was three months ago. Last weekend, he married someone else."

"So why do you still wear it?" he asked.

"I guess I was hoping he would come back," she said. "But now I wear it for protection. And just to remind myself that love"—she took a deep breath—"and marriage are possible."

They were both quiet for a minute. Finn measured the invitation in her voice. A tugboat far out on the river let off a long hollow sound.

"When he moved out, did you find someone else, too?" Finn asked, wondering if he was asking too many questions.

"Nope." She raised her chin and looked out over the water.

Finn smiled and leaned into her. He breathed the scent of her light, flowery perfume and the sweet smell of her skin. She turned her face toward his.

"One thing, John. Don't pretend. Don't tell me things are one way if they're not," she said. Her fingertips brushed below her throat. "It hurts me here."

"Hmmm," he mumbled.

As soon as his lips were on hers, she felt longing struggle with reason, like a cat in a sack.

Finn's tongue was against her teeth. He slipped one hand from her thigh to her right breast. Then he dampened one finger inside her lips and traced the outline of her chin while his other hand moved over the length of her body. As she touched the bristly nape of his neck, he pressed into her as if he were a drowning man and she was the only thing that could save him.

Kate heard his breath coming hard now and she felt desire run down her body like rain on a window.

She opened one eye and looked down the long promenade. She imagined Finn, pants around his ankles, plunging into her as the dog walkers of Brooklyn Heights strolled by.

"Let's go," she said. "Hotel room."

"No, my apartment."

By lamplight, Finn looked disheveled and his lips were red. He kissed her again. Hips pressed together and clothing in disarray, they walked to her car. When they rounded the corner to Henry Street, they noticed flashing yellow lights.

"My God, that's my car," Kate said as the tow truck pulled by with her black Tercel.

Finn checked his zipper, placed his hand under his arm to steady his revolver, and began to jog after the truck, waving and shouting. The driver would have to stop at the end of the block, Finn thought.

He reached into his pocket and flipped open the black leather fold that held his shield and waved it as he ran. Instead of slowing down, the driver picked up speed and blew through a yellow light.

Finn began to sprint, his feet slipping on the damp stones, his breath growing ragged. He edged closer, shouting and pounding on the rear tire well. His chest was bursting from the strain and he knew he couldn't keep up the pace much longer.

The driver adjusted his rearview mirror for a full look at Finn, then pushed the truck into third and strained the engine into fourth. The wheels spun, spitting a fine coat of grit that covered Finn from shoulder to knee.

Under the Victorian streetlight at Pierrepont, Finn slowed and then stopped, heaving and sagging with his hands on his knees. He could hear Kate's heels clicking as she ran to catch up with him, but he watched the tow truck until it was lost in the flow of traffic along Clinton Street. Then he looked down. His white shirt, jacket, and trousers were filthy.

"Ah, fuck it," he said. "Fuck it."

Finn drove Kate the full width of the borough and combed through two muddy car lots before they found her black Tercel in the Bedford-Stuyvesant car pound.

By the time she paid the fee and her outstanding parking tickets, the faint black smudges under Kate's eyes had grown darker and her smile had begun to look tight. He kissed her tamely as the lanky Department of Transportation security guard shone his flashlight on them and said good night.

32

o, when do we get to eat? I want my baloney sandwich. How come we haven't seen the AY-DEE-YEH yet?'' complained Marcus Ralphson, the larger of the two prisoners Finn was guarding.

Finn shifted in the hard plastic chair, resting his elbows on his knees, and tried to tune out their incessant whining. Although the waiting room at Centre Street was bleak and chilly, Finn was feeling warmer than he had in weeks. It was as if he had received an infusion of hopefulness. He smiled inwardly, remembering Kate's look of incredulous confusion at dinner two nights ago, like a baseball fan in the cheap seats with a pop fly heading her way.

Some things have changed, he thought. He had never pressed a woman for a date. He waited for them to come to him. His ex-wife used to call him the quiet type.

"The law says you got forty-eight hours to arraign us or we go free, so you'd better hurry your white asses," Marcus said.

Finn looked at the two men. Between them, they probably had been to Central Booking as many times as Finn. Before ADA Priscilla White bustled away, she had shown him their rap sheets. Both had arrest records spanning more than eight pages.

Ralphson, the meaner of the two, had been arrested for sodomy and assault when he was fourteen and by twenty-six had been arrested for a breathtaking array of crimes, ranging from grand larceny to attempted murder.

He had a gleaming psychopathic look to him that made Finn wish Aviles, the arresting officer, had rear-cuffed his hands rather than pinning them in front.

The second prisoner, Paul LeShawn, a thrice-convicted robber, apparently met Ralphson a few hours before they decided to stick up a bodega. A worn crack addict, LeShawn's career as a cat burglar was hindered by a badly mangled leg, which gave him an awkward limp. His wrists were so thin that the steel handcuffs hung off him like bracelets.

Finn started at the sound of a chair scraping across the dirty floor. The two men were sitting together whispering.

"Yo, Mr. Officer, sir," said Marcus Ralphson. "It is about time for me to get out of here."

Finn looked at him and realized for the first time how solidly Ralphson was built. His upper arm was about the size of Finn's thigh.

It was only when Marcus Ralphson stood up that Finn saw how much his face resembled Marvin Plank's.

With his lips pressed into a thin line, Finn motioned for him to be seated. Ralphson lowered himself into his seat, but Finn saw that he was still tightly coiled.

"This Central Booking stuff is just bullshit," said Marcus, his voice dropping to a mean hiss. "And we're not going to take it."

LeShawn piped up on cue. "Yeh, we ain't gonna take it."

Finn was having trouble breathing. He felt his scalp contract like a tight hood. He recognized it as panic. He realized nobody had walked by the small gray room in over an hour.

"We could get you if we wanted," said Ralphson, bragging to LeShawn, who nodded enthusiastically.

Finn felt Marvin Plank's hand touch his chest. He remembered his eyes. They looked just like Marcus Ralphson's. He felt a fear so great that it was like a physical repulsion, pushing him away from the prisoners.

"Front cuffs? Shit." Marcus Ralphson stood up again and theatrically extended his beefy arms. "I could throw my arms over your head like this. I'll get LeShawn to help me. Then I'll grab your gun and shoot you with it."

LeShawn giggled nervously.

"We could do it together, we could," said Ralphson, peering at LeShawn. "There's two of us and one of you."

LeShawn nodded enthusiastically and rose to his feet, still bent at the middle, like a rag doll. "We could fuck him up," he said and giggled again.

Finn felt the cold floor of the abandoned Bushwick apartment. He heard children playing and he heard a low drone that became louder. It was a prayer. He touched his lips, but they were not moving. And the sounds disappeared.

"Sit down," Finn said evenly, grateful his voice didn't waver. "And shut up."

Both men sat coiled on the edge of their seats.

Finn felt sweat beading in the small of his back. He knew he should draw his gun, but he thought of the ferret-faced inspector at the Firearms Review Board and his hand dropped back to his side.

"At the count of five, we're going to get you, both of us together," said Ralphson, taunting him. He started counting. "One, two . . ."

Finn was sure no one would hear if he called for help. If he took out his gun in such a confined area, there was a fair chance, working together, the two men could take it off him. If he shot and missed, he would be standing in front of the review board before he could call the precinct and be out of a job in less than twenty-four hours. If he shot and hit one of them, not even the union could save him. The brass would feed him to the newspapers, who would have a field day, reporting that a detective shot a handcuffed man to death. He felt the hairs on the top of his arms vibrating. And what if he dropped the gun in the struggle? Then one of them would grab it. Then they would shoot him with it. He wondered if anyone would hear the shot.

"Five!" shouted Ralphson, with the exaggerated enthusiasm of a high-school quarterback taking a snap from the center.

LeShawn leaped up looking excited and confused, but Ralphson merely jerked forward before settling back into his chair, laughing.

"Maybe we let you live five more seconds," said Ralphson casually, and he began counting to five again. "Ready? One, two . . ."

Finn stood up and forced himself to walk toward the two prisoners. He was sweating and his movements were slow and thick. He felt like Diver Dan scouting out the ocean bottom.

He reached out and grabbed LeShawn's cuffed hands.

"Whattaya? Whattaya? What are you going to do? What are you going to do?" chattered LeShawn.

"I'm going to let you go," Finn said, looking straight into Le-Shawn's twitching face. "I'm going to loosen your cuffs so you can slip them off. Then I'm going to let you escape out that window. It's three or four floors, but there's a ledge and a landing. You have a damn good chance of making it."

He began to fish for the cuff key, then he turned to Ralphson.

"But as soon as he's out the window, I'm going to push you out after him and say you fell trying to follow LeShawn's escape."

For a second, Marcus Ralphson seemed to retreat somewhere inside himself. LeShawn looked confused, then surprised, and was giggling as he proffered his cuffed hands.

"Paul LeShawn, SIT DOWN!" roared Ralphson. "Sit down or so help me God, you'll be a dead man before the day is over."

LeShawn, who had long ago surrendered his will to addiction, was flexing an atrophied part of his brain.

"Let's go, LeShawn. Four stories isn't that much. The ledge is wide enough for you to walk on, even with a limp," said Finn, bringing out the key so LeShawn could see it.

"You take one step toward that window," shouted Ralphson, jumping from his chair, "you never walk again as long as you live. Promise."

LeShawn's face was a swirl as he glanced first at Finn and then at Ralphson. He looked as if he might explode.

Suddenly, the door swung open and ADA Priscilla White walked in, trailed by a glum corrections officer. LeShawn immediately dropped his wrists and Ralphson took a step back.

She looked surprised that the three men were standing, but didn't break her stride. She whipped out a clean manila folder as the four men tried to make room for each other in the small room. "We'll get statements and ship these two out to Rikers," she said. "Then we can all go home."

33

The police have been harassing me for two years," wailed the man with the thick Russian accent. "I can't take it anymore. You HEAR? NO MORE!"

Kate pulled her ear away from the receiver and continued to write a police brief on the arrest of an arsonist who was in love with a topless dancer. First he followed her home. Then he wrote her real name on a building across from the Doll House Lounge, where she worked. Then he set the Doll House Lounge on fire.

"You're my only hope. You have to help me. Please. Please."

Kate wrote. *A Bronx man was arrested in his home and charged with arson for allegedly setting fire—* "Nah, too stiff." She paused and listened to the man's crazy tirade. Then she interrupted. "I'm sorry, there is nothing I can do for you, and I really do have to go," she said.

There was silence on the end of the phone, then a voice echoed over the line: "Then FUCK YOU!"

Kate hung up and began the arson story again, distracted by the loud boastful tones around her. Wilson was standing in her section of the newsroom and Grant had risen from his chair to talk to him.

"I love her," Steve Reardon, 48, told the detectives
who arrested him in the Bronx apartment he shares with

his elderly mother. "I think, given the chance, she would
learn to love me too."

She pressed the "save" key on her word processor.

"My sources tell me that the detectives handling the Severing
homicide are close to an arrest," Rob Grant was boasting to Wilson.
"I was out last night with some police brass who said an arrest was
expected this morning, this afternoon at the latest."

Kate felt an electric jolt, then fear. She recovered, thinking
quickly.

Grant had to be lying. He may have been drinking with police
brass, but she had come damn close to having sex with the lead investigator on the case. If they were preparing for an arrest this morning, she would have known about it.

"You heard anything about this?" asked Wilson, turning to her,
hostile. Grant's lips curled upward in a smug, satisfied grin. "There
are a lot of reporters on this story. I'd hate to lose our edge."

Finn had kissed her at the car pound. He said he was going home,
not back to the precinct.

Kate eyed Grant and turned to face Wilson. "Last time I checked
was about two-thirty this morning, and they weren't even talking
about a short list of suspects. The police brass may be telling that tall
tale to Grant, but my sources are actually working on the case. And
they tell me they aren't ready to make an arrest."

Grant's head flew back as if she had slapped him. Wilson looked
at them both carefully and walked away without saying a word.

Avoiding Grant's death stare, Kate picked up her ringing telephone.

It was the Sailor, perennial front-runner for Loon of the Week.

"I saw what ya wrote, ya communist," he began for openers.
Kate called him the Sailor because he once mentioned, between in-
sults, that he was a merchant marine. He also talked like Popeye would
if Popeye was a mean, angry drunk.

"You're all the same, you leftie commie bleeding hearts," he
rasped. "Maybe if you got raped, you wouldn't stand up for the vermin that run through the streets."

"I might have known it would be you," Kate said, resigned to
bantering with the Sailor for a few minutes before filing her story.

Over many months, she had learned that if she didn't talk to him, he would call her repeatedly, tying up her line all night. ''What is it, a full moon already?''

''Don't give me any of your guff, you yellow-bellied cock-sucker.'' Kate could tell he was warming up for a long harangue.

''Listen, Pops, don't you have anyone to talk to? Don't you have someone else to call? A member of your family or a friend?''

''No,'' said the Sailor, meekly. ''I left my family when I left Ireland. And I never made any friends here t'all.''

A silence dawned over the line.

''I'm sorry,'' Kate said, amazed and genuinely sorry for him.

''Ah, never mind,'' he said, and hung up.

Just then, a clerk ran up to her desk. ''Radio,'' he gasped. ''Radio says ten people shot, seven likely to die in the Bronx.''

Forty-five minutes later and perilously close to the final deadline, she was trying to put the finishing touches on the story about the Bronx shooting. One of the night editors stood by, wringing his hands and rocking like a Talmudic scholar, correcting punctuation as she wrote.

Within twenty minutes of the shooting, the police department's Public Information office had issued two contradictory versions of the crime. The first version had police walking into a shoot-out between drug gangs. The second said that police officers trying to apprehend a drug dealer had in fact shot three innocent bystanders, who were now dying at a nearby hospital.

''You can't have it both ways,'' Kate shouted at Stephen Rissolli. She could hear the television blaring behind him and imagined him slumped in his gray cubicle in the public information office. The night editor at her side was squeezing his hands to his temples.

''Unless you come up with the official version of what happened in two minutes, so help me God, I'll quote you by name,'' Kate said. '' 'Department spokesman Stephen Rissolli said, ''I don't know what the fuck is going on.'' ' End Quote. Two minutes.''

She slammed down the receiver.

In front of her stood a small, familiar-looking elf, with a face like an old tree trunk, wearing a bulky tan coat and a green knit cap.

''Can I help you with something?'' Kate asked. The figure pulled off the cap and a profusion of wiry white hair sprung out. It was Ellisa Severing.

"I didn't expect you, Mrs. Severing," Kate began.

"Please," Mrs. Severing began, her voice quavering and thin. "I need to talk to you."

Kate looked helplessly at the night editor, who stalked away.

"Can you wait for a few minutes? I have to finish another story."

Mrs. Severing nodded and sat where Kate pointed, at one of the empty terminals.

Kate's telephone rang again. "Stephen, what? What? Well, put me on hold and find out! Stephen. Steve. Ste— Shit."

She looked up, suddenly remembering Mrs. Severing. She gave her a shrug and punched more numbers into the telephone.

34

Dominick felt almost weightless as he was carried along by the flow of people exiting the subway to the street. It had been almost a year since he had been in the city, longer since he had walked through this part of town. He had always considered himself a neighborhood guy, finding the crowded sidewalks of midtown an unrelenting reminder that everyone had a place to go except for him.

Maybe that was the root of his problem, Dominick reflected: He was too much of a neighborhood guy. But that was about to change. He was working on a big story for the most important newspaper in the city. It could lead to anything. Maybe he'd catch on with the paper, then use it to get his own television show like Geraldo Rivera or Howard Stern.

Outside of the *Daily Herald* offices, Dominick shifted a paper cone of tiger lilies to his injured hand, pulled a cassette out of his pocket, and snapped it into his Walkman. Frank Sinatra cutting loose on "That's Life" blasted through his earphones. He always saved this song for special occasions, and this trip to see the reporter was becoming one.

> That's life
> And funny as it may seem,

> Some people get their kicks
> Stomping on a dream.

As he pushed through the doors of the *Daily Herald* building, the jazzy riff seeped into his soul. Unconsciously, Dominick listed to the left and caught his toe on the back of a high-heel shoe. The blonde in the shoe stumbled, righted herself, and cursed Dominick before she walked on. For a second, Dominick stood stricken. The music was reduced to a background buzz. His good hand plunged into his jacket pocket and his fingers laced around the large hunting knife he had brought from home. But then he could make out the lyrics again and Frank seemed to be singing just for him, calming him down, reassuring him.

> I've been a puppet, a pauper, a pirate, a poet,
> a pawn and a king.
> I've been up and down and over and out,
> and I know one thing.

"Can I help you?" a dull-eyed security guard was asking him. Startled, Dominick held the flowers in front of him as if he was warding off a blow, causing yellow pollen to drift from the tiger lilies onto his anorak.

"Oh, flowers. Who for?"

Dominick lifted one earphone of his Walkman.

"Gotta see Kate Murray," Dominick croaked.

"Murray, thirtieth floor. Use the service elevator."

> Each time I find myself flat on my face,
> I pick myself up and get back in the race.

Sinatra was telling him to be confident, be strong, thought Dominick as he got off the elevator. He didn't know which way to go, so he walked through the double glass doors marked DAILY HERALD. He wasn't sure what she looked like, but when he found her he would just stick out his hand and say, "How do ya do, I'm Dominick."

It was something Frank would do.

The newsroom was almost empty. "Where is Kate Murray?" he asked a harassed-looking receptionist.

She pointed to a couple sitting in the far corner of the newsroom. The older half of the couple, a wizened woman, faced Dominick without seeing him. In front of her, twisted toward a computer screen, was the second woman, though all Dominick could see was a spout of dark hair on the back of the woman's head. He switched the Walkman off and listened, his nose quivering in the air as if he were smelling, rather than listening to, the woman doing the interview.

That voice, throaty, sometimes harsh. It was definitely her. Dominick had to stop himself from whooping and rushing toward her.

Kate! Kate! he wanted to shout. *Here I am.* He wondered if she would let him kiss her and decided it was too risky in the office. He walked toward her. His heart was pumping like a jackhammer and something was stirring below.

He was twenty feet away from her when she turned to pick up her ringing telephone, pulling a thick hank of frizzy black curls off her forehead with her other hand.

He stopped, a confused sputtering sound inside his head. It was the girl from the Captain's Table. The one who wasn't a stripper. The girl who had watched him from the bar. What was she doing here?

Then he stood solid and still. It was Kate. She had seen him, looked him over, and pretended not to know him. Something inside of Dominick felt singed, then began to burn in earnest. His hand slid into his anorak until his fingers touched the smooth blade of the knife. He held it in his hand, feeling the cool blade grow warm. He wanted to plunge the blade into his heart. Oh, Kate. Oh, Kate.

He watched her pull back another hank of hair, chatting. Oh, Kate. Oh, Kate.

He wanted to cut her throat.

He felt himself crumble. He dropped the flowers on the floor and fled.

35

By the time Kate filed the story, a few seconds before the six-thirty deadline, Mrs. Severing was shifting around uncomfortably, like a dutiful parishioner in the front pew.

"It's about my daughter," the old lady finally began, timid but resolute. "I've tried to be patient, but I feel that her soul will not rest easy until something is done."

"I think the police are working on it, Mrs. Severing." Kate waited. She wondered if Mrs. Severing really wanted to know the truth.

She tried to be gentle. "But honestly, Mrs. Severing. I think the more time elapses, the less likely they are to find the person responsible."

Two tears coursed down a deep wrinkle in Mrs. Severing's cheek. Kate looked on helplessly.

"But the person is still out there, free, and my daughter is dead," she said.

Kate's head was aching. "I'm sorry," she said.

Mrs. Severing sat with her head down, brushing the tears into her coat as they fell from her cheeks. Kate could see her shoulders shaking in silent sobs.

"She was my only child. My little girl," she moaned.

Kate couldn't think of anything to say.

Mrs. Severing unfurled a white lace handkerchief from her pocket, pressed it to her eyes, then pulled herself unevenly out of the terminal chair.

"It's fine for you here," she said, gesturing to the newsroom. "For you, life goes on. But please don't forget me." She put her finger to her skinny chest. "Please don't forget that my daughter is dead."

36

He sat at the shadowy end of the Forty-second Street subway platform, half obscured by some pipes, the filthy, cold cement slab under him. Tears were running down his face and collecting under his chin. But Dominick was not even aware of them. His dream was gone.

A skinny junkie with a plastic bag packed with cans approached him and tried to make conversation, but Dominick just snarled and the man glided away. She had broken his heart. She had watched his humiliation. She had probably laughed. She wasn't going to help him. She thought he was a jerk. No one was going to help him. It was always the same. When he asked a girl out, she didn't say "No," she said "Never." Even ugly Suzy only slept with him because he paid for her drugs. The city was full of happy couples holding hands. When was it going to be his turn? His thoughts were getting louder and louder until he thought the top of his head would fly open like a hatch. When he opened his eyes, he saw that the din came from a topless car filled with trash that had pulled into the station.

Out of nowhere, a small tan cat, its fur clumped together with soot, walked delicately by Dominick. He reached down and petted the cat.

All he wanted was a normal life, he thought, stroking the cat's soft dirty fur while it sniffed a small pool of teardrops. Dominick's other hand tightened on the hunting knife. He scratched behind the cat's ears and watched its pink tongue flick out, sampling the tears. Steadily Dominick moved the hunting knife into position. When it was one inch from the cat's neck, the little beast raised its heart-shaped head. It touched its delicate damp nose to the deadly point and walked off.

Dominick pulled back the sleeve of his coat and traced blood-red letters on his forearm with the blade. K A T E.

37

Nearly every racket in Brooklyn took place in the basement room of Castle Harbor, which, in truth, was neither a castle nor a harbor but an old brick bar in Sunset Park. It was home to so many NYPD parties that most people in the neighborhood thought of it as a clubhouse for drunken cops.

Although someone had hung up a few crepe-paper streamers and a mirrored ball, Castle Harbor maintained the ambience of a soup kitchen, with worn Formica tables ready to collapse under so many meaty elbows.

The dowdy waitresses, who had worked every promotion and retirement party there for the last fifteen years, knew the police department better than the chief of personnel. They eyed the men nervously, like deer near a highway, ready to scamper away when alcohol extinguished too many basic inhibitions.

Finn loosened his collar, listening to his friend Sergeant Bobby Clifford tell his favorite party stories.

"So we're listening to the wiretap and sure enough, he starts it again," said Clifford, who worked in Brooklyn Narcotics. "We couldn't believe our ears. The guy is setting up heroin shipments from Hong Kong and at the same time is making obscene telephone calls to the Home Shopping Network. I mean, he's talking to those little old ladies in Iowa, saying, 'You've never had it unless you had it with an Italian. I'm hung like a salami.' "

The detectives from Organized Crime slapped one another, roaring until the tears came to their eyes.

Finn smiled, having heard the story four or five times already, and put his hand on Clifford's shoulder.

"Clifford, you wouldn't believe what happened to me today," he began.

Clifford nodded at him, but his attention was drawn to blond-haired Dennis McCarthy.

"Yeah. But tell them the best part. One of the day operators' names is Ida. And she loves listening to him. He starts calling the Home Shopping Network and asking for her by name." McCarthy was a lieutenant in Organized Crime. "I mean, she's about sixty years old, but she can't get enough of this Italian Stallion stuff. Gets all her friends on a party line so they can listen to him talk about what he's gonna do with 'em in bed. Four or five old ladies and a half-assed wiseguy from Brooklyn. It got so he had the Home Shopping Network on rapid dial. He called them ladies two and three hours a day."

"No wonder I could never get through," complained Roger Royson, a detective from Sunnyside, Queens.

"But when you do, be sure and ask for Ida," said Clifford.

The crowd of men burst out laughing again.

It was Tommy Nichol's promotion party, and though Finn knew him from the neighborhood and the academy, he hadn't seen him since he was transferred to Ozone Park. Nichol was being promoted to captain and was leaving Ozone Park for a more dangerous precinct in the Bronx.

Finn wandered away from the men, pumping hands with Nichol, who was already red-faced, and Johnny "Dino" Marino, whom Nichol hated since Marino married and divorced his younger sister. Marino hugged Nichol, handing him a dripping pitcher of beer.

Marino had been trained as designated shooter on the hostage negotiation team. During a hostage situation, Marino, armed with a high-powered rifle and a laser scope, found the best vantage point. If the hostage-taker moved to harm his victims, Marino was supposed to shoot him in the heart.

Although he trained often, Marino rarely fired a gun outside the police firing range at Rodman's Neck. But those few times when he did work, he inevitably walked away from the hostage scene with an insatiable appetite for teenage girls.

"When they're young, everything is new. Everything," Marino was telling Nichol, his former brother-in-law. "You want to tie 'em up, hey, they don't mind. They never did it before. They think it's something you made up."

Fat Tony collided with Finn.

"Hey, Tony, you get anything back from Motor Vehicles under that name I gave you?"

"Christ, what are you, the King of Overtime? You just got back from five hours at Centre Street and you're still thinking about work?" he said, laughing. "You make the overtime, you buy the drinks."

Fat Tony had dressed for the occasion, Finn noted, wearing a white net shirt under a plaid sports jacket.

Finn pressed. "No, Tony, serious. Did you get any hits on that name, Donatti? Dominick Donatti?"

Tony looked at him strangely.

"What's the rush? You going to bring this woman back from the dead? Relax, man." He watched Finn's face fall. "You're too much." He whistled. "You really want this bad. Okay, I got it. Five hits altogether, one under the spelling you gave me. From Gravesend. The list is on your desk."

Finn nodded.

"But what's the hurry, my man? This isn't like you."

Finn wanted to talk to him about the review board, but quickly decided to tell him about Marcus Ralphson instead. He was just warming up to the story when another narcotics cop reached over Fat Tony's shoulder and tugged a tendril of chest hair poking through the net. Fat Tony only grinned, pulled up his shirt, and ran his hand through the thick black rug that grew on his chest.

"A poor girl's mink," he said.

Even Finn laughed at that one, but when he turned to talk to Fat Tony, his partner was already pushing through the crowd to get to the keg.

Out of the corner of his eye, Finn saw Stan Wochowsky pouring himself a pitcher, too. Wochowsky had been avoiding him since their trip to pick up Marvin Plank.

"How ya doing, Finn?" he asked nervously. He talked slowly, as if he were overcoming a speech impediment. "Good to see ya."

"You too, Wochowsky."

The two men sipped their beers and eyed each other uncomfortably.

"I don't know if I ever told you how sorry I—" Wochowsky began.

But Finn cut him off. "Forget it. I'm okay. It was nothing."

"I know, but I heard about the Firearms Review Board. I mean, that shouldn't have happened to anyone. . . . "

"Forget it. It doesn't matter now anyway," said Finn.

"The kid, Marvin Plank, pleaded guilty. He could have gotten three fifteen-year sentences, but his lawyer dealt it down to one three-and-a-third to fifteen."

Finn saw Plank's eyes glimmer against the brick wall of the apartment.

"How's the wife and the little Wochowskys?" he said, noticing how relieved Wochowsky looked to change the subject.

He listened to Wochowsky, talking like a 45 played at 33, ramble on about his kid's second-grade teacher. Finally, they were overtaken by a hooting gang of Public Morals Division detectives, all wearing T-shirts emblazoned with the word *Tufthunters*.

The noise of the party had become deafening. One of the PMD detectives, Joe McConville, slapped Finn on the shoulder. "Can you believe that fucking Flaherty is heading for Florida, the miserable scumbag," he said, spilling beer on his shirt.

Finn was stung.

"Oh yeah, no kidding," he said unsteadily. "He was always talking about doing that."

"Well, he's leaving next month. He sold me his little outboard."

Finn started to push his way to the cold cuts, but got jammed against a wall when a space was cleared to accommodate a loud, five-man drinking contest. Suddenly, there was a cry, and the crowd surged forward as Nichol punched Marino in the mouth. Finn kept moving, feeling his way past some coats along the wall and out the emergency exit.

The air on the quiet street felt clear and cool. Finn found his car, rolled down the windows, and began to drive.

He cruised aimlessly, trying to think of the things in his life that made him happy. He had been a tough little kid, street-wise and wild. Back in South Brooklyn, stickball was his passion. High school seemed like a blur; even his short courtship with his ex-wife Sandy didn't leave him with any lasting glow. It was the police department that had finally given him grounding, and at first, working as a beat cop in Bushwick seemed like the best job a man could have. Getting his gold shield made him proud. He couldn't think of a thing since then—an experience, a conversation, even a good meal—that had made a significant dent in his memory. The odd thing was that until Marvin Plank tried to kill him, he had never thought of himself as an unhappy guy.

For some reason, he remembered dating a beautiful auburn-haired girl named Mary Pitchard, from Mary Immaculate High School, who taught him how to kiss. Standing in front of her father's row house in Sunset Park, she would mouth him passionately until her mother began furiously blinking the light near the front door to signal that Mary's curfew had passed.

Finn's heart grew large with the recollection.

Sitting behind the wheel of his father's Dodge, he'd watch her round ass totter through her front door. He remembered the elation of being seventeen with every hormone in his bloodstream tingling and the whole night in front of him. He drove that car through the Brooklyn streets singing along to the AM radio until the gas tank was almost empty.

He was so lost in the memory that he didn't think about Kate until he stopped in front of the Chrysler Building. It looked shiny and quilted, like an old-style toaster, compared to the tall modern building where Kate worked.

He settled into the weave of the car seat, as if he were on a regular stakeout. She had told him on the telephone that she'd be working until midnight on a project and it was only a little after eleven. Finn checked the time again as two men pushed through the revolving doors of the *Herald* building and bid each other good night. College graduates, Finn thought. Then he watched a janitor, an old black man with a halo of white hair, check in.

Finn flexed his knees, checked his watch again, and got out of the car.

The hound-faced guard in the lobby gave him a big smile when Finn flashed his shield and asked for directions to the thirtieth floor.

He stepped off the elevator and walked down a brightly lit hallway, smiling at the white-haired janitor who was wringing out a dirty mop in an industrial bucket on rollers. Every desk in the newsroom seemed blanketed with paper and the empty computer screens blinked like they were already expecting tomorrow's news.

He felt like he was behind enemy lines. Since his third day in the Academy, the brass had drilled the phrases into his head. *Just say no comment* or *Call Public Information. Never talk to a reporter about police business. Never tell the newspapers what's going on.* He had seen cops with balls big enough to walk through a puff of gunpowder, straight into the line of fire. But he had never met one with the nerve to walk into a newsroom.

He followed the rhythmic tapping sound made by a computer keyboard.

In the wide newsroom, Kate looked younger and her wrists seemed thin and delicate, like a child's. Behind her, a wall of windows summoned the light of the buildings farther down Park Avenue. About twenty feet from her desk, Finn saw a paper cone of flowers on the floor. He stooped, checked that they were fresh, and then held them out to Kate.

"Flower delivery, ma'am."

She looked up, startled.

"John, what are you doing here?" she said, reaching out to take the flowers and smiling. "How nice of you."

He looked down at her. "I had a bad day," he said. Then he closed his eyes. When he opened them, she was staring, waiting for him to speak. He smiled. Then he pulled her toward him.

He kissed her for a long time. She tasted a little bitter, like coffee, but he didn't care. He lifted her out of the chair and set her down again on the warm radiator against the cold black glass, thirty stories above the street.

"What are you doing?" she said quietly. "Someone might come in."

He kissed her again.

"I'm terrified of heights," she said, turning to look down at the cars moving along Park Avenue.

"Me, too," he said. Then he placed a finger on her lips.

"Two men said they wanted to kill me today," he said.

"Are you okay?" she whispered.

"I don't know."

He undid one button on her blouse and then another. He heard the rollers of the janitor's bucket but he didn't stop. He leaned down and kissed her neck, then slid lower.

"Somebody will see us," she hissed. But she seemed to run out of air when he unhooked her bra and ran his hands over her breasts.

He marveled at the fleshy length of her. He touched her face again, running his finger along her lips and tracing a damp line to her left nipple.

He noticed that her breathing had grown more rapid. Then he thought he heard the casters on the industrial bucket and the scraping sound of a door closing.

He looked around and saw the janitor's back. Finn paused until he disappeared down an interconnecting hallway.

Kate leaned back, her knees touching him on either side of his thighs. He felt the pressure inside himself build. He slid his hands up her short skirt. His fingers met the elastic garter to her panties, and he hooked them under the lace at her hip. He followed the lace around to the front and smiled when he felt her quiver. She was gripping him harder with her thighs as his fingers began moving lightly over her pubis.

He could hear his own blood pounding in his head and feel it, like tremors before an earthquake, building through his groin.

The next sound was the janitor's bucket dragging across the floor again.

He looked up and saw the man's fuzzy head poke through the door. With his free hand, Finn waved. The old man smiled and disappeared.

Finn bit her shoulder. He stroked her leg, pushing her panties further down. Her head was tilted back. He stood up and arched over her, leaning his hands against the windows. He pushed himself into her, struggling to grab hold. Finally, they were moving and sliding together. He delved deeper until a ragged sound tore out of her chest, then he came and for a few moments he was lost.

When he opened his eyes, she was looking up at him with a loose half-smile on her face. He leaned his cheek against the cold window and stared out at the city.

He realized that he was looking at a scene from an old movie. *King Kong.* He had seen it at a neighborhood theater in Bay Ridge. In the movie, the ape climbed to the top of the Empire State Building, which hadn't changed at all since the film was made.

Kong clung there, free and defiant, while the crowd clamored below. Airplanes dove at him and soldiers fired rockets, trying to knock him off the building.

When he was a child, Finn was frightened of Kong and he sided with the soldiers. But tonight, he felt sorry for him. The ape must have been terrified, with all those people hating him, trying to hurt him.

He looked down at the mass of Kate's curly hair. Of course, the ape never showed that he was afraid. Instead, he bellowed and beat his chest, and maybe, secretly, even though he was afraid, he was happy deep down. He had a woman he loved tucked safely in the warm meaty pillows of his hand.

o that's when I decided," said Finn, swallowing a dry hunk of
turkey sandwich as he stared straight ahead through the windshield at
the Cork and Barrel. "I decided, I'm finishing this case, then I'm
leaving the department." He was trying to make his voice sound reasonable, but it was wavering and threatened to bounce an octave.

From the driver's side of the dark sedan, Fat Tony began to choke
on his baloney sandwich, then he gulped a Coke to clear his throat.
He seemed not to notice that a tear of brown cola dribbled from his
nose.

"What d'ya mean? You can't leave just like that." He heaved
forward in outrage as he struggled to face Finn. "You only got fourteen years. I mean, I could see if you were a hairbag, still walking
some shit beat, but you and me"—he wiped his nose with the back
of his hand—"we got a tit job. You know that."

"Don't tell me again how good we got it," said Finn, holding up
his hand. "I know. I know. We go to work, we get paid, we stay out
of trouble. We got no one on our backs."

"Right," Tony said enthusiastically. "That's why I walked the
beat for six years in Crown Heights, trying to keep the West Indians
from carving the hearts out of the Hasidim. So I could get a job like
this one."

"I'm not saying it's not a good life," Finn said. "I just don't think it's for me. Okay? Maybe I got to do something else."

"Like what? Become a brain surgeon? How about joining the circus? Or maybe a run for Congress? You'll end up working for some pathetic private security operation, guarding a gas station, and getting shot to death in a two-bit stickup."

Finn said nothing as he watched a desiccated little man stagger out of the Cork and Barrel.

"Did you hear me, Johnny-boy? This is reality talking," Fat Tony said mockingly. "I should have known you were off the deep end when you started working time and a half on this bullshit homicide. You've really changed. First it's DMV, then we're in a cold car outside a warm bar because you think some punk might be connected to the guy you think might have killed Severing except you don't know why or how or what have you. Keep this up, they won't let you put in your papers, you'll get discharged on a psychiatric. And you can tell that to your reporter girlfriend." Momentarily exhausted, Tony stopped, then said, "Shit," in a long-drawn-out exhalation that reflected the full measure of his disgust.

"Fuck you, Tony. You still don't get it. Six weeks ago, a seventeen-year-old put a gun to my head and pulled the trigger. Two weeks later, I'm fighting for my job in front of the Firearms Review Board like I was the one that did something wrong. Wouldn't that make you think?" He stopped as if he expected Tony to answer. But Tony just continued to stare at the Cork and Barrel. "It made me think, all right. It made me think that I wanted this case cleared and I wanted to get the hell out."

Tony's eyes never moved, but he made his voice soothing, like he was talking an emotionally disturbed person off a windowsill. "I would think about kicking the ass of the union delegate who let me walk into that meeting, but would I leave the department? Hell no."

Finn wanted to look at him, to make sure Tony took in what he was about to say, but he found he couldn't turn his head.

"Well, it made me think something else," he said finally. "It made me think that I started in the department with nothing, and I got nothing now. Except then I was a kid and that was all right. Now I'm a man, and not a young man either."

Tony was silent.

Finn reached up and grabbed the back of his own neck, massaging the muscles that were strung like cords below his ears. "I just gotta get something for myself before it's too late."

Fat Tony stuck the nail of his fat forefinger behind his eyetooth and pried off a bit of his dinner.

"But just changing things isn't necessarily gonna be a change for the better," he said.

Finn, touched by the mildness of the response, turned to smile at Tony. But his partner grunted and extended his chin.

"There he is, Dominick the Boy Wonder."

They watched as he staggered out of the bar and headed unsteadily up the street, like he was wading into a strong current.

Finn checked his watch, then squinted, watching Dominick weave under the streetlight. They had followed him to the bar from his home in Gravesend, but he had been in the Cork and Barrel so long that Finn had almost forgotten what he looked like.

"You sure it's him?"

Fat Tony didn't answer.

They sat in silence as Dominick, his thin jacket opened to the cold night air, stopped near the shadow of the alley next to the bar and clumsily attempted to unzip his fly.

"It's him," said Tony.

"Look at his hand," said Finn in agreement. They got out of the car, quietly closed the doors, and walked toward Dominick until they stood about two feet away from his hunched back.

Finn cleared his throat.

"Can't you see I need some privacy here?" Dominick snarled. All of his attention was directed at the clear stream issuing from his crotch.

Fat Tony raised an eyebrow to Finn, who said nothing.

"What ya gonna do, mug me when I'm taking a piss? That's a new one," said Dominick, turning around, his bruised hand still clutching his genitals. "Jesus, it's the cops. What are you, Public Hygiene Division?"

"Actually, we wanted to ask you a few questions," said Finn.

Dominick squinted at the two detectives as he awkwardly tucked his pale penis inside his pants. A large wet spot spread across the front of his jeans.

"It's after midnight and I need to get home and sleep this off," he said. Finn noticed that he looked slightly cross-eyed. "Why don't you give me your card and I'll call you?"

"Why don't we take you down to the precinct and let you sleep it off there?" said Tony. "You'd have the cell to yourself." He waited a beat. "Except for a big nasty queen we call Vlad the Impaler."

Dominick started to protest, but Tony had already grabbed him by the arm and was hauling him back to their sedan. Tony hoisted him on the hood of the car. Dominick looked young and vulnerable against the expanse of dark metal shining under the moonlight.

"So, Dominick, what happened to your finger?" Finn asked consolingly. It was an effort to speak kindly to Dominick, since everything about the man, from his weird unfocused eyes to his overwet lower lip to his mangled hand, filled Finn with disgust. He had grown up with guys like Dominick—weasly, weak boys who lived off their mothers until they found another woman willing to let them freeload for a while.

"You come all the way here to ask me that?" Dominick whined. "It got broken, but it's almost better."

He reminded Finn of something mad and mean trapped in a small cage.

"Didn't I go to high school with you?" Dominick asked, smart-assed. "Didn't you play football with a guy named Daitch?"

Finn ignored him. He wasn't sure if a guy like Dominick could know anything useful at all.

"We heard you might know about something that happened in Bushwick," said Tony.

"Heh, what do I look? Black? I don't know Bushwick."

"We heard you might know something about a homicide there," said Finn, watching him steadily.

"I don't know nothing about nothing," said Dominick, his face suddenly filled with cunning, despite the alcohol.

"You little prick. We know all about you," said Fat Tony, enraged.

Dominick said nothing, giving Tony a defiant red-eyed stare.

Finn felt they were getting warmer, but he needed a sign, a slip, something to make the tie to Dominick more concrete.

"Listen, Dominick, we don't want to make problems for you. But you might be in trouble."

Dominick looked doubtful. "What kind of trouble?"

"In trouble with the Spanish," said Finn, casting. He saw fear flicker through Dominick's eyes.

"I don't know any Spanish people. There are none in Gravesend."

Finn felt the fish nibbling on the bait, but knew he was still far from being hooked.

Dominick made no effort to hide an enormous belch. "Just say I am in trouble. Are you here to protect me? Right. Sure." The cold wind was making Dominick's nose run, and he sniffled almost continuously.

Tony, unable to contain himself, cuffed Dominick lightly on the side of the head. "Listen, you little skell, what are you on? Probation? Parole? We could make things very tough for you."

"Ah, screw you," Dominick said, weaving slightly, even though he was sitting. "Arrest me and let me call my lawyer, or I'm out of here."

Finn felt momentarily peeved at Fat Tony for being so abrasive, but he kept looking at Dominick steadily, hoping to reestablish the rhythm.

"Listen, a very nice lady got killed in Bushwick. A nurse. We may need your help," said Finn.

"Don't break my heart," said Dominick. "I take care of my business. You take care of yours. I help you and the next thing I know, I need help myself from Jacoby and Meyers to get out of Brooklyn House of Detention. I know how cops work. You can help me by staying away from me. Okay?"

The fish wasn't going for the bait. Finn said nothing. Fat Tony, stomping his foot with impatience, raised his hand to hit Dominick again.

"You better not," Dominick said quickly. "You ever hear of the First Amendment? I got protection."

"Wha?" said Fat Tony.

"Me and my girlfriend. We got protection from the First Amendment. We got the power. We got the love. We do what we want."

"The William Kunstler of Gravesend. What the fuck is he talking about?" asked Tony, his arm still raised.

Finn looked at Dominick closely.

"Your girlfriend?"

But Dominick was already leaving. "Fuck you, police," he said.

He slid off the car hood and stumbled a bit, drunkenly deciding which way to walk.

Fat Tony and Finn watched him go.

"What a waste," Tony remarked.

"Think he did Severing? Think he knows who did?" asked Finn, his mind whirling.

"Who knows?" said Fat Tony as he wearily opened the driver's side door. "Who knows?"

39

Something about the homicide in the Bushwick brownstone was bothering Finn. In the first place, the victim, Graveyard Jones, had been dead for several days. Interviews with the neighbors indicated that while the young skateboard wizard lay dead on his living-room floor with his chest cavity draining out onto a dirty rug, his faithful customers had shuffled in and out of his apartment looking for drugs. It was only this morning, when the stench became overpowering, that the super called the police.

But there was something more. It was this block, Finn decided, that made the hairs on his arms stand on end.

"Tony, have we ever been on this block before for anything big?"

"Yeah, this is the block where the old Jewish grandmother was taken hostage, you know the one I'm talking about," said Fat Tony, for the benefit of the young cop standing to Finn's right. "She woke up and found the robber in her house and he took her hostage with a plastic gun. It took a few hours to get the negotiating team in place, and in that time, the old lady and the skell got to be friends. She made him breakfast. She told him being a robber was too dangerous for such a nice young man. She promised to help him find a real job. She even asked the hostage negotiator to call her grandson to see if he could find a job for the mutt in the garment business." Tony bit off the end of his short cigar. "Then, after all that, the robber traded her for two cigarettes. What a day that was."

Both cops laughed appreciatively.

For the thousandth time that day, Kate's smile drifted through Finn's mind.

After staking out Dominick, he dropped by her house around one A.M. He expected her to be sleeping, but she was making telephone calls on a shooting in Howard Beach.

"What if it's a mob hit?" she asked him, panicked, as he made them both hot chocolate in her kitchen. "I can't blow it."

After watching her get nowhere, he called a buddy from the academy who worked in Howard Beach and found out the victim was a ninety-year-old Asian man.

"Unless it was the Gambinos' laundry man, I don't think you have to worry," he said, pulling the comforter over them both. Before drifting off to sleep, their heads touching, she told him a daydream she had that evening about attending her own Pulitzer Prize awards dinner. She didn't say he was part of the daydream, but he thought her telling him about it was a hopeful sign, as if her plans for the future might include him.

So he described a daydream of his own—walking out of the 83rd Precinct station house one last time. He told her what he couldn't tell Tony, that he wanted a job that would give him a chance to become himself again. A job, he had added silently, where Marvin Plank was just a distant uncomfortable memory.

This morning, she was all business again, quizzing him about different suspects before lapsing into her caressing five-note laugh.

"What's new on the Severing homicide? When do you expect to have an arrest?"

Finn didn't mention Dominick or the stakeout. He didn't want her to know he had used her information.

"Listen, Kate," he interrupted. "You got to be careful who you talk to." He was trying to keep his voice light, thinking of the way Dominick said "my girlfriend." "You got to try to avoid trouble."

"Listen, Detective," she said with mock toughness. "I'm a crime reporter. I look for trouble."

He tried again.

"You don't know about some guys . . . like Dominick." He was trying to keep it casual but the name was echoing in his head. "They're not like you. They're like animals and they're only after one thing." He hated himself for sounding like a hairbag. "Well, maybe two things, but believe me, they aren't like guys you know."

She had listened politely, helping him put on his coat, but he could tell she didn't understand. He couldn't make the thing that was clutching his gut let go.

"Haven't we done a shooting or a homicide on this block before?" asked Finn, scratching his head.

"Not one of ours," said Fat Tony.

The Crime Scene Unit had arrived, so Finn and Fat Tony let them in and then stood outside, preventing disoriented drug addicts from walking into Graveyard's apartment.

Flaherty had always said, Finn thought to himself, that most of police work is just standing around.

He glanced at the numbers above the door, then he looked toward the corner, at the twisted green and white street signs, Halsey and Wilson, decorated with worn-out sneakers.

Halsey and Wilson, he murmured, then smiled, flashing on an image of Kate on the Promenade. He looked at the street signs again. Dominick. Gusano. Graveyard Jones. He remembered when he had last heard this address mentioned.

"Give me a minute, I got to make a call," he said quietly to Fat Tony and began running toward the steel-hooded pay phone outside the laundromat.

Finn dug into his pocket, but didn't have any coins. He walked into the laundromat.

"Could you change a dollar for me, please? I need money for the phone," he said to the ancient attendant.

"No speak English," she replied in a weak, aggrieved tone. Two bony crackheads staring into a dryer snickered.

"I need to use the phone," he practically shouted. Then he pulled out his badge. "Police business."

The woman stared at him impassively, then shrugged, dug into a fold in her worn apron, and handed him four quarters.

Finn hurried outside and tried to insert a coin, but the telephone was broken.

"It don't work. Try down the block," said a black man clutching a Thunderbird bottle that looked like it was half full of urine.

Finn walked quickly toward a bodega fortified on three sides with Plexiglas and covered with stickers for canned beans. The telephone was bolted to a thick steel pole, but the handpiece was connected to the body of the telephone by a single frayed red wire. A small explosion had ripped away the coin return slot.

Finn's heart was pounding as he ran down Knickerbocker Avenue and spotted three telephones, one of which appeared to be in reasonable shape. Three young men, their round heads straining inside their hoods, stood expectantly by the phones, with their hands sunk into their front pouch pockets.

Finn raised his badge and watched the three men backpedal toward the corner, where they broke into a run.

His hands trembled as he pushed the quarter into the slot.

The receptionist answered in one breath, "*Daily-Herald*-hold-please," then he heard nothing. He shifted his weight anxiously from one foot to the other, until he heard a dial tone. He swore, then pushed another quarter into the phone, dialing Kate's home number.

He tried to make his voice sound calm as he spoke into her answering machine. But the strain made him sound like a nervous adolescent.

"Hello, Kate, I may have some interesting news on the Severing homicide. I need to talk to you. But listen, you know you told me Dominick followed Gusano to Halsey and Wilson? Well, do me a favor. Don't take any phone calls from him. And for God's sake, don't meet him unless I'm with you. There's been a homicide right here. Right in front of the building he was staking out."

40

Detective Second Grade Tom Loeb followed the messenger with his oyster-colored eyes as he tossed a load of envelopes into the In basket of the Ballistics Unit. The rest of his five-man squad groaned and continued to gnaw on their bagels and bialys. Loeb ignored them, wondering idly if the precincts were starting to ship bullets to Ballistics by the pound.

Every Monday morning, the messengers showed up with a weekend's worth of glassine evidence envelopes. Inside each envelope was a gun found during an arrest or a slug pulled out of a wall or a corpse. Every Monday morning his colleagues groaned.

Beyond a grunt or a scowl, Loeb rarely acknowledged the men he worked with. They were useful, he was occasionally forced to admit, like so many drones in his hive, but he never engaged them in conversation. He couldn't imagine them having anything interesting to say.

Without a word, Loeb threw his coffee away and grabbed a handful of envelopes containing bullets. His colleagues began their customary argument over which morning talk show should be blasted from the small, dented television set that dominated the lab. He grunted a few times as he slipped on his Walkman, selecting the aria from Wagner's *Tristan und Isolde,* then tugged absently on his walruslike mustache and sat down in front of his double microscope.

He had worked in ballistics for twenty-three years and considered himself not an investigator, but an artist. True, he worked in a drab city building instead of a sunny loft. But with five kids and a wife, he couldn't leave Jericho, Long Island, for the Left Bank of Paris.

Besides, Loeb liked the job. He'd been fascinated with guns since the early morning of September 17, 1964, when his father handed him his first BB rifle in the hills behind their Vermont home. Loeb remembered the thrill, the Godlike feeling, that came from standing on one side of a pasture and causing a bottle to shatter on the other side.

He still felt exactly the same way whenever he pulled the trigger, whether he was squeezing off a round on an exotic Dutch M-16 assault rifle or a garden-variety nine-millimeter semiautomatic. The kick translated into a rush of raw power traveling up his arm to his shoulder until his chest contained, not the frail pump of a mortal man, but the heart of a lion.

"What have we here?" Loeb murmured to himself, looking over the voucher sheet included in the envelope. The kids in the precincts, the ones the prosecutors would respectfully refer to as the arresting officers during the trial, didn't know shit about bullets these days. They couldn't tell a .38 from a .45. And if they ran across a hollow point .38 that had deformed into a .65 glob of lead on impact, forget it. Sometimes they just wrote down "1 (one) slug, unknown." Didn't even want to guess.

He grunted in disgust. The paperwork said the bullet Loeb held in his hand had been found in the body of a gunshot victim named Graveyard Jones. Graveyard, snorted Loeb. What ever happened to Mikey or Bob?

Loeb stuck the slug on the gummy slug holder on his microscope, illuminated it with a conical lamp the size of a baby fist, and bellied up to the machine. It was a nine-millimeter Lugar slug, sprung from a copper cartridge exactly nineteen millimeters long. Before the slug entered the barrel, it had measured exactly .355 inches in diameter, a fraction larger than the gun bore. When it was launched from the gun by the force of exploding gunpowder, it squeezed through the bore, and should have picked up the barrel markings like a stamp. But instead of having six even ridges called "lands" moving to the right, imprints from the striation along the barrel, the slug had been wiped clean of class characteristics.

Loeb grunted and tugged his mustache again. Somebody had tried to drill the barrel to make the bullet untraceable. He tsked quietly to himself. The note from the detective asked him to try to match the bullet with another Brooklyn homicide. This one was a female, Margaret Severing.

Loeb pushed himself away from the double microscope, ignoring his colleagues who were having a tug of war with a World War II Remington shotgun that had just come in. He walked to the bullet catacombs, where slugs that caused death were removed from glassine, placed in yellow envelopes, and left to gather dust forever.

Severing. Severing. The lovely Mrs. Severing. It was a musical name. Like bells jangling on a cold winter night. He slid open the green file drawer and pawed among the yellow envelopes. There was nothing where the bullets that killed the lovely Mrs. Severing should have been.

For the first time that morning, Loeb spoke. And when the sound came out of his mouth it was a roar.

"Plimpton. PLIMPTON!" he hollered, and a pasty-faced man stumbled around the corner, his face a hurricane of anxieties.

"Wha-wha-what is it, Detective, sir?"

"WHAT HAPPENED TO THE SLUGS THAT KILLED MARGARET SEVERING?" Loeb shouted as he pointed at a confused jumble of envelopes in the drawer.

Plimpton, whose head seemed too large for his wrinkled neck, drew his lips into a tight line and squinted at Loeb. "Severing?"

Loeb only glared.

Quaking, Plimpton dipped his skinny arm into the drawer and tentatively checked a few names. Then he drew a yellow envelope neatly marked SEVERING, MARGARET from the heap.

"Ah," said Loeb, stretching his features into a grateful grin. But Plimpton, who saw only a harsh, sarcastic leer, hurried away. Loeb stared hard after the little man. Then his attention was diverted by the opening notes of the aria and he turned on his heel, making clucking noises as he brought the envelope back to his double microscope.

It was a nine-millimeter Lugar as well, free of class characteristics. No lands. No grooves. You could tell that without a microscope. Loeb's heart began to pound. He stuck the Severing slug on the other slug holder and adjusted the light. He fine-tuned the focus, bringing the images of the two bullets closer and closer.

Although both guns had the lands and grooves rubbed clean,

the drill bit had left certain markings in the barrel which were now impressed on the soft lead of the slug. He moved the images closer until he appeared to be looking at two sections of the same bullet. The beauty of it almost brought tears to his eyes. Leontyne Price's voice trilled and dived, caressing the outline of the cold steel. It fit. The two slugs were fired from the same gun.

"Mona Lisa," Loeb cried out, then began to chuckle. "Perfect as a picture."

41

Dominick pushed himself off the bar stool at the Cork and Barrel and walked unsteadily to the telephone. He pumped in his quarter and dialed Kate Murray's number.

The same man's voice answered.

"It's me again," Dominick said. Then he belched.

"I gave her your messages," Grant said. "I guess she's still out on a story."

Dominick's good hand moved unconsciously to his chest and his fingers picked up the faint pulsing of his primary arteries. His heart was swollen and sore and pressing against his lungs. When he thought of seeing Kate in the newsroom he felt sick. He struggled to suck in another breath. He knew there was some logical explanation. And he needed to hear it from her.

Dominick tried to focus on the red Budweiser sign hanging in the window. He could see the sleet, like red acid rain, falling behind it.

"Hello?"

"I need to talk t' her," he began, almost begging. "What are you, her secretary or something? Why don't ya get her to call me back?"

"I'm sorry. I'm working on deadline. Good-bye," Grant said.

"Wait!" Dominick practically screamed.

"What?"

Dominick was trying to think, but the sound of his own voice was echoing in his head. "Do ya have another number for her? Like a home number? It's a life or death thing."

There was an empty pause, then Dominick heard a low chuckle.

"Sure," Grant said. "Get a pen. Here it is."

Dominick's heart leapt. He gestured wildly to Vinnie, who handed him a red grease pencil he used to mark dates on the liquor bottles.

"Thanks, man, thanks a lot. I don't know how to tell you how much I . . . " Dominick bubbled.

"Just don't tell her where you got it," said Grant and hung up.

Dominick continued to babble his thanks even after the telephone began to make a raucous sound. Then he staggered back to his bar stool.

42

s Kate edged the car through the rain and the midtown traffic, she tried to forget the family she had just left in Flatbush. A nine-year-old girl had been wrapping presents under the Christmas tree when a bullet shattered the living-room window and split her head. Now the child's mother lay, almost unconscious with shock, in her daughter's pink-lace-trimmed canopy bed.

"Don't you let the media into my house," the mother had screamed from the bedroom as Kate stood dripping on a plastic door-mat whose raggedy red letters spelled WELCOME. Kate took a deep breath. A tough one. While the girl's aunt smiled uneasily, Kate stepped through the half-opened door. "We don't want our tragedy to sell your newspapers," she heard the woman say.

In a low voice, over the roar of game-show laughter, Kate began her pitch.

"My editors want me to write a story explaining how such a terrible thing can happen to good people. How the neighborhood can destroy its best hope for the future," said Kate, nervously hitting her best lines. She felt like a snake oil salesman. Then she thought of Grant's "Ode to Sparky" and pushed herself to go for the hook. "Do you have a picture of"—to save her life, she couldn't remember if the victim's name was Kimba Skinner or Carley Skinner—"the poor little girl?"

The aunt went down the hall to the child's room to confer with the mother. Kate followed, taking note of the schoolgirl drawings pinned on the refrigerator and the stuffed animals strewn around the bedroom. The girl's mother, her face pressed into a pillow, was ignoring the aunt, who had crouched down to speak with her.

Kate spoke directly to the mother's back.

"Mrs. Skinner, I'm sorry to intrude on your tragedy," she began. "But the whole city feels for you in your time of pain."

Most of the time, this preachy stuff worked, but as the woman turned to face her, Kate sensed a warning bell about to go off. Unconsciously, her forearms crossed over her midsection.

"Get out, you vulture!" she screamed at Kate, who drew back in fear. She could see that the woman, her face smudged with tears, would strike her if she could free a hand from beneath the pink bedspread. "You were not invited here. You can't help me now, my little girl is dead."

Kate had been backing up while the woman spoke and was already out of the dead child's room, but the mother's screaming was getting louder as she hoisted herself up from the bed. Without warning, the aunt, who had been keeping the mother calm, joined in with an angry, inarticulate wail.

Kate backed down the hallway toward the living room, bumping into something unyielding. Without looking, she tried to step past it, but it moved with her. Kate spun around.

Behind her the dead child's father, prematurely gray and worn, sat rigid and silent, his wheelchair wedged between the door and the television set. As Kate offered an automatic condolence, she saw that his eyes were full of intelligence and brimming with hatred.

"I guess I'd better go," said Kate. The mother's voice grew louder. "I'll kill you if you don't get out. Get out!"

For a second, Kate stared directly into the father's glowering eyes. "Again, I'm sorry," she said.

Then Kate reached down and gave the wheelchair's metal frame a shove, moving it back six inches as she darted for the door.

Without a picture, and only a single usable quote from the grief-stricken mother—"My daughter is dead!"—she knew the story would run somewhere after an analysis of the city budget. Wearily, she phoned the details to rewrite.

As she parked her Tercel in between a van and a beat-up Cadillac,

Kate decided that she had the worst job in New York. Well, not exactly the worst. The lowest of the low, she had decided long ago, was the guy whose job it was to sit in the Plexiglas booth in the Lincoln Tunnel monitoring traffic and breathing car fumes far below the surface of the Hudson River. But hers was close.

She checked her watch, then jumped out of the car and dashed up the steps of the Plaza. She found her mother, dressed in a Bill Blass day suit, sitting under a thatch of potted palms. The room was humid, like some Raj tearoom in India.

"Don't run, dear, it isn't becoming," said her mother, proffering her heavily rouged cheek.

Kate brushed it with her lips and sat panting slightly while a raft of violins behind her began sawing through Vivaldi's *Four Seasons.*

"You're looking terrific, Mother," Kate said jauntily, noting that her mother had chosen her second-best ladies-who-lunch outfit to wear on the hour-long journey from her meager home in Mamaroneck to the Plaza Hotel.

Her mother sniffed and picked up Kate's hand. "You need a manicure."

Deflated, Kate felt her face burn and she hunched her shoulders protectively. Her right leg began an involuntary rocking under the table. She felt young, fat, and vulnerable.

She picked a soup spoon off the damask tablecloth. It took her a few disorienting seconds to realize that the spoon was oversized and she was still grown up.

She smiled with effort.

"I've been under a lot of pressure at work," she said, feeling like she was apologizing.

"I don't know why you bother with that job anyway," said her mother.

"Well, don't worry," said Kate, feeling aggravated. "I may get fired. I'm holding on by my fingertips and if I lose this job, I'm not sure how I'll pay the rent." She paused, hating herself, but craving sympathy. "If you have some secret trust fund set up for me that you never mentioned before," she added with a bitter laugh, "it's time to break the good news."

Mrs. Murray pressed her spotted hand to her throat. Kate noticed that she had dragged her bright red lipstick crookedly over her upper lip.

"What about getting married?"

"What about it?"

"It was good enough for me," said her mother proudly. "Instead of chasing ambulances and hanging around the ghetto." She said the word in two syllables: *get-toe*. "You'd be much happier."

"You'd be much happier," Kate said.

"When I think of what your father would say if he could see you ... I think it may be a blessing that he's ... he's ... gone." She dabbed her dry eyes and sniffed.

Kate flashed. "It wouldn't matter to him," she said. "He always told me, 'Don't be afraid to be ambitious.' "

"Why do you want to talk about that?" her mother asked, a note of accusation in her voice. "Why do you always bring up your father when you know it hurts me so?"

Kate took a deep breath. She hadn't brought it up, she wanted to shout. She hadn't even looked at the menu and she was already mad enough to walk out.

But her mother had unexpectedly veered onto another of Kate's least favorite topics.

"So, who is keeping you so busy you don't have time to get a manicure? Are you seeing anyone?" she asked, fluffing and settling in as if she expected to hear a long story. Kate fought a teenage impulse to tell her mother about John Finn.

Silence spread like a stain across the table.

It would make her mother so happy to hear that she was dating. But she couldn't imagine telling her, right here under the palm trees at the Plaza, that the fish she had chosen from the wide, wide sea was not a doctor or a lawyer or even a graduate of a private New England college.

She thought of Finn's round buttocks, pale like the skin of a new potato. She felt his strength, like the surf, as he surged against her thighs. She tried to sound casual.

"I've had a few dates with a guy," she said.

The waiter appeared, his oily hair pressed into flaps bisecting his head and his tuxedo-style uniform drawing attention to his sunken chest. He left them a pot of jasmine tea and a seasonal fruit plate— canned peaches, hard bright green kiwi, and three burgundy grapes— for her mother and a towering slice of chocolate three-layer cake for Kate.

"I know how much you like chocolate," said her mother, reaching across the table to harpoon the cake with her slender fork, while Kate picked at the frosting.

"Fattening," her mother said with relish. "So what does he do?"

"Who?"

"This boyfriend of yours." A little bit of chocolate clung to her upper lip.

"Ah, it's not serious," answered Kate evasively.

"Where did you meet him?" she demanded.

Kate reached across the table and tried to spear a grape, but it rolled off the table and onto the marble floor.

Kate felt trapped. She quickly calculated. "I met him at work."

Her mother raised her eyes to the rococo painted ceiling. "A newspaperman?" she said, as if Kate had told her he was a leper.

"Why don't you date a doctor or a lawyer? Your father was a lawyer when I met him." She was warming up to the topic. Without her father's genial, softening influence, her mother had become a web of interconnecting prejudices.

Her father came from lace-curtain Irish stock and was raised in Brooklyn. Kate's mother, who was raised in Madison, Connecticut, was fiercely proud of her Anglican ancestors and kept a little scroll in her drawer, complete with gold stamp and wax, certifying a distant connection to a long-dead English duke. Not even her father's success as a corporate lawyer could convince Kate's mother that she hadn't married beneath her.

"When I think that we raised you in Scarsdale and sent you to the finest schools in Westchester County, only to have you find a man who probably drinks too much and chases ambulances and calls it a living . . . " Her mother shuddered.

"Mother, my whole life we lived in Mamaroneck, not Scarsdale." This was a timeworn disagreement between them. Her mother, full of unexpected vanities, told lies to disguise the ordinary life she led. "I went to Mamaroneck High School. The public high school. I can even show you. It's written in big letters on my diploma."

"You could make an effort to find someone more . . . presentable," her mother hissed.

Kate was furious and, feeling like a spiteful adolescent, she drew back the bow.

"Mom, he's not a newspaperman"—she let the arrow fly—"he's a cop. A homicide detective, actually. Lives in Brooklyn. Carries a gun."

It was too much, Kate realized, momentarily disappointed. Her mother blocked out her words entirely. She seemed focused on the violinists as they played a classical arrangement of Sinatra's "New York, New York." Kate felt relieved, knowing her mother would never ask her about this particular boyfriend again.

Mrs. Murray began rooting through her Fendi bag, which Kate knew was usually stuffed with tissue paper and kept in her top drawer near her grandmother's pearls. She was making comments half under her breath and for a second Kate wondered if she remembered she was sitting at high tea at the Plaza.

Suddenly, Kate noticed that her mother's generous mouth, so often pressed in a hard, disapproving line, was like a string, puckering the bottom of her face. Her hair, which had turned gray shortly after her husband's funeral, looked receded and thin. When she bent over her purse, Kate could see that the hair at the back of her head was uncombed and slightly wild. For a second, Kate saw her mother as a fragile old lady, terrified of icy steps, delivery boys, and the harsh winter wind.

Kate felt a lump in her throat and she wanted to press her face against her mother's second-best jacket, but the table stretched wide between them. Instead, she leaned forward and touched her mother's hand.

"I'm sorry, Mom, I really am," she said. "I don't know what has gotten into me. It's the pressures of my job and the kinds of stories I've been covering."

Her mother looked up uncomprehendingly. "Here," she said triumphantly, unfurling an envelope full of tattered news clippings from the local paper. She began shoving them across the table to Kate, one at a time. They were wedding announcements.

"See. Here. I knew you'd want to see these. You went to school with this girl. She played in the orchestra with you. Janice Shapiro. Married last year. Her mother says she is pregnant and as big as a house."

Kate felt a weariness roll over her like heavy machinery. But her mother seemed animated, beaming down at the awkward, formal portraits that accompanied the wedding and birth announcements, like a grand matriarch at a family reunion.

"Here's another. Wendy Swenson. You remember, she played tennis. She married that nice boy who took her to the prom." She paused for effect. "He's a lawyer now. You remember the one. And here's another."

43

Gusano watched the Manhattan streets spin by and thought about how much he loved the feel of money in his pocket. Not just a handful of change wearing away at the white pocket liners. But real money. Green cash. So much that his billfold refused to fold over properly and bulged, like a woman's breast, under his jacket.

Business had been good, he thought with satisfaction. He had eliminated the nurse and the drug dealer, two big problems, without a fuss. Montoya was pleased. Gusano was wealthier than he had ever been in his life. If only his grandmother could see him now.

As the driver pulled to a stop in front of the tan Upper East Side high-rise, Gusano had already found the door handle. After working hard in Brooklyn, Manhattan seemed like television. The buildings sparkled, the women looked alluring. Even the dogs came on expensive leather leashes. This is what his talents had prepared him for. Manhattan.

He got as far as the doorman before he remembered the gift, tied with a deep red bow, still on the backseat of the car, and went back to retrieve it. Women love presents, he thought smugly to himself, riding up in the elevator. A beautiful gift often opened the fleshy door to a beautiful end of the evening. His carnal feelings combined with the weightless ascent of the elevator, making his hips jut out. He allowed himself a short, sensual groan before smoothing his double-breasted jacket and arranging his face in a smile.

Montoya had recommended this escort service, Sophisticated Ladies. Very attractive and discreet, he had said. Already Gusano knew that such an evening would not come cheap. Five hundred dollars to arrange a date with what the operator called "a special someone," and that didn't even include sex.

Not that he cared about the money, he thought quickly. He liked his work, but much more than job satisfaction, he loved what the money could buy.

The apartment door was opened by a pale-faced young girl a few years away from puberty, who eyed him with open hostility.

"Is your sister at home?" asked Gusano, peeking playfully into a living room crowded with black leather furniture, as if his Sophisticated Lady might be hiding.

"I don't have a sister," replied the girl, then opened her mouth to reveal a row of silver-colored braces and screamed, "MAAAA! He's HEEEERE! And he talks funny, like the doorman."

He smelled the Sophisticated Lady before he heard her spiked heels in the hallway. He held the present in front of his heart, so she would see it as soon as she rounded the corner.

She looked older than he had expected. Her hair was an obvious yellow dye-job and cut too short. She wore tight jeans and a red sequined jacket and was somehow harder and more pinched-looking than most Latino women. As she smiled, Gusano saw that she had dark maroon specks of lipstick on her teeth.

"For you, madame, with my compliments," he said, bowing slightly at the waist as he extended the present.

The woman smiled warily, and awkwardly introduced herself as Sueanne. She said Gusano's name, which he'd given as Velasquez, smiling all the while but sucking in her cheeks like she had mango pulp stuck in her molars. When she turned to introduce the child, the girl lunged forward, grabbed the gift, and began tearing off the ribbon.

It was a Venetian glass perfume bottle, perfectly molded into a translucent jewel shot with blues and greens. He had found it earlier in the day at a store called Barneys when he was picking up two new suits from Montoya's tailor on Twentieth Street.

Although the bottle weighed nothing, and was smaller than the palm of his hand, it had cost him over a hundred and fifty dollars.

"It's an empty bottle," the child said, aggrieved, and shoved it toward her mother. But Sueanne was still smiling at Gusano.

The bottle never made it to her hand.

When it shattered, it almost sounded like water splashing on the fake marble floor.

"Sorry," Sueanne said lamely as the child wordlessly skipped to the other room.

"It was nothing," Gusano said. Then he composed himself and smiled. "Shall we go? I have a car waiting."

In the elevator Gusano tried to reformulate his plans for the evening. Unused to non-Latin women, he had planned on something very American and elegant—dinner at a popular but expensive jazz club in Greenwich Village and the rest of the evening in a midtown hotel room. But Sueanne was wearing jeans—too casual for the club—and she was talking breathlessly about another club, called Limelight, where she often went with her friends who also worked at Sophisticated Lady.

"I mean, it's really, really great," Sueanne was saying over and over, settling back into the leather car seat. "You work all day with a bunch of stuffy lawyers, saying, 'Yes, sir, No, sir. I'll kiss your ass, sir.' Then you get on that floor at the Limelight and dance until blood leaks out of the toes of your shoes."

Gusano felt his stomach lurch. "Driver, the Limelight," he said.

"So, you are a lawyer?" Gusano asked.

"Nah, silly. A secretary. An executive secretary. What do you do?"

Before he could answer, Sueanne began to prattle about one of her girlfriends, another Sophisticated Lady, whose last date, she said, was a drug dealer.

"Can you imagine? But you're not Colombian, are you? What did you say you do?"

"Dominican," he said stiffly. "I run a private security concern."

Before she could question him further, the driver pulled up in front of a grand-looking church. The crowd, standing patiently on the stone steps despite the cold, parted as Gusano and Sueanne stepped from the limousine.

Sueanne tugged playfully at his hand, pulling him toward the church. As Gusano followed, he was surprised to hear ear-splitting music coming from inside. Before he completely registered his outrage at how this House of God had been defiled, Sueanne disappeared inside. He tried to follow her, but his path was blocked by a blond boy, wearing lipstick and an oversized tuxedo jacket. The boy silently motioned for him to join the crowd standing in the cold night behind a red velvet rope.

Gusano was so stunned, he didn't think of shooting the boy right away. By the time he reached into his jacket, he realized there were too many witnesses, so instead of pulling out his nine-millimeter, he handed the boy twenty dollars. The kid didn't blink. With his face burning, Gusano dipped into his wallet and pulled out a fifty-dollar bill and stuffed it into the boy's breast pocket. Then he pushed his way past him and walked through the doors.

By the time he found Sueanne, he was sure that the vibrations of the music or an angry God Himself would soon reduce the church to rubble.

"Isn't this great?" screamed Sueanne, who was gulping a mixed drink in a plastic cup. Gusano only stared. Small men with huge shoulder pads bumped into him and never even looked his way as they pushed through the crowd. A woman with outsized breasts flung the tresses from her long red wig over her shoulder, whipping Gusano's face and stinging his eyes.

Suddenly, the music changed and became even louder. Lights began flashing and couples dressed in cheap black clothing swarmed the dance floor. Sueanne began throwing her weight from one foot to the other, causing her breasts to leap almost to her shoulder.

His manhood shriveled like he had waded into icewater. To make matters worse, the incessant din and the bright lights were starting to remind him of prison. He felt the old tension in his body, and was ready to beat anyone who threw a punch in his direction. He touched the nine-millimeter under his jacket.

"Why don't you dance?" shouted Sueanne.

But Gusano was blindly pushing his way to the door.

He flagged down the first livery cab and headed back toward Brooklyn. Speaking too loudly for the quiet of the car, he instructed the driver in Spanish to stop at a liquor store on Atlantic Avenue. The driver nodded wordlessly and pressed the car across the Manhattan Bridge.

44

Kate had eaten all the green M&M's and was summoning the energy to leave the couch to get another beer when the doorbell rang.

"Go away," she shouted above the television.

She lumbered into the black-and-white tiled kitchen, where she saw the telephone answering machine blinking insistently next to a pile of unpaid bills. She vaguely rooted through the white cabinets, then got another Michelob from the refrigerator and, grabbing a tattered corner of her sweatshirt, tried to twist off the cap.

"Oww, shit," she said, examining the inside of her thumb. "Why does Michelob design the twist-off tops for lumberjacks?" she asked no one.

The doorbell rang again, two long bursts.

As soon as she saw Finn, she became acutely aware that her face was stained with tears and she was wearing paint-splattered sweatpants and a threadbare button-down shirt purloined from James.

"What are you doing here?" she asked him.

Finn's eyes took in the beer and a small smudge of chocolate on her cheek.

"Why don't you check your answering machine? I've been going crazy trying to reach you," he said.

"I've been hiding," she responded. He followed her into the apartment, which looked pretty much the same as the last time he had been there. Maybe a little messier. It was furnished with an assortment of cadged furniture and nice antiques. The feminine feel of the room, lace-paneled curtains and expensive-looking rugs, was diminished by large overfilled bookcases and stacks of newspapers on the chairs and floor.

"I left a dozen messages for you at the office, too," he said. "I was so worried."

She flicked off the television and threw herself down on the over-stuffed couch. Above her was a silver-framed picture of an older man Finn assumed to be her father. Finn sat on the corner of a blue striped easy chair covered with week-old newspapers.

"I didn't know where you were," he said, embarrassment mounting in his voice.

Kate drank some beer. "I was with the mother of a dead kid in Flatbush, pretending not to be a ghoul. Then I was with my own mother, pretending I don't care that I'm thirty and single and all my friends are married. My mother," she said. Her voice got louder. "Call the waiter who serves tea at the Plaza if you don't believe me. The one with the stain on his tuxedo. Then I was in the newsroom long enough to hear about the Publisher's Awards dinner, held at the Rainbow Room, to honor Rob Grant, not Kate Murray. So what do you have to tell me? Some good news?"

As he told her about finding Graveyard Jones, Kate began eating the yellow M&M's.

"Didn't you say Dominick watched Gusano go into a building at Halsey and Wilson?" Finn repeated.

"Coincidence," she said abruptly. "If Dominick knew Gusano was in a killing mood that night, I doubt he would have followed him. Dominick looks like a wimp and he sounds like a deranged child."

Finn recalled the look in Dominick's eye when Fat Tony was badgering him. He thought it was fear, but after seeing Graveyard Jones's dead body, it seemed more menacing. *My girlfriend,* he'd said. *My girlfriend.*

Finn tried again. "Why that block? Why that apartment building? Estimate the chances of that being dumb luck," he said. "Don't you see? This guy could be more than your Loon of the Week. He might just be a witness or he could be ordering the hits. Or maybe, just maybe, he's the killer."

She looked at him blankly.

"I want you to lay low for a while. Change your routine. Don't go to work. Don't take calls from Dominick. Maybe you could stay at my place for a few days until we pick up Gusano and Dominick."

Kate put her beer on the table next to a coaster and rubbed her head.

"What do you mean? Just skip work, just like that?" Kate asked.

"Skip it, go on a leave, quit. I don't want you anywhere unprotected."

"Oh, for God's sake, stop thinking like a cop," Kate said irritably. "Nobody's coming after me. I'm just a pimple on the ass of this whole Magilla."

"This is no joke, Kate." *My girlfriend.*

"You've been watching too many cop shows," she said. "Take a break. Things like this don't happen except in the movies. I'm a reporter, not some kind of crime fighter."

Finn looked at her. Then he looked away.

"I could get fired for telling you this," he said slowly. "But we've developed some information on Gusano and Dominick, connecting them to the Severing homicide."

Kate's eyes widened. "They work together?" she asked breathlessly. "How? Why? I don't understand."

Finn inhaled and continued.

"There's some concern downtown, at headquarters, that you might have become a target," he said.

"I don't understand."

"Of the organization that Gusano works for."

Kate stared.

"You mean like a death threat?" she asked.

Finn nodded.

"We can't put you under a police guard until the paperwork is done, but I wanted you to know."

Kate let out a shriek and walked quickly into her bedroom. Finn followed behind.

"What are you doing?"

"Calling the city desk." She was suddenly animated.

Finn just stared.

"Are you kidding me? I'm calling my editors. This could be the best thing that ever happened to me." She spoke into the phone.

"Hello, Cyrus. Yeah. It's Kate. Get me Wilson. Interrupt the meeting if you have to."

She covered the receiver with one hand and wiped her eyes with the sleeve of her sweatshirt. She gave a triumphant laugh.

"When you piss someone off enough so they threaten your life, you don't just win a Publisher's Award, you get nominated for a Pulitzer," she said. "This is great. I'll probably get page one with this story."

Finn took a sip of her beer.

"God, they're going to go crazy with this. Crazy." Then into the telephone: "Cyrus, put me through to his office. It's important!"

"If you go with the story, I'll be off the case," said Finn quietly. Kate looked at him, confused.

"Hold on a second." She covered the telephone, calculating.

"Okay. So, officially, we'll get the chief of the department to confirm it. But off the record, you've got to confirm this to Wilson now so we can get page one. Tell him what you told me."

Finn began backing away until he bumped up against the wall. He waved his hand at the telephone. She covered the receiver again.

"Don't fool around, my boss is on the line."

"YOUR boss? You're going to cost me my job."

She said into the telephone, "Hold on just one more second."

"We can't do it this way," he said quietly.

"Why not?" she said. "This is a great break for me."

"We just can't," he said. "It's not solid."

Her eyes didn't move from his face.

"You mean it's not true."

She uncovered the telephone. "Wilson. I'll call you back." Then she hung up.

Finn walked toward the bay window, pulling back a panel of lace curtain, and looked out at the rain turning to diamonds under the streetlights.

She noticed for the first time that the check of his suit was too large and not matched at the seams. It was poorly cut; the pants pulled tight across his thighs and the jacket rode up as he moved.

Finn turned and walked toward her.

"Look, this isn't funny," he said mildly. "I don't want to see you get hurt."

She said nothing.

"If you don't want to stay at my apartment, stay with a friend. Go stay with your mother. But take a few days off from work. I mean it."

"Just like that," she said.

"Just like what?"

"The lie," she said, looking almost startled, as if something was waking her up.

He shrugged.

"It's not a lie, it's avoiding a problem."

"And I'm supposed to trust you?" Her lips curved upward, smiling but angry.

"Look, Kate, I'm sorry. I'm sorry, all right?" he said impatiently.

But Kate continued as if he hadn't said anything.

"We agreed on the Promenade. No lies. Lies will get me fired. Lies will break my heart." Her voice was getting louder. "You promised, but in the clinch, you act like a cop, not my lover."

"What about you?" he spun back. "The first hint that you have a front-page story and you're ready to throw me to the dogs. You're so busy acting like a reporter, I'm surprised you even remembered we were friends."

They squared off and glared at each other without saying a word.

Finn broke first.

"Okay. Okay. What I did was stupid," he said quietly. "But what if something happened to you?"

Kate turned and plucked his coat off the easy chair. "I think you should go now," she said, handing it to him. Her voice was flat and precise. "It's been a long day and I'm very tired."

"Let me buy you dinner."

"No, I'm not hungry."

"What about tomorrow night?" he said. "Let's go to Rockefeller Center and see the Christmas tree."

She shook her head. "I have plans." Then she added, "Maybe some other time."

"Look, let's not make this the end," he began, desperation in his voice. But her hand was already on the brass knob.

He knew anything he said would make her angrier but he couldn't stop himself. "You can't always tell what you're up against. Please be careful."

Without a word, she ushered Finn out into the night.

45

Kate poured herself two inches of Scotch and set the tumbler next to her half-finished beer.

"Worst day of my life," she mumbled to no one, grabbing at the remote and stabbing through the cable channels.

"It's not solid," she heard him say over and over. "It's not solid."

Carelessly, she poured more Scotch in the glass.

"Don't want you to get hurt," he said.

"You're the one doing the hurting," she slurred at the television.

She got up, took another beer out of the refrigerator, belched mildly, then changed her mind and put the beer back. She noticed the answering machine blinking, reversed through the lengthy messages, and switched it to Play.

She walked unsteadily back to the living room, sprawled on the couch, and listened to the voices fill the room.

Her mother confirming their date. Nina. Finn. The landlady asking about the storm windows. J.J. Finn. Mary. Finn. Nina. Finn. Finn.

James said he needed more space. Finn said it wasn't solid.

She had just settled into a half-sleep when she heard an unfamiliar voice on her answering machine.

"Kate. Kate. Are you there? It's me. I need to talk to you. It's me.'' There was a long pause and Kate could hear a jukebox and muffled shouts from a barroom. ''Everything feels wrong now. I don't know what t' do. I need to talk to ya.'' Kate sat up on the couch. There was a long pause and she could hear him breathing. ''I'll try to get in touch.'' Then there was silence.

46

Dominick was so numb from a Quaalude he bought from Vinnie's little brother that he thought it might be Kate, dressed in a tan trench coat, leaving her apartment. The temperature had dropped and the light rain was turning to sleet. He pulled the brim of his blue Yankees cap over his face and zipped the dirty gray anorak up past his chin. With only his eyes visible, he jumped off the top step of the stoop where he had been sheltered by a small overhang. He ran across the street to meet her.

"Kate! Kate!" he called. By the time he got close enough to get a good look, he realized that it was a man in the trench coat. He slowed to a walk and hunched his shoulders inside his coat as he watched the man get into a car. He moves like a cop, Dominick thought, a pissed-off cop. He wondered what a cop would be doing in Kate's apartment. Dominick walked unsteadily up to the car and knocked on the window.

Finn rolled it down halfway as he eased the car into drive.

"Hey, man, what time is it? You got a watch?" Dominick asked. His words were slurred together and muffled by the coat covering his mouth. The cop looked familiar, like a guy who played football at Dominick's high school.

"Beat it," Finn said without looking up.

Dominick put his hand on the top of the window, trying to get a better look. There was something about this guy, this cop. He'd seen him before.

"Yo, man, I'm just asking what time it is." The guy refused to acknowledge him and Dominick had to jog alongside the car to keep up. He could see the cop was really angry. He reached his hand a little farther into the window.

Instead of recoiling from his reach, the man looked up, quickly taking in Dominick's cap and dirty coat.

"Unless you want to do the Centre Street shuffle, you best get the fuck away from my car."

Recognition made Dominick's knees go weak. It was the same cop that had stopped him outside the Cork and Barrel.

The cop didn't recognize him. Dominick moved away from the car and let his hand drop, satisfied.

He waited until the car was out of sight. Then he bounded up the steps to Kate's apartment. He shivered in the cold night air. He had to talk to her. To find out why she had gone to the cops without him. He wished he had a credit card or a screwdriver so he could break the lock. Impatient, he was about to shatter the small pane of glass near the handle with his fist when a police car nosed around the corner. Quickly changing directions, Dominick pulled his jacket tighter and, hoping he looked innocent, trotted down the street.

47

Police Officer Daniel Owens didn't like working someone else's case.

In the first place, nobody brought you in on a case to offer your opinion. Usually, a detective needed some extra manpower to run down a skell. Something a rookie three weeks out of the Academy could do much better than a veteran like himself.

In the second place, you never got any overtime on a job like this. To a supervisor, one set of legs was as good as another. They would simply pull a guy from the next shift to start where you left off.

All in all, Owens didn't want to drag this one out.

The way Fat Tony had explained it, they were looking for a white guy named Dominick who hung around with a Spanish killer named Gusano.

Owens had been assigned to the 83rd Precinct for seven years. Although he had learned little about the neighborhood in that time, he had figured out that the only person who kept tabs on the Spanish population of Bushwick was Montoya, a local narcotics trafficker who worked out of a bar on Gates Avenue.

Owens hitched up his baggy blue pants, pulled down low by the bulk of his gut, and got into his car and drove to the bar.

If any other white cop had opened the door of El Fuego, at least five patrons would have made a twenty-yard dash to the men's room and squeezed out the small shoulder-high window into the back alley. But Owens was different. When El Fuego's patrons saw his gray-blond hair, they returned to their newspapers.

Everybody knew Owens wouldn't arrest you, especially in the morning when a collar was unlikely to bring in overtime. One afternoon about a year ago, three high-school dropouts had dared each other to get arrested by Owens. The most courageous of them walked up to the broken-down cop, unzipped his fly, and pissed on his scuffed shoe. Owens merely dropped his lower lip, made a disgusted sound like "Aawww," and wiped the top of his shoe against the calf of his trousers.

"Where's Montoya?" Owens asked the bartender, who everyone in the neighborhood called See No Evil.

"We got lots of Montoyas here. It's a common name, like Smith and Rivera," said See No Evil, pushing two beer glasses over dirty wet brushes.

"Well, then, I guess I'll just sit down and wait for him," said Owens loudly. "I might end up being here all day."

See No Evil looked at him for a second, then glanced at Gusano, who was drinking coffee at the back table. "Montoya won't be back for ten days, he's in Colombia. Perhaps you could come back."

Owens sighed.

Then he walked heavily over to a table of coffee drinkers and spoke loudly, as if the volume of his voice would make them understand English.

"I'm looking for a Caucasian male named Dominick Donatti," he announced. "And a Hispanic known as Gusano—like worm, but in Spanish."

The men looked at him sleepily. Gusano, whose expensive woolen suit covered his barrel chest and a nine-millimeter, closed his eyes slightly to indicate boredom.

"Some detectives want to talk to them. We think they have been doing very bad things. The white guy has been saying the Spanish guy may even have done a homicide or two."

One of the group raised a hand to his mouth in mock horror.

Owens flipped one of his cards onto the table.

"Please call the precinct if you hear of anyone who might go by those names," he enunciated again. "The white guy's named Dominick, and the Hispanic's named Gusano."

Gusano waited for the door to slam behind Owens before he spoke.

"That foolish boy," he said. "First his finger. Now his life."

48

Kate always felt a sense of reverence when she walked by the giant menorah above the front desk of the Beth-El Nursing Home in Borough Park. This time of year, the ancient symbol of perseverance was leavened by the nine-inch Christmas tree wrapped in blinking lights that stood on the main desk. Beth-El housed both Jews and Gentiles, but the ancient black security guard greeted all white people by shouting "Shalom!" with a resonant, Southern drawl.

"Shalom, Mr. Washington, how are you today?" Kate called out.

"Just fine. Just fine. Shall-home to you too, honey," he answered.

Today was Ballroom Dancing Day. Kate scanned the room, watching the couples tenderly move each other across the floor. She didn't see Edith anywhere, but her eye was drawn to a little man who sprang across the room as if he were on fire.

She waved at him.

"She's in her room," he called out between breaths.

Kate nodded and walked quickly down the long hallway.

Through each open doorway, Kate could see dioramas of human aging. Two ancient men sitting in chairs with movable armrests, watching "The Price Is Right." A bent old woman leaning into her walker, her fingers outstretched toward a framed poster of the Louvre. Another man, his translucent skin stretched over his skull, lay on his bed, hovering between life and death, a plastic oxygen tube in his nose.

Kate knocked on the half-open chipboard door.

"Come in, darling. I was just napping," said Edith faintly.

At ninety, Kate's grandmother had shrunk to the size of a child and was so thin she barely depressed the bedsprings.

"What were you dreaming about?" Kate asked, kissing Edith's forehead. Edith was still beautiful, even under the harsh overhead light.

"I was dreaming about my husband. Your grandfather. I was remembering the day we moved into our first home and his brother, Kenneth, was bitten by a tiger."

"What tiger?" She looked at Edith carefully.

"Well, it was before the war and Kenneth had left Ireland and gone to Germany to give a lecture in physical science. Afterward, he went with some colleagues to the Munich zoo." Raised in a lively intellectual and staunchly Catholic family in Borough Park, Edith spoke with a forceful vocabulary and a thick Brooklyn accent. "A tiger escaped and went right for him. Bit him on the throat."

"The same day you moved?"

Edith considered. "He had probably been bitten a few days before, but we got the telegram from the hospital in Munich on moving day saying he would probably die."

"What happened?"

"Your grandfather went into mourning. Everyone came over to pay their respects, but they had to sit on the floor because the furniture hadn't arrived. After three days of mourning, we conceived our first child. Your uncle Albert. Conceived in sadness."

"Then what happened?" Kate asked, leaning comfortably on the bed.

"By the time I was ready to have the baby, Kenneth had completely recovered and was sitting at our dinner table, eating everything in sight, as he did in those days. He had two big scars running around his neck." She drew two fingers under her chin.

Kate waited for her to continue but Edith's eyes closed, remembering.

"So we named the baby Albert."

"Why?"

"After the tiger that almost ate your great-uncle."

"The tiger's name was Albert?"

Edith looked at Kate. "Haven't I told you this story before?"

Kate shook her head.

Edith motioned for Kate to help her into a chair. As her grandmother shifted, Kate wondered how her wasted little bones still managed to support her body. Ever since Edith retired from the printing shop she ran in Borough Park and dropped out of Democratic ward politics, she got smaller, yet something inside her shined brighter and brighter.

Edith reached into a bag attached to the chair's movable armrest and brought out the week's worth of Kate's articles. With a gleam in her eye, she unfolded each clipping, asking questions about the victims, the suspects, or the police investigations.

"Mr. Heisler, you know, Room 401, is very interested to know if they caught the man who killed the nurse."

"Not yet, Edith. Soon."

After they discussed all the articles, Edith carefully transferred them into a bulging scrapbook. Then she looked into Kate's face with concern and her spidery fingers swept back a piece of her granddaughter's hair.

"Why don't you tell me what's wrong?"

Caught off guard, Kate tried to smile.

"It's complicated."

Edith sat very still.

Kate sighed. "Work isn't going well. I made a mistake. I got into trouble. Now it looks like I might get fired."

"I see," said Edith. Then she waited.

Kate pulled back her hair and rubbed the end of her nose with the palm of her hand. Without warning, the picture the *Herald* had run of Amanda Sanders, the two-year-old sex-abuse victim, spun through her mind and she felt her stomach clutch.

"I don't know what is wrong with me. I'm trying so hard to get ahead at work and nothing is going right."

"What else?"

"I started seeing a man. I thought I really liked him, but then it turned out . . . I don't know."

Edith waited.

"See, I met him through work, on a story, on the Severing homicide."

Edith nodded. "He's a police officer?"

"Detective. And he seemed to like me, except he can't accept that I work for the *Herald*. He always says, 'Be careful. Watch out for this one. Watch out for that one.' Like I can't take care of myself." She decided not to tell Edith about the crazy phone call on her answering machine. "Then, just the other night, he accused me of acting like a reporter instead of his lover."

She shot Edith a look to see if she was shocked, but Edith was unfazed. Kate gave an inward smile. Edith was the hippest ninety-year-old she knew.

"So it seems like I can't make anyone happy. Not my bosses. Not my lover. Not even Mrs. Severing's mother." Kate rubbed her forehead.

Edith rested her dry, papery hand on Kate's arm.

"And that's the problem. You're trying to make everyone else happy."

"What do you mean?"

"I'll tell you something that it took me four decades to learn. We have a lot more control of our lives than we think."

Kate waited for her to explain.

"What you need to do is figure out what you want. What *you* want. Not what your boss wants. Not what your detective wants for you. What you want." She lifted her fist, which was the size of a dried apple. "Then go get it."

"I'm trying," Kate began, helplessly.

"Well, not in the right way," Edith said crisply. "You have to focus. If you are going after the story, don't worry about the man. If you are going after the man, let the work pile up for a few weeks. You'll get what you set out for. But just be sure it will make you happy once you get it."

Edith leaned over and brushed another strand of hair from Kate's face.

"Well, I know I want a man in my life, Gram," Kate said, using the name she had used for Edith when she was five. "But I think this detective and I are just from different worlds. Maybe it could work out, but I don't know."

"You'll figure it out, I promise," she said, crooning softly, like a lullaby. Then she straightened up and sucked on her teeth.

"I've got something for you," she said, fishing around in her bag again. "Here. A book Mrs. Shulman gave me. It's called *Women Who Love the Wrong Man*. No, that's not it."

She squinted at the book and Kate made a mental note to ask the doctors to check Edith's eyesight.

"*Women Who Love Too Much,*" Kate read, mystified why Edith and Mrs. Shulman would concern themselves with modern mating rituals.

"There's been quite a fuss about this book. Both Oprah and Sally Jesse Raphael did shows on it when it came out. We take turns in our group reading it out loud."

"So what do you think about it?"

Edith gave a dismissive wave.

"Pure nonsense. Women need to get smart. Open an IRA. Buy property in their own names. Make a decent wage. Get state-funded child care. Pass the ERA Amendment."

"Edith, you old lefty." Kate smiled. "The ERA was rejected a long time ago."

Edith sniffed. "Time they brought it back, too."

Kate could see why Edith had been a formidable Democratic Club secretary.

They were interrupted when a fleshy woman on the far side of seventy-five stumbled giggling into Edith's room and hid behind the open door. She was pursued by the wizened little firecracker Kate had seen on the dance floor. He put his hand on her ample waist.

"Barney Silverman, you stop that this minute," the woman said, laughing.

"Don't tell me you're still a virgin?" he replied, and they lurched off together down the hall.

Edith smiled and shook her head.

"Those two can never keep their underpants on," she said, half-marveling. Then she turned back to Kate, her eyes bright. "Tell me about this mistake on your job. Maybe we can think of a way to put it right again."

49

Finn bisected Manhattan as he walked from the designated police parking lot outside One Police Plaza to Battery Park City. Though it was an unseasonably warm morning, the streets were empty.

Coming from Bushwick, he felt like he was walking into a futuristic model city. The buildings were already erected, but humans hadn't evolved quickly enough to find a place in the plan.

When he entered one of the greenish glass buildings, Finn realized that Battery Park City's office towers were connected by tunnels. Secretaries in pumps and Federal Express men pushing handcarts chose the soft industrial rubber flooring of the tunnels over the rough pavement and cutting Hudson River wind.

He sat in Richard Rondon's lucite-and-glass waiting room thinking about Kate, her face shifting with anger, handing him his coat. He had never had that kind of fight with his ex-wife. When Sandy was mad she sulked in the bedroom and wouldn't come out unless he begged. Kate had accused him of acting like a cop. Finn measured the accusation and decided she was probably right. All the girls he'd dated since his divorce had ex-husbands, brothers, or fathers in the department. They were used to it. They knew what to expect. They were resigned to it. Liked it, even. He wondered if, like the hairbags who hung around the station-house desk, he had forgotten how to treat civilians.

He checked his watch and saw that forty minutes had passed. He got up and walked over to the secretary, then asked her to remind Rondon that he was here.

"Mr. Rondon is in a meeting," said the secretary, who had close-set eyes lined with dramatic makeup under a pile of red hair. She said the word *meeting* as if it was something grave and irreversible, like *coma*.

"If you could just remind him," said Finn, looking at his watch and smiling uncomfortably. "I have another appointment."

The secretary checked her phone list and looked back up at him, her face blank.

"I'm sure."

Finn smiled again, his dry lips sticking slightly to his teeth, and sat back down. He stared out the enormous picture window at the vacant lot below. He tried to stop thinking about Kate, imagining himself looking out this window every day instead of the small dirty precinct panes. His mind drifted back to Kate, so he tried to concentrate on locating the exact spot where, in 1989, Joey "Cheese" Iacco, a Gambino crime family underboss, buried three members of a Genovese heroin operation.

Three gray-suited men, the shoulders of their jackets tailored into angles to prop up their soft bodies, walked through the reception area. To Finn, their laughter sounded like Brooklyn dogs barking: first one, then another, then all together. They probably didn't work for Rondon because the entire twenty-seven years Rondon had worked in the police department, the cops who worked under him laughed only once. The Day Rondon's Men Laughed had become something of a legend.

Two years before he retired, Rondon's wife had convinced her husband to take a winter vacation to Jamaica. Despite his own dark forebodings about racial uprisings and voodoo, Rondon had returned with a bright red sunburn and a surprisingly gentle afterglow. Early in the trip, their hotel room had been robbed, he admitted. The Jamaican thieves had stolen his traveler's checks but left his expensive camera, which he used to take a deck of snapshots during the rest of his vacation.

It wasn't until he reclaimed his pictures from Fotomat and was passing around the shots of his slack wife in a beach chair and palm trees near the surf that he saw the photograph that would forever change his reputation. The picture had been taken in his Kingston hotel room and it featured two black asses. Stuck snugly in those rear ends were toothbrushes, one belonging to Rondon, the other to his wife.

While Rondon commandeered a marked police car and sped, lights and sirens blazing, to his Nassau County home to throw out the toothbrushes, Rondon's men, who hated his guts, laughed until one police officer pissed in his blue trousers and another called EMS for oxygen.

Rondon's situation had clearly improved. From his current office, Finn could see the spikey western edge of Manhattan as it followed the Hudson to midtown. The morning sun was bright, and as he sat waiting for Rondon, Finn watched two square white sailboats, like moths, circle on the river.

The secretary finally shepherded Finn to the door.

"John Finn, it's been a long time," said Rondon, looking up from his wide desk. There was warmth in his voice, but the cool expression never left his face.

He beckoned Finn into his office and offered him a chair that turned out to be much too hard to be comfortable.

Sitting at attention on Rondon's left was a fresh-faced young man whose finely tooled wire-framed glasses hid hungry eyes. Rondon introduced him as Chester, his assistant, and Chester gave Finn a brief nod.

"Thanks for seeing me, Chief Rondon," Finn began.

"Not 'Chief' anymore." Rondon smiled. "Not since I traded the PD for Paine Webber."

"And a very prestigious job at Paine Webber," Finn said. He thought of the wild party thrown at Castle Harbor the day Rondon announced his resignation.

"I always thought the work I did at the police department was prestigious, too," said Rondon.

The blatant invitation for more flattery almost made Finn laugh.

"Especially your initiatives on auto theft," said Finn. "You certainly brought the department into the modern ages in that area of law enforcement."

It had been Rondon's idea to stop cars at major intersections and place drivers under arrest if they couldn't produce proper registration. The newspapers had a field day with the idiotic plan, which took detectives away from investigating homicides, assaults, and rapes while causing epic traffic jams. The mayor had called a halt to the plan in less than forty-eight hours.

Rondon took the compliment, ran a hand down the front of his well-tailored suit, and ah-hemmed modestly before a look of suspicion crossed his face. Chester smiled at his boss like a proud son.

"Now, don't go pulling my chain, I'm still your superior officer," Rondon said. "I assume you've come crawling here because you want a job."

Good old Rondon, friendly to vicious in the blink of an eye.

"Well, sir, I am interested in exploring opportunities outside the department," said Finn. He sounded like some kind of mealy-mouthed banker. "Not that I'm thinking about leaving. But you know what they say, twenty years can go by very quickly."

Rondon picked up on the lie immediately.

"Is Internal Affairs about to put you up on charges or are the streets getting too tough for you? I say, 'Fight back.' " He held up a liver-spotted fist. "I spent twenty-seven years on the job, and not once did I know fear."

Rondon again, Finn thought. General Patton of the clerical workers. The closest he'd ever come to a line-of-duty injury was a paper cut.

"Yes, sir."

"But it's a difficult world out there." He pointed to the harbor. "You have to be hard. But here, it's different." He gestured around his office. "To make it here, you have to be . . . me."

Finn's eyes moved across Rondon's face. He wondered if his ex-chief was getting senile.

"Yes, sir."

"You come here looking for a job, but consider my point of view. Why should I hire you? You're not a chief. You're not commanding a division. You probably don't even have a degree from a four-year university." He paused, waiting for a response. Finn nodded. "The world is full of disgruntled detectives. Do we need them at Paine Webber? I don't think so."

Chester was relishing every word of his boss's lecture, and Finn imagined himself rupturing Chester's larynx by punching him in the center of his skinny, pale throat. Finn was sweating under his collar.

He felt the walls of Rondon's office move in on him. He was a cop. He would be a cop until the day he retired. Then he would be a retired cop. He fingered the knot of his tie. There was no way out.

Rondon pressed a button under his desk, stood up, and walked to the burled-wood door. Finn saw that for all his expensive tailoring, Rondon's suit was bagging and hung on him like a tired old uniform.

Finn remembered sitting with Kate on the Promenade and swallowed hard. Desperation cut through his voice like a chainsaw.

"Well, sir, the last time we talked, you told me to drop by. I thought you might—" Finn was cut off in midsentence as Rondon's secretary opened the door. Rondon gave her the smug, knowing look a man gives a woman whose head has been between his knees.

"So I did and so you have. And I thank you for coming." He extended his hand and Finn shook it mechanically. Chester bobbed his head and smiled.

"Sweetie, show Detective Finn out, please."

Finn was stunned. The interview was over, finished, almost before it had begun.

"By the way," Finn said, turning to face Rondon. "We locked up some Jamaican burglars last week. They mentioned your name. Something about a robbery in Kingston."

A look of disgust, then fury, leapt across Rondon's face.

Finn turned to go. "Thanks for your time, Chief."

50

hy do you want to go to this stupid exhibit, anyway?"
croaked Kate as she lay supine on her oatmeal couch, clamping a
tattered blue throw pillow over her face like an icepack. "I thought
your BMW would turn back into a pumpkin if you crossed the Brooklyn Bridge."

"*The New Yorker* said the Brooklyn Museum had put together
the best Gainsborough show yet," said Nina, busy making coffee in
Kate's kitchen. "Even better than the one at the Met, and the Met
show was out of this world."

"I must have missed that one," Kate said. Then she felt bad about
being so sarcastic.

After covering a four-alarm fire in Crown Heights until four-thirty
A.M., Kate had stripped off her soot-stained clothing and fallen asleep
on the couch. Now, four restless hours later, she felt as if she had
been crawling through a gritty black tunnel instead of napping in her
living room.

She took shallow, cautious breaths, as if inflating her lungs to
their full capacity would prove too exhausting. Although her vision
was partially blocked by the pillow, she saw that Nina wore a pressed
white shirt and forest-green wool slacks. She watched without speaking as her friend threw the day's papers onto a stack near the blue
easy chair.

"Ugh. You smell like a campfire," Nina said, wrinkling her nose and holding out a cup of coffee. "After you take a shower, I've got something I need to tell you."

Moodily, Kate pulled back a swirl of hair.

"I hate covering fires. You stand on a cold sidewalk in six inches of dirty black water listening to people screaming inside an inferno," said Kate, her voice dull from sleep. "At around three-thirty this morning I'm complaining to my photographer that my new shoes are getting ruined."

She paused. "One pair of brown suede Kenneth Cole ankle boots: dead at the scene. Oh yes, and four children burnt beyond recognition. Christmas lights plugged into faulty wiring."

She paused and looked up. Nina looked confused.

"The *Post* said it was arson," Nina said, looking at the tabloid. "They carried it on page one. 'Father Kills Four Children in Brooklyn Arson.' "

"Arson," Kate said, suddenly awake. "Goddamn arson?" She lunged for the papers. "The fire marshal told me they didn't know how it started."

Nina grabbed another paper and poked her finger against the front page.

"The *Times* has arson, too. They quote police department spokesman Stephen Rissolli. The *Daily Herald* ran it on page seven. Their story doesn't even mention arson."

"I know the *Daily Herald* doesn't have arson. I wrote the goddamn story. I didn't know it was goddamn arson. Goddamn Rissolli," Kate groaned.

She threw herself onto the couch and buried her head under the pillow again. If she had a coffin, she would have pulled the lid over herself.

"Wilson is going to go crazy when he sees this," she moaned.

"Kate, it's not the end of the world," Nina began, but was interrupted by Kate's answering machine intercepting a telephone call on the second ring.

With wide eyes, they listened to Kate's recorded message. Then they heard the beep.

"Murray, this is Ridgeway." The voice sounded gruff but reasonable.

For a second, Kate and Nina relaxed.

Then the voice on the machine exploded. "PICK UP THIS FUCKING TELEPHONE, Murray. IT WAS ARSON. ARSON!" Ridgeway was roaring. "PICK UP THE PHONE, YOU DUMB BROAD, I KNOW YOU'RE IN THERE."

Kate lunged for the telephone.

"Yeah. I saw. Right. Arson," Kate said, staring into the telephone. "Yeah. Yeah. You're right. Of course. Right." Kate shrugged into the telephone, then slowly hung up.

"What did he say?"

"He wants another story on the Crown Heights arson," said Kate miserably.

"What else did he say?"

"He said if I don't have something new on the Severing homicide by the first of the week, he's giving the story to Grant and moving me to the obituary desk." Then she threw her legs over the sofa. "I've got to get back out to the scene in Crown Heights. Cover the arson angle."

"Just give me a second, before you go."

"What? For God's sake, Nina. I don't give a damn about Gainsborough. Don't you get it? I'm about to lose my job." Kate was pulling on her coat and thrashing under the couch for her shoes.

"Kate, I'm going to have a baby," Nina said quietly.

Kate's mouth was frozen in a little O of disbelief.

"But you just got married."

"Right. Now I'm pregnant."

"Hand me my bag, will you," demanded Kate.

Nina held it a few inches from Kate's fingers.

"Kate, tell me congratulations. Say, 'That's wonderful, Nina, do you want a boy or a girl?' "

"Is that what I'm supposed to say? Okay. Congratulations, Nina, great. I hope it's a girl."

"Don't be a bitch, Kate." She tossed the bag on the couch. Kate grabbed it and scrambled toward the door.

"Why did you have to do that?" Kate asked accusingly, pulling on the door handle. "Get pregnant. Hah. I'm not used to the idea of you being married. Now I have to deal with this, too."

"So it's about you again. Your story. Your job. Your broken heart. Your getting used to my marriage. What are you going to do. You. You. You."

"I got to go, I'll phone."

"Kate, if you can't stay with me a few minutes now, don't bother calling me."

But Kate, pretending not to hear, was already in the foyer.

"Slam the door when you leave," she called from the foyer.

She loped over the first two stairs with a single stride and stopped on the third stair. She turned her face toward the wind. Then the tears came.

51

From his red Nissan, Gusano watched Dominick as he sat at the lunchroom counter, a meatball hero stuck in his mouth. Some men are just lucky, they can eat anything, Gusano thought somberly as he fingered the waistband of his worsted pants. He shifted his weight to the other side of his buttocks, rhythmically tightening and relaxing the muscles in his legs to improve his circulation.

Gusano had been following Dominick since early this morning and, after several hours, had concluded that Dominick would eat anything.

Now it was late afternoon, and in the last two hours Gusano had watched Dominick swallow two doughnuts from Coffee-To-Go and a fried-egg sandwich on a kaiser roll from a deli. Earlier, while standing near him at a bank of telephones on Bedford Avenue, he had listened as Dominick left messages for a woman named Murray while consuming three Snickers bars from C-Town. Less than an hour later, he watched Dominick leave McDonald's with a chocolate shake and french fries. Gusano, listening to his empty stomach growl in protest, wondered if Dominick's ancestors had been raised with goats and had adopted their eating habits.

He adjusted his black cashmere coat and stared at his own deep black eyes in the rearview mirror. Dominicans were a more self-respecting race than these mutt Europeans, he concluded, adjusting his tie and smoothing his holster strap, which wrinkled his pressed shirt.

A beautiful young Latino girl walked past the car. She was wearing tight black pants and her bangs were dyed, sprayed, and brushed back into a stiff brown coxcomb. She saw Gusano's little grooming gestures and smiled. In a second, Gusano was out of the car, standing by her side.

"Madame, forgive me my courage, but I know we must be introduced," he said, bowing slightly from the waist. It was a line from an English language tape he had memorized in jail.

The girl's smile faded and Gusano saw she was Italian, not Hispanic.

"Git the fuck out 'a my way," she said.

Just then Dominick came out of the restaurant and Gusano, his eyes glittering, quickly got back into his car.

52

Dominick paced back and forth in front of the black Tercel, muttering to himself. He had been ringing her bell since about sundown, hoping to intercept Kate before she went out. But as the hours rolled by, he was convinced that she had somehow eluded him.

By now, the traffic was dying away; the Saturday-night revelers had arrived at their destinations hours before. Even the dogwalkers, who randomly patrolled the flagstone sidewalks, were nestled safely in front of their television sets.

But as the city noises faded, the roar in Dominick's head grew louder and louder.

"Come home, Kate. Come home to me," he called out softly, but the words were lost in an anguished moan.

Dominick lifted his hands from his pockets and blew on them. The cold was making his fingers stiff, and his broken finger, now healed except for a tender gnarl of bone below the first knuckle, gave a remote ache.

Agitated, Dominick skipped up the steps and rang Kate's doorbell again, then swiveled, stalking back to the car. A swirl of broken leaves, gum wrappers, and soot curled around his feet, and the miniature urban twister gave Dominick an idea. He broke the window of her Tercel with the handle of a screwdriver he carried and climbed in.

As soon as he was settled in the front seat, he felt calmer. Something about the pliant black leather made him think of Kate. He took a deep breath. It was like the air that had been around her was clearer, easier to breathe.

With a little grunt, he began rifling through the glove compartment. A green plastic parking permit, a five-borough map, a half-dozen pens. He grunted again and reached in farther. With a flourish, he pulled out a slim plastic box which he assumed was a small tape recorder. Instead it held four Tampax wrapped in crackling white paper. He felt himself blushing to the roots of his hair. He would have to get used to these intimate little discoveries, he chided himself. But it wouldn't be easy. He was raised in the old school, where men were men and women just didn't leave things like this lying around.

Where was she? Why had she stopped taking his calls? His mind skipped over the same questions again and again. His desire to see her had become a physical need, like a hunger or a terrible thirst. He wanted to set their plan in motion. He wanted to take her to the Cork and Barrel. He wanted to slap her until her eyes crossed for betraying him to that cop. Then he would hold her in his arms and tell her the most important thing—that he loved her and needed her by his side.

He pulled out the screwdriver again, then took a length of rope, a cassette, and a roll of electrical tape out of his pocket. He jammed the screwdriver into the steering column, then switched on the heater and the tape deck. He pushed the cassette into the deck. He reached under his left buttock and lowered the seat until he was lying almost flat and stared up through the sunroof.

"In the wee small hours of the morning," Sinatra sang.

> While the whole wide world is fast asleep,
> You lie awake and think about the girl
> And never ever think of counting sheep.

That's what he loved about Sinatra. His voice could reach through all the terrible and confusing things that were happening to him and make his emotions flow along with the song. This one made him feel more lonely than the last man alive.

Almost to distract himself, Dominick reached down for the zipper of his jeans. He pulled up the elastic of his underwear with his almost-healed hand. It was, after all, only a broken bone, he thought, trying to cheer himself. He gave himself a squeeze and tried to press the image of the three-pronged garden tool from his mind. One more week and his finger would be as good as new. In a week, he would have straightened out this mess with Kate. They would be working together for the newspaper. They would go after his enemies together. Expose them. Make them squirm. Make them leave town. Just like on ''60 Minutes.''

Dominick settled back against the headrest and looked out onto the empty street.

> When your lonely heart has learned its lesson,
> You'd be hers, if only she would call.
> In the wee small hours of the morning,
> That's the time you miss her most of all.

When he was done, Dominick felt depressed. He zippered his pants and climbed into the backseat. He would hide in her car until she came home tonight and then grab her as she unlocked the front door to her building. Nothing too violent, he just wanted to make a point. He settled across the seats so he had a clear view of the street. He stared without blinking at the steps where he would greet her.

53

Kate stood outside the painted white door, listening to the sounds of an old Prince record and muted laughter, debating whether to ring the bell or go home. When you're in a bad mood there's nothing like a party to make you feel like dying, she thought.

James would have insisted she go in. They were his friends, anyway. The Young Turks, he used to call them. Success stories of the 1980s. People who came to New York with the single, sole intention of making money.

Kate was heading back to the elevator when Ellen Von Dam, one of the top photographer's agents in the city, threw open the door and began to shout.

"Why, there you are!"

Von Dam, born Ellie Fostovitz, had grown up in New Jersey, and though her marriage to society photographer and avowed homosexual Clarence Von Dam had lasted less than a year, it had put a margin of mystery between her new image and her perfectly conventional middle-class upbringing. Two years later, she brokered just about every photographer whose work had appeared on the cover of *Vogue*.

Ellie blew air kisses on either side of Kate's face and beckoned her into her enormous SoHo loft.

Almost every white square of wall was hung with photographs, lithographs, and paintings from the neighborhood's hottest artists. A

Chuck Close self-portrait hanging in the living room moved the eye to a Schnabel crockery collage, which in turn drew attention to a small but cleverly lit Warhol hung near the exposed kitchen. But Kate couldn't stare at the art too long, because clustered in between the paintings were the Young Turks.

"Help yourself to everything," Ellie said, pushing a glass of wine into Kate's hand. Kate took two steps forward and tried to join a small cluster of people talking about a Japanese banking scandal.

" . . . but because of those shenanigans, the bank fell. And there was a run on the main branch in Tokyo," said a man who described himself as a venture capitalist. Kate thought he was good-looking and tried, subtly, to catch his eye. "The police had to call in the riot squad. Then the president of the bank committed suicide because he had lost his honor."

Two couples broke into laughter. "Oh, that's terrible," Kate said, and the couples laughed more.

"No, no. That's great," said the venture capitalist.

His date, who was wearing a dress Kate had seen in the window at Saks, turned slightly, looked Kate over but did not smile.

Snubbed, Kate drifted off, helping herself to an enormous grilled shrimp from a silver tray. As she stuffed it into her mouth, she thought of a homicide she had covered a month ago in Flatbush. A crack-addicted mother of four had been shot to death. Visiting the woman's dirty home, Kate had watched a seven-year-old try to feed his hungry, squalling newborn brother a neon-yellow Twinkie. There was no other food in the house.

Kate allowed a waiter to refill her wineglass.

Feeling invisible, Kate wandered to another room, where, under a giant Roy Lichtenstein, a hired pianist was playing Cole Porter songs on Ellie's grand piano. Oblivious to the music, a prominent art dealer Kate recognized from the Styles section of *The New York Times* was holding court.

In the next room, which was given over to African and Brazilian tribal art, a senior editor from *Vogue* was talking to a production editor from *Vanity Fair*.

"I mean, one week she has Seven Sisters written all over her—a Fair Isle sweater and a copy of *To the Lighthouse* in her top drawer. The next week she moves to the East Village and gets a tattoo," said the *Vanity Fair* editor, who had thick bangs covering her forehead.

"Well, my assistant has color-coded every file in my office, but she will not answer the telephone," said the *Vogue* editor, who wore round wire-framed glasses. "So I am constantly raising my voice an octave"—she feigned an outer-borough accent—"and pretending to be my own secretary. It just doesn't seem right."

The two women looked at Kate, who smiled in a way she hoped was sympathetic.

"I wish I had an assistant sometimes," she said lamely.

The *Vogue* editor gave Kate an appraising look.

"Really?" She waited just a second too long, then added, "What is it that you do?"

Kate grabbed at a tray of triangular spinach pies as a waiter glided by and stuffed one into her mouth, so her next words were garbled. "I'm a crime reporter for the *Daily Herald*."

The *Vanity Fair* editor drew back as if Kate had said she committed crimes instead of covered them.

"Well, how interesting," she said, again halting long enough to change the meaning of her words.

But the *Vogue* editor leaned forward. "You must see a lot of tragedy," she said.

Kate was flattered at her interest. Maybe Nina was right. She should do more networking. Kate knew that many magazine careers had been started with a few witty remarks at a cocktail party. "Yes, I do," she said. "I cover a homicide almost every day."

"That's why I stopped reading those sleazy tabloids," the editor pronounced. "Too much violence."

Kate's smile turned stiff and began to crack.

"Excuse me, I need to go find my date," she said, gesturing behind her.

As she turned around, she saw the back of a familiar head. She smiled eagerly, then her fingertips went cold. She knew the nape of that neck. It was James. He was facing a thin-nosed woman with a geometric haircut that made her perfectly balanced face look like a sculpture.

His blushing bride. Kate's arms laced around her midsection. She thought she might vomit.

She blindly dodged past a cluster of people and through a doorway until she found an empty bedroom with a double bed piled high with coats. Locking the door behind her, she lay back against a long sable, letting it fall over her shoulders. She sucked in a breath, slightly dizzy from the exotic perfume that clung to the fur. It smelled like success, she thought. Like the whole party, it reeked of self-assurance and entitlement. The right husband. The right job. The right friends.

"Are you sick?" asked a deep voice.

Kate hadn't even noticed a dark-haired man watching television in the corner.

"How do you feel?" he asked again. Kate noticed the delicate frames of his glasses and his exquisitely made two-toned shoes.

"Inadequate," Kate said before she could stop herself. "I mean, yes, I was feeling a little sick, maybe claustrophobic. . . . " She was fumbling. "Such a nice party, interesting crowd—"

"With a lot of attitude," he finished for her. Then he laughed.

Kate looked at him closely. He had beautiful eyes, wide, sensuous lips, and a long, well-shaped nose. She wondered if he was gay.

"Well, you look more than adequate, you look wonderful to me," he said.

"I do?"

Kate noticed that he spoke with a slight accent. She looked directly into his eyes and saw the clear invitation. Definitely not gay. She smiled, flattered.

"Tonight I'm celebrating," he continued smoothly. "My uncle has been named to a cabinet post in Argentina, my country. And I landed a big account for our agency in New York. A great big loft full of interesting people. But who can I share this happy moment with?"

Kate thought of James. She couldn't go back out there alone. She couldn't go home to an answering machine full of hang-ups. She struggled off the coats and stood up to introduce herself.

"We'll leave this party now," he said, throwing his arm around Kate as if they were cousins or old lovers, and steered her out the door. "Let's go out and paint the city red."

54

Dominick was standing alone on the stage, looking into the rectangular silver microphone, while hundreds of women screamed, "Dommy! Dommy!" He smiled gratefully, opened his mouth, and began to croon.

But then the cheering voices began to sputter as a toxic cloud filled the auditorium. The swooning turned to coughs and then death rattles as the airborne infectious waste pressed the life from the women. Then there was silence.

Dominick squinted into the footlights, blinded.

"Is anyone still alive out there?" he shouted, his voice trembling.

Through the swirling cloud, a grayish figure began to emerge, becoming clearer as it moved down the center aisle. It was his mother, a giant version of his mother, getting larger as she got closer. And she was screaming.

The silence and intense cold woke Dominick. It was dawn. The car battery had run out, shutting off the heater and the tape deck. The cramped way he slept had cut the circulation to his left leg, so he stumbled when he pulled himself out of the Tercel.

He half-crawled up the stairs of Kate's building and leaned on the bell. No answer. He leaned on it again. Nothing.

He sat down, flexing his toes, wincing as the feeling pumped back into his leg. He stood up and rang again.

He was mystified. Where could she be? Then he felt the sickness creep over him. She had stayed out all night, he thought, feeling his rage grow stronger until his head began to buzz. She had spent the night with the cop.

55

Kate exhaled small white balloons of frozen air into the bright cold morning. She stomped her feet slightly to drive the chill out of her toes as she walked.

Anxiety had jerked her awake shortly after dawn. She set Federico's alarm clock so he would make his plane to Argentina and left him, doe-eyed with sleep under his blankets. It was too early for the subway trains to be running regularly and she didn't feel like waiting for a cab on an empty street in TriBeCa, so she decided to walk home.

She looked up and down the vacant sidewalks. Nothing moved. She wished she could get rid of this creepy feeling, but she kept hearing Finn's words. *Be careful*. Her answering machine wasn't helping matters. For the last three days, all she got was hang-ups. Sometimes she heard street sounds, barroom shouts, or heavy, irregular breathing. But never any messages. If it kept up, she'd have to get a new number.

A garbage truck rumbled by and a three-hundred-pound sanitation worker made kissing and smacking noises at her. She scowled at him as she crossed Reade Street and headed toward City Hall.

Fred, it turned out, was an advertising executive who commuted twice a month from Buenos Aires to New York. His girlfriend, he told her after a full bottle of wine, waited for him there. He was lively and charming and lighthearted, but she doubted she would see him again.

The little smile, which was creeping across her face, faded when she thought of Finn, standing in her apartment twisting the lapel of his wrinkled coat. She suddenly felt guilty and worried, as if sleeping with strange men had become an addiction. She thought of a young divorcée, stabbed to death in Queens. Detectives had simply gone through her crowded address book, calling her lovers, until one of them confessed to the killing.

She rubbed her eyes, suddenly feeling empty and tired. Her hand unconsciously locked over her midsection. Sometime last night, she had decided: As much as she liked Finn, she would never go back to him.

Kate sighed and kept walking, listening as her footsteps made a hollow sound on the walkway of the Brooklyn Bridge.

The sun was rising over the projects east of Chinatown and the wind was blowing around the island out to sea.

She put her hands on either side of her head, like blinders, and looked toward Staten Island, imagining she was a Dutch settler seeing the majestic waterway for the first time.

Then she moved her left hand so she could see the rusting docks and defunct Navy yards in Brooklyn, imagining the longshoremen and metal workers groaning and spitting and pissing as they unloaded and repaired the boats tied to the bustling pier.

Then she moved her right hand and her eyes traversed the Financial District, flat expanses of glass and steel, a monument to money, which started at the tide and ended in the clouds.

On the lip of the vast panorama, she thought of all the people who had been murdered and forgotten in the city. She imagined their souls, trapped in a spiritual inversion, floating above the city in a ghostly miasma. She quickly cataloged the stories she had written about murder. An insignificant number in the face of the vast army of the dead.

She thought of all the people who had killed and never been caught. Their stories whispered in the steamy subway breaths that billowed upward from manholes and cracks in the concrete. She imagined stories that were told but then forgotten, inscribed on the discolored marble cornerstones of skyscrapers, then obscured as each passing year laid down a fine oily coat of grime.

She thought of the glib, slippery sound of lies and the brutal howl of rage that rips from the chest of a bereaved mother. And she heard the thunder and whine as the driver of a sixteen-wheeler jammed on his worn brakes somewhere on the FDR below.

She thought about how far she would have to travel and how lonely it might be. And when her heart was grinding, she remembered Mrs. Severing. She knew what she had to do. She had to write another story about the woman's daughter.

The current of Kate's thoughts shifted abruptly, and she traveled back through her college years. She saw herself talking hopefully to one man after another while their eyes followed some other woman across the room. She remembered how she wished with all her heart that she was the one their eyes followed.

She skipped to a comforting fantasy she'd replayed over and over. It was a daydream of her own wedding day. In it, she stood, frozen in time, draped in a long white veil. Her gown rustled and the organ music played. Next to her, like a groom on a cake, stood James.

Instead of being warmed by the daydream, she felt a gust of wind travel up her spine. James was married. She flashed on his wife's perfect haircut. It was never going to be. She was setting her life on a different course.

She twisted the ring James had given her, and to her surprise it slipped off easily. She held the ring in front of her like a kaleidoscope, looking first at the Navy yards and then at the buildings of lower Manhattan. Then she flung the gold circle out in front of her, losing sight of it long before it hit the water.

The wind suddenly made the cables vibrate. She wondered what the hell she was doing, standing alone on the Brooklyn Bridge, like a space traveler, lost in the cold silent leagues between two galaxies.

56

Dominick drove along the Belt Parkway, his eyes scanning the paved track that ran to the right of the road. He noticed a young mother on a thin-framed ten-speed bike gliding ahead of her young son on his sturdy-looking dirt bike. A broad-chested man with a Tom Selleck mustache jogged fifteen feet ahead of his girlfriend, who looked as if she was about to drop. The sun was beginning to set behind the Verrazano-Narrows Bridge, but for Dominick the peaceful scene only highlighted his inner panic.

He was exhausted from his broken sleep in Kate's car last night, but he was so angry and distraught, he couldn't nap. Even a Quaalude chased by beer at around noon gave him no relief.

Out of the corner of his eyes he saw shadows darting toward him, although he told himself it was nerves. He was ravenous, but since this morning, everything he ate came up violently before it even settled in his stomach.

He took a deep calming breath and let it out slowly. He noticed the tall reeds that separated the shoulder of the road from the bay and made a mental note that if he ever managed to kill his mother or the cop he saw coming out of Kate's apartment, he would leave their bodies in those weeds.

Kate. He said her name out loud and felt comforted.

It was dark by the time Dominick pulled onto the JFK airport service road. He had driven past many miles of weeds and was satisfied, like generations of gangsters before him, that few things meant to be lost would be found in the Jamaica Bay swampland.

He sighed loudly when he saw the low, bunkerlike building marked ANIMAL QUARANTINE. Dominick didn't see the red Nissan lagging behind him.

He pulled up to the loading dock and blew his horn a few times until one of the corrugated metal doors rolled up.

Inside, high up on the loading dock, stood a tall dark-skinned man with the fierce, sculpted features of a chess piece. A T-shirt stretched over his enormous frame, outlining shoulder muscles that stood out like coconut shells stuck between his skin and the cloth.

"Hiyado," said Dominick, smiling nervously.

The man only grunted, then picked up a large plastic bag and tossed it at Dominick.

Dominick caught it awkwardly and stifled a scream. Under the translucent plastic he could see a child's face. His scream died away when he saw the face was small and furry and the eyes were flat and yellow. A teddy bear. Dominick shifted his grip and the teddy bear's face lit up.

"Will ya look at that?" said Dominick. "That's the greatest toy I've ever seen."

He tried to tear open the plastic to get a closer look at the bear, but the guy on the loading dock was grunting again, heaving another bag in his direction.

Dominick hurriedly began packing the bags of teddy bears into Big Mike's station wagon. They worked silently until the car was packed. Some of the bags had split and the bears were lighting up on their own all over the car.

"These are going to go over big for Christmas," said Dominick when the man had thrown down the last bag. The physical activity had calmed him and Dominick held one of the sightless bears up to his face.

"Nice toy," he said, inhaling the formaldehyde scent of the fake fur.

He heard the man chortle and turned around to laugh with him, but the man was lying on his face, his arm tucked at an ugly angle beneath him and a pool of blood spreading from his neck.

The man gagged, made a small gasping sound, and then Dominick heard nothing but the wind over the swamp and his own whimpering breath.

He crouched down, but didn't know what to shield himself from.

Slowly, he reached up and opened the door. He threw himself into the car and almost blacked out from panic when he realized the keys weren't in the ignition.

In the rearview mirror, he could see the bears blinking a warning. He pushed his good hand into the pocket of his skintight jeans trying to find the keys. Then he heard the sound of breaking glass as the passenger's-side window collapsed into fragments.

Dominick turned around and saw an empty Nissan behind him and to the right he saw Gusano leveling a large gun made larger still by a silencer.

A bullet whistled by, leaving a red burn on his forehead.

Another bullet dinged the steering wheel and tore through the tender spur in Dominick's broken finger.

Dominick whipped the keys out of his pocket, jammed them into the ignition, and threw the car into reverse. He had driven about ten feet when he felt the blinding pain, like his hand had exploded.

Gusano crossed his arms over his chest, like a Hispanic Mr. Clean, and calmly watched his target drive off.

*　　*　　*

Dominick was still mumbling when he reached the turnoff to Big Mike's warehouse.

"Twelve more shopping days. Twelve more days for great savings," sang a woman on the radio. Dominick angled his head and felt a rush of relief. It was Kate Murray singing the song, using the radio to communicate with him. She was trying to explain everything. He turned up the sound. She was giving him advice, trying to tell him what he needed to do.

The jingle ended and Dominick flicked off the radio, splashing a thin stream of blood over the dashboard. Immediately, his mind was filled with black thoughts. He was sure that there was a connection between Gusano and that cop at Kate's house. He put his finger in his mouth and bit down. How could Kate, the woman he loved, have sold him out? He stared at the blinking bear in the front seat. Then he saw it as an enormous grizzly towering over him. The bear raised a heavy paw and with his glinting five-inch razor-sharp claws carved out Dominick's heart.

"Why, Kate? Why?" he howled, letting his sobs whip out the broken car window with the wind.

Dominick knew he needed to get inside Mike's warehouse, to hide out. He gripped the steering wheel, which was sticky with blood, and tried to concentrate on driving. He longed to sit near the espresso machine and listen to the men brag about girls and swag. He needed to get in there where it was safe, away from that crazy killer. Most of all, he wanted Kate Murray to be with him, but he was afraid to go to her house again. Afraid Gusano might find him before he found Kate.

Tears ran down his face, mixing with the moisture dripping from his nose. A little bit of drool formed a cold puddle on his shirt.

Dominick turned the final corner to the warehouse and screamed.

The loading dock was blocked by a dozen cars with flashing lights. Not just police cars but vans from the Environmental Protection Agency and trucks from the Chemical Hazard Unit. Sanitation officials in orange hard hats swarmed between the vehicles and three men dressed in space suits were on the loading dock, prying open the door of one of the meat trucks.

Dominick began to bang his head on the steering wheel. Sharp cries came from deep within him on each impact.

Big Mike stood still, watching the circus, hands behind his back, passively waiting to be handcuffed. Birdie was already cuffed to a federal marshal and the two Megadeth boys, one with a vivid bruise on his cheek, lay spread-eagled over a police car.

57

Grant nervously fingered the cellophane wrapper of his cigar as Kate pounded on the keyboard. Even before it was filed, her story was creating a stir in the newsroom, and Kate noticed Grant couldn't stop squirming. His eyes closed into slits as he watched Wilson, his Hermès tie flapping, trot over to ask her yet another question about Margaret Severing. When Wilson left, Grant lit his third cigar of the day and Kate gave him a dirty look as the smoke drifted lazily over her desk.

> So far, police have linked at least two killings to the drug organization that controls several blocks of the crack trade in Bushwick. The nurse, Margaret Severing, was the first victim. A part-time drug courier, Graveyard Jones, was the second.

As she wrote, tension buzzed in her neck. It was a good story. It was a great story. With every paragraph she felt herself take a quantum leap toward the Publisher's Award. And she knew, with cold certainty, she was making a choice. She was using Finn, publishing information he had told her in confidence. Burning a source—a source she had slept with. She felt slightly dizzy, wondering for a second how many professional ethics she could breach in a single story.

But she pressed on, tapping out the words. It would never have worked anyway, she reasoned. They were too different. Fat Tony was right. Finn worked for the police department. He would never understand that she was a reporter. A damn good one, too.

She scrolled through the story, editing and making adjustments. She sealed up something soft and sentimental inside her, willing her heart to become solid, like a rock.

She pressed the button and filed her story.

And hour later, Wilson himself wrote the headline: DRUG HITMAN STALKS BROOKLYN, smacking his lips with satisfaction.

"Good job, kid. One of these days you'll be a great crime reporter," he barked, scanning the room. Kate imagined sprinkling him with lighter fluid and striking a match.

Wilson's eyes focused on her again. "Keep it up," he said, "you might even get a merit raise."

Kate grinned appreciatively at Wilson as he strode away. In her mind, she hastily blew out the match.

She could tell that Grant was furious when she overheard him confide to a new blond intern his suspicion that Kate was sleeping with a police official. Then he gave Kate his hearty congratulations.

Kate rode the adrenaline, yet something was missing. She tried to find J.J., but her desk had already been emptied out. She called Nina, but there was no answer, so she left a message.

She made a few calls to set up another story for tomorrow and opened her mail. At 7:30 she was still at the office, and she wasn't sure why.

Driving down the FDR, she craned her neck to see around the masking tape and plastic she had rigged up as a makeshift window. They should give the death penalty to the creeps who boosted cars, she fumed. It was true, her car wasn't actually stolen. Someone must have spooked the little criminal before he drove it off. But somehow he had shorted out her battery, forcing her to call Triple A for a jump, and it was going to cost her $100 to fix the window and fix the ignition. Little bastard. She jammed the play button on the tape deck to blast Patsy Cline and clear her head before she hit the traffic on Flatbush Avenue.

"I'll be lovin' you, always," Kate warbled while the tape hissed.

She pulled onto the entrance ramp of the Brooklyn Bridge and almost drove into the traffic divider. Instead of Patsy, she heard a familiar crooning. It was Frank Sinatra, his voice like a gin-soaked onion at the bottom of a martini glass.

She felt a cold breeze go down her back. She had never owned a Frank Sinatra tape in her life. Nervously, she checked her rearview mirror. Maybe someday this would make a good "only-in-New-York" story: "Later that day, I turned on the tape deck only to find that the car thief had left his tape behind. Ha. Ha."

She hit the eject button with so much force that she broke her nail, and she began to gnaw at the ragged edge. She could hear her heart pound, and on her forearms the tiny pale hairs were standing on end.

When she got home, she ran from the car to her apartment. She walked directly to her blinking answering machine and yanked its plug out of the wall. She wanted to talk to John Finn. She dialed his number but hung up on the second ring. What was she going to say?

Then she pulled on sweatpants and a sweatshirt and cleaned every inch of her silent apartment, trying hard not to notice that she lived alone.

58

Jeff Kubrick was the one who first saw the article linking Grave-yard Jones to Margaret Severing. He was just getting off his four-to-midnight tour when he picked up the first edition of the *Herald* to check the daily Lotto number, hoping for the thousandth time that he could finish paying off his Bronco before the transmission gave out. He flipped to the third page and determined that as usual his number hadn't hit. Then he glanced at the banner headline, DRUG HITMAN STALKS BROOKLYN: POLICE LINK TWO.

He sprinted back to the station house and handed the paper to Garvey, who immediately dialed Finn.

At the same time, Mark Troutman was waiting in his black Regency, on Queens Boulevard, for his mistress to come out of Liggett Drugs with contraceptive cream so they could have sex before he went home to his wife. He waited impatiently, watching boxy-shouldered men hoist square stacks of newspapers off a truck. He checked his watch, then handed one of the men change for a paper.

By the time Maria Gillette, reaking of tester perfumes, returned to the car with a tube of ORTHO-GYNOL in a brown paper bag, Trout-man was no longer interested in sex.

By 8:30 A.M., Kate's story was the lead item on every radio and television broadcast. Forty-five minutes after the police commissioner called Troutman to chew him out, Troutman pulled Finn and Fat Tony off the case. Glowering at the two men behind the desk, Troutman reassigned Finn to administrative duty and placed him on disciplinary probation. Fat Tony made faint growling noises as Troutman alternately gasped and screamed. Finn, looking pale and shaken, said nothing.

59

Finn scanned the rows of families crowded into the blond wood auditorium at police headquarters, but he couldn't spot Joe Flaherty. It wasn't the best time for him to be at headquarters. He certainly didn't want to run into any police brass. But he was here for a reason. Finn knew his old partner wouldn't miss his only son's swearing-in, and he wanted to say good-bye.

"Let us pray that God will guide our young men and women who will this day become members of the New York City Police Department," intoned Father Mahon, the chaplain.

The crowd, like a motley congregation, bowed their heads. Finn lowered his chin, but his attention was drawn to a coffee-colored child in a starched white dress whimpering in her mother's arms. He wondered if she was too young to remember what would probably be the biggest day of her father's life. These days a black man could end up as chief of patrol, Finn thought, while Irish guys like him stayed detectives in Bushwick. Times were certainly changing.

Finn remembered Flaherty telling him about his early years on the force, when the department was almost entirely Irish. In every precinct at least three men answered to the name "Kelly" when it was shouted out at roll call. Now, at least a third of the new recruits were black or Hispanic. Flaherty had predicted it, complaining bitterly over a beer at Mann's that the department was going downhill. Tough-minded and racist to the starchy root of his soul, Flaherty had put in his retirement papers the day the mayor appointed a black commissioner.

It's a new day in the department, Finn thought, feeling tired and old. And it's high time for me to be gone.

He scanned the new recruits seated on the stage in front of the enormous American flag. He hadn't seen Flaherty's son in a few years, so it took a minute to spot him in the front row. He was amazed that Little Joe, whom he had never seen out of a football jersey or a rumpled T-shirt, looked so sharp in his shiny black dress shoes and white gloves.

It was the police commissioner's turn to address the crowd. He took the podium and smiled at the wives and parents before launching into a stiffly written speech about responsibility and community service.

Finn noticed that the crying child had begun to fidget again. He smiled at the little girl as he let the PC's words float over him.

He thought of his own swearing-in. His mother had worn a well-ironed dress that she would never admit she had bought at a second-hand store. His father, with the slight confusion that comes with age, applauded wildly when his only son took those long slow strides across the stage to salute the PC and collect his certificate. He had felt so alive, so full of promise, the day he became a cop.

Finn heard the PC say "honor" and "bravery" and "the ultimate sacrifice." Instead of comforting him like a timeworn prayer, the words depressed him. No one talks about the lucky ones who make the ultimate sacrifice and don't get killed, he thought. No one cares if you spend the rest of your years in the department, doing your job, scared to death, pretending you're alive when all the time something inside of you has shriveled and died.

He imagined himself standing up and throwing his arms out to the crowd. "This is not the kind of life I wanted," he ached to shout. "I wanted to be a hero, but this job has left me with nothing. Now I'm middle-aged and all alone, trying to find out who killed a Bushwick nurse"—his windpipe hurt with the effort of keeping silent—"and even that's been taken from me."

Just then the child wrestled free of her mother. In her soft white shoes, she quickly covered the wide expanse of the auditorium floor. She headed straight for the recruits, passing the podium without a glance. The PC, stunned by the divergence in his carefully choreo-graphed ceremony, paused. The abrupt silence startled the child, who stared at the sea of blue uniforms, horrified, suddenly aware that six hundred people were watching her.

"DDAAAADDDEEE!" she cried out in panic.

Finn watched in astonishment as Little Joe effortlessly extended one white-gloved hand and scooped up his daughter.

As she pressed her cheek into her father's stiff blue jacket, the audience relaxed. The PC ahemed, made an unscripted comment about the department's efforts to recruit younger females for the Academy, and returned to his speech.

After the ceremony, Finn found Little Joe and was introduced to his wife, an elegant black woman.

"Where's Big Joe?" asked Finn, after he snapped a picture of all three with their Instamatic. "He wouldn't miss this for the world."

Little Joe looked uncomfortable and said nothing. Finn felt the blood wash from his face, and he knew his old partner was dead.

"I don't know how to tell you this," began Little Joe, "but Dad had a heart attack last week. He's still at St. Mary's in intensive care. They say he's on the mend."

Finn almost laughed in relief. "You know Joe wouldn't have died before you became a police officer," he said. He was interrupted as a group of new officers pushed by, clapping Little Joe on the shoulder and kissing his wife.

*   *   *

By tradition, funerals, promotions, and swearing-in ceremonies were celebrated afterward back in Bay Ridge at Mann's, a plain, noisy bar on 82nd Street. Forty-five minutes after the recruits became cops, the place was packed.

Brand-new police officers opened the top buttons of their dress uniforms and stood against the chestnut bar, drinking shots of rye and short glasses of honey-colored beer. Their wives and girlfriends, loos-ening up after a few tense hours in the city, took their places at the tables.

Finn sipped his beer and stared at Little Joe's wife, guessing she was probably the first black woman to get served at Mann's. After a few beers, just looking at Little Joe's wife made him feel hopeful, like anything could happen.

He thought about Kate for the thousandth time, wondering if she was all right. It gnawed at him and made him queasy inside. He tried to imagine her here. She would be safe and sound with him, drinking at Mann's. Kate, with her college girl talk and her big newspaper job, next to Little Joe's wife. Why did she write the story? Why did she have to be so pig-headed? Anger welled up in him, and he took a long gulp of beer to tamp it down.

Sullivan, a beefy red fireman who had once planned a career in pro-football, and Gallagher, a transit cop with a master's degree in applied mathematics, were holding pints of beer at eye level and laughing. Finn scanned the crowd as he ordered another ball and a beer.

"John Finn. God it's great to see you." Suddenly Blinky Givers was there pumping his hand.

"So, the prodigal son has returned," said Finn, grabbing Givers's arm. He saw that Givers had already polished off several drinks before he'd arrived at Mann's.

Finn and Blinky, too small for St. Sebastian varsity football and too tongue-tied for debate, had spent their afternoons after school driving through Brooklyn in Blinky's aunt's Impala.

As a teenager, Blinky, nicknamed for his debilitating facial twitch, had amazed Finn with an uncanny aptitude for getting laid.

"Life's still treating you well, I see," said Finn, fingering the lapel of his friend's expensive suit. Blinky had failed the civil service exam and become a stockbroker.

"But I'm remembering the Lord at collection time," said Givers, doing a near perfect imitation of Father Bob, the headmaster at St. Sebastian.

"How's the department?" Givers signaled the barman for another round. "I've seen your name in the papers. First you're a hero cop. Now you're tracking down a serial killer?"

Finn winced. "Nah. I got thrown off the case. Too much publicity." Finn felt bitterness come over him again. How could Kate have screwed him so badly? "I'm thinking about retiring early," he said. "How's the market? Think there is a future in it for me?"

"Nah. It's down the tubes. Stick with the department—at least the pension's a sure thing," said Givers. "How's the family?"

"Grand, just grand," said Finn.

Givers paused, twinkling. "You remember my old aunty Mary Catherine?"

Finn began to smile again. "Sure. How is she, Mary Catherine?"

"She's not well," said Givers, pausing for effect, "not well at all." He let a few a few beats go by. "In fact, she's dead."

They sagged with laughter at their old joke.

Sullivan, who appeared to be making a boastful gesture with his hand about a foot from his crotch, looked up and smiled. Thomas Walsh, a promising St. Sebastian graduate who had left the priesthood after ten years for a desk job with the city, fell off his stool and landed, soft and logy, on the muddy tile floor.

Finn pulled hard at his beer, trying to scour from his memory Troutmouth's livid face and Kate's disappointed frown. He wanted to still the anger that was turning to remorse as the weak afternoon sun faded and the faces around the bar became longer and the voices became louder.

All of a sudden it was after 10 P.M., and Finn felt the drink, like a heavy hand, grip the back of his neck. He ordered another round, but as they downed it, the bar seemed to crumble in the center before righting itself again. Then he and Blinky were half walking, half dragging each other out of Mann's and wobbling unsteadily down 82nd Street.

They circled up toward the school, talking halfheartedly about old teams and then animatedly about turning forty. Finn felt almost like a teenager again, trotting alongside Blinky, but he was dizzy with beer and heavy with confusion.

"What are you going to do once you leave the department?" asked Blinky. "Got any plans?"

All the feelings Finn had momentarily stunned with beer back at Mann's leaped up and tackled him. Finn staggered, but he couldn't shake them off. "I was thinking about getting married again," he said thickly, amazed that the concept had reached his mind and mouth simultaneously.

Givers stared at him in mock surprise. Under the street lamp, Finn noticed his friend's cheek tremble and saw how tightly he still fought to control the muscle spasms in his face.

"Congratulations," said Givers, producing a pint of whiskey from inside his jacket. "Who's the lucky woman?" he asked, slurring slightly.

"I didn't say I'd found the right woman," said Finn, taking a sip and passing the bottle back. "Just said I was thinking it was time I settled down." Finn belched quietly. "Again."

Blinky gave him a glassy smile, then put his lips to the bottle.

Finn stared down Colonial Road, trying to construct an imaginary home movie. It opened with a shot of the brick row house he shared with Kate. Then a shot of Kate eating breakfast. Pan to the children sticking spoons into milky bowls.

They could be happy together, he told himself firmly, even though he couldn't muster up a single frame of the two of them together. The exertion was pushing his head to his chin, and a voice was telling him it was impossible. She didn't care about him enough to hold off on her newspaper story, and now he was practically out of a job. She'd never stay with a cop, anyway. She'd end up with a college man. A rich guy from Manhattan. A banker. A lawyer.

He shook his head again, suddenly frustrated and wild. He imagined himself walking out of the 83rd Precinct with the man charged with killing Margaret Severing in tow. The camera flashed, and small children from the neighborhood drew back in fear.

Next he saw himself walking through Battery Park City, dressed in a suit, without a badge. But when he looked down, he was wearing a synthetic security guard uniform, and a large clumsy radio squawked on his hip instead of a gun.

He blinked a few times in the streetlight, trying to remember what he had planned to do after he left the department. Kate. Everything about her irritated him, and he couldn't love her more. He wanted to hold her more than anything in the world, and he didn't know if he would ever see her again.

They stopped in front of a late-model black Jaguar, and Givers took out his keys. "Blinky, you son of a bitch, look at these wheels," Finn said, punching him lightly on the shoulder.

They talked about cars, before Givers swung himself into his Jag and started the motor. Finn watched the car glide down the block out of view. He turned, stumbling slightly. He was dangerously drunk, but he didn't care. "What am I going to do?" he asked aloud.

He began to walk, not ready to head home but not wanting to go back to Mann's either. He felt the frozen sidewalk through the soles of his sneakers, and the thin blade of the night wind. He felt like Adam, standing with the apple core in his hand, vulnerable and naked, longing for things he couldn't name.

Finn stopped and arched his back, trying to look for stars. Instead, he looked straight into the streetlight until the space in back of his eyes began to ache.

Maybe his courage had failed him. Or his faith in his own survival. All because of Marvin Plank. This thing that was torturing him had begun the day he had almost died. That frantic memory, seeing himself lying on the floor of the abandoned building, came at him like an arrow. This feeling would never stop, he thought, until he had killed Marvin Plank. Until he had ended Marvin Plank's life just as surely as Plank had ended part of his. Finn's throat opened and he wailed, but not from fear. It was a deep turbulent, keening sound of mourning.

60

It was almost dawn when Dominick made it home. All but a few of the blinking bears had exhausted their batteries. Whimpering slightly, he picked up one of the live ones and carried it with his good hand like a shield as he ran from the station wagon to the front door. His mind was moving in small circles, like a kite in a storm, and he knew he needed to cut through the confusion in order to take the next step.

The light was on in the kitchen. His mother sat with her bare feet on the table and large white balls of cotton stuck between her toes.

"Dommy. What happened?" she shrieked as he stumbled in. "The police were here looking for you. What happened to your head? What happened to your hand?"

Dominick threw the bear on the table with a grunt and headed for the bathroom, slamming the door behind him as a warning to his mother not to follow.

The bullet had left a bright red welt on his forehead that started as a channel where it had touched the skin and ended as a light scratch. The deep end of the wound was tinged with black. His knees went soft when he thought how close he had come to death. He studied the bloody section of his finger and saw white chips that he recognized as splinters of bone.

His mind flashed to the man on the loading dock and the dark red stain that leaked from his body.

His mother was rapping insistently on the door. "Dommy. Dommy. What happened? Why do the police want to talk to you? Tell your mommy. Tell her," she urged.

Dominick tried to make his voice steady. "I'll kill you if you don't get away from that door," he tried to say, but the threat was lost in racking sobs. He collapsed onto the pink nubby toilet seat cover, listening to his mother's voice growing fainter as the roar in his head grew louder.

The roar had subsided by the time he left the bathroom, freshly scrubbed, a large blue towel wrapped around his waist. A wad of electrical tape was wrapped around his injured finger.

His mother rushed to the hallway and fastened herself to his arm.

"Dommy, Dommy. What happened?" she asked as he walked, dragging her, toward his bedroom.

Dominick sounded surprised. "Nothing, Ma. Why?" He dropped his shoulder, trying to loosen her grip.

"Who did this to you? Who?"

Dominick's hand went to the top of his head, like a man anxiously charting progressive baldness. He could feel his skin, cold and slightly clammy. He shrugged.

But his mother insisted. "Dommy. Your forehead. You have a bullet hole in your forehead."

He looked at her, surprised. "Ma. You got a clean shirt for me? I'm going out."

"Where are you going? Out? Your hand. Your head. You should go to an emergency room."

"Ma. I have a date," he said, shaking her off his arm. She stared after him as he ambled down the hall to his room. He snapped a Sinatra tape into the boom box and twisted the gleaming volume nob. He picked up a black plastic comb and, with the tip of his tongue sticking out in concentration, parted his hair slightly to the left of center. His lips were cracked and dry and he could hear birds warbling somewhere inside his head. Letting his towel drop, he rummaged around in his top drawer, coming up with a crushed tube of Clearasil, which he dabbed on several spots to disguise the angry-looking gash on his forehead.

Humming along with Frank, he reached into another drawer and pulled out a can of deodorant, spraying his underarms until they were caked with cool white powder. He took a deep breath and said, "Ah, fresh," like the guy in the commercial. He found some acne astringent and poured it over the electrical tape on his finger. As his eyes watered in pain, he considered what to do about his hand. He knew the blood would soon leak through the tape, and he didn't want to scare off his best girl. But he wasn't sure he could get a better bandage on without help.

He pulled a black leather glove over his mangled hand, admiring the effect. It was perfect. He looked like a race car driver, a magician, an assassin.

Next came the problem of underwear. His good hand cupped his balls protectively, weighing one and then the other, as he tried to pick a pair. He rejected the boxers with hearts in favor of some sleek black spandex jockeys. What a stud, he thought admiringly, as he looked down at the way the jockeys drew up his genitals in a fine display.

His mother appeared at the door carrying a white shirt with large pointless epaulets. She looked so scared that Dominick laughed. "Here, give me that, Moms. What's the matter?"

She smiled at him, still uncertain. "You going out with Suzy?" she asked.

"Not Suzy, Mom. A date. A real date," he said, pulling the shirt over his head without unbuttoning it. "A very nice girl. You'd like her. She's a reporter for the *Daily Herald,* the newspaper. I think we're going to get engaged."

His mother was stunned, then effusive.

"Oh, Dommy. I'm so proud of you. You've made your mother so happy."

61

Dominick strolled down the wide avenue that divided the expensive apartments from the cheap ones in Park Slope. Even though the winter sun was barely breaking through the clouds, the street looked nice. He'd been walking for what seemed like hours but he wasn't tired. He was hopeful. He and Kate could be happy here. His days of confusion and fear were over, he thought, touching the gun which sat snugly in the deep front pocket of his gray anorak. Love was on his side.

As he moved down the sidewalk, he felt bathed in the warmth of a giant spotlight. He was more powerful than Big Mike. Bigger. He felt substantial, respected, filled with the dreams and ambitions of a man on the rise. He rubbed his thumb with the forefinger on his good hand, trying to pin down the feeling. Then he had it. He felt like Frank Sinatra.

A small orange cat leapt from the stoop when he walked by. Dominick nodded. Even animals could sense it.

He couldn't wait to see Kate. This time she would find him irresistible.

He had already stopped by her apartment, but this time he didn't ring the bell. Instead, he searched under the stoop until he found a brick to break the pane of glass near the door handle. He was about to shatter the glass and let himself in, but he had reconsidered. He wanted everything to go just right. He left a Christmas bear by her door and set off to buy her some flowers.

Walking down the wide avenue, he smiled. He knew he had done the right thing. Frank Sinatra wouldn't have broken into Ava Gardner's apartment with a brick.

Dominick imagined Vinnie the bartender's face if he walked into the Cork and Barrel with Frank Sinatra. He was so caught up imagining the two of them sauntering into the dark, cool bar that he didn't notice he had passed a small chrome-and-enamel coffee shop called Purity. For a moment, the smell of frying meat, piped through the exhaust fan onto the street, covered him in a greasy cloud.

Stricken, he fell against a telephone pole, then pushed off and stumbled, blind, into a small knot of people. He crouched behind an old blue Ford Fairmont, gagging as the poisoned meat fumes filled his nose. But suddenly the gritty Brooklyn wind was on him, and when he sucked in a lungful, the meat smell was gone.

He pulled himself upright and staggered down the street. In his panic, he had grabbed the gun. A few blocks from the Purity, his heart began to slow, and he crept back to center stage. Even meat, rancid and full of toxic germs, couldn't get him. He was invincible. He didn't notice men placing protective arms on their girlfriends and mothers with strollers giving him wide berth as he approached.

He came to a corner, but instead of crossing, he stood dazzled by the buckets of flowers stacked in front of the Korean market.

He remembered the tiger lilies he had brought to give to Kate on their last date. No good. Tiger lilies were the kind of flower Big Mike might get for his mistress. Kate deserved better than that. Dominick shifted his weight from one foot to the other, considering.

Roses, red roses. That's what he needed. Roses were the kind of flowers Frank would get Ava Gardner. Solid. Substantial. Classy.

He directed the guy behind the counter to wrap up a dozen, then added another dozen before the man had stapled the newspaper around the flowers. Two dozen red roses, he said, snapping his fingers three times; shoo-be-do-be-doo, he hummed to himself. It was the kind of thing Frank would do.

As he crossed the street, Dominick noticed that the roses were wrapped in an old edition of the *Daily Herald*. He smiled, thinking it was a sign from God. He tilted his head, reading the headline circling the twenty-four stems. DRUG HITMAN STALKS BROOKLYN: POLICE LINK TWO. The story that followed was written by Kate Murray.

His lips moved slowly as he read the story. She described him as a white mentally disturbed male. She said he was wanted for questioning. She wrote that detectives thought he was the link between the killings.

The wind blowing through the brownstone canyon almost obscured the sound of Dominick's scream. He pulled the pistol out of his pocket and blew two round holes in the yellow CAUTION DEAF CHILDREN sign before running down the street toward Kate's apartment, two dozen roses still tucked under his arm.

inn pounded on the door so loudly that one of Kate's neighbors, dressed in a faded housecoat, came to the top of the stairs to see what was going on.

"Never mind, Mrs. Rosen," Kate said mildly, yanking him through the door. "He's a friend."

"He looks like a cop to me," Mrs. Rosen sniffed as Kate shut the door.

"I didn't hear you ring the bell," she said. She bent down to pick up a gray teddy bear. It probably belonged to a neighborhood kid, she thought, and brought it inside for safekeeping.

"I'm off the Severing case," he said flatly.

"I heard," she said. "Would you like something to drink? I have soda or beer." She was moving nervously toward the kitchen. He grabbed her arm and looked in her face.

"I said I'm off the case," he repeated, more slowly this time but louder.

Finn had come to get her back, but now something was slamming around inside of him. He didn't know what to do next. It was like trying to interrogate a suspect who couldn't see or hear.

She pulled her arm away.

"Why did you write the story? Revenge? Is that what you wanted?"

"I made a choice," she said, controlled.

He figured right away that she was sleeping with another guy. But it didn't matter, he was too far gone. He was clenching his fists so tight his palms began to ache. "Did it save your job? Do you think you will get an award for this? Maybe even your fucking Pulitzer?"

She shrugged, looking at him without expression.

"I can understand how angry you must be."

Finn jumped at the opening.

"Understand? Understand? You don't understand anything." Rage was making his voice shake. "Fourteen years I have invested in this job. Getting up every morning, driving to Bushwick, trying to do my job. Then you walked into my life, you with your stupid newspaper job, and just about wrecked everything I've built for myself."

"I wasn't trying to wreck your life," she said blandly, without apology. "I made a mistake getting involved with you. I think we both can see that now."

Finn's brow was still folded, but the anger went out of him with a puff. She was dumping him.

"What?"

"I should have realized it when you asked me to dinner. I never should have let it go any further."

For a few seconds, Finn had no idea what to say. He was lost. In two more minutes, he would be standing outside her door. Then he would be driving away from her apartment. Further and further away, and he would never have a reason to come back.

His eyes fell on her bookshelf, the stack of newspapers, the prissy New York City Ballet poster she had framed above her couch.

He was reaching down inside himself, probing blindly, grabbing for something buried deep. Something to make her understand.

"You know, two months ago I was a different guy," he said. The strain was making his voice sound tentative. "Two months ago I wasn't trying to do these things that seem so . . . out of reach. I knew what I was. I was a detective, second grade, running down felons in Bushwick with Fat Tony. Maybe I wasn't happy"—he shrugged— "but I wasn't sad. But suddenly"—he thought of Marvin Plank and took a long breath—"I get a look at my whole life in a single afternoon. And I realize I'm not happy, I'm not sad. I'm not anything at all. And it's just not enough.

"In here, see, it's like I've been dead." He pushed his thumb against his chest. "And now I'm alive. Things are changing." His voice was almost a whisper, pained but steady.

She stared at him without blinking.

"Because all this is going on, it's hard for you to see exactly who I am. So I just wanted to tell you. I'm John Finn." His voice was getting stronger. "And out of all the guys in New York City, out of all the guys you ever knew and the ones you still have to meet, I'm different." He couldn't look away from her if the house was on fire. "Because I'm the one who wants you."

He felt exhausted. He wished he could just curl up on her couch and sleep for the rest of the week.

Finn filled his lungs.

"So, I guess that's all I have to say."

Her eyes flickered.

"Except one other thing."

"What?" she asked, barely breathing.

"There's some sneakers hanging over the wires in front of your house."

"What?" Kate asked, looking slightly disoriented.

"Size-ten Adidas."

"How do you know the size?" she asked, unsure whether to smile or not.

"I threw them up there before I knocked on your door."

"What was your wish?"

"I wished that you'd take a chance on me."

She smiled, and for the first time something in her face softened. When he reached for her, she didn't resist. Then she was saying something sweet to him, something he needed to hear. Her words felt wonderful, like cool water poured over his confusion and fatigue. And her lips were at his ear, murmuring. He put his hands on her shoulders, turning and collecting her, pulling her close.

63

She shouldn't have gone to the police, he thought as he watched the cop leap up the steps to her apartment. That was her first mistake. She had ruined everything. No wonder the police wanted him for questioning and a madman was shooting at him and his name was in the paper. He should have known better than to trust her. He knew it.

He'd have to make her promise never to do anything like that again. Never.

He walked down the block from her apartment, turned a corner, and stepped into the wide alley. He waded through neat bags of garbage and stacked newspapers, counting the buildings until he was under her window. His hands were numb with cold, but he silently moved three dented garbage cans against her building until he had built a crude aluminum platform. Leaning against the building to stop himself from shaking, he climbed on top of the cans. Through Kate's window, ineffectively shielded by lace curtains, he watched, without breathing, the shadows moving inside.

Dominick listened to the sound of traffic and a trumpet being played badly several blocks away. He saw a leaf, brittle from the winter chill, skitter across the pavement and heard it whisper down the alley.

He felt dizzy, and anticipation made it hard to breathe. He exhaled, relieved, when the top of Kate's head appeared in the window, bobbing forward. He decided not to knock on the window, afraid that she might scream and alert the cop. So he waved the flowers in semaphore, vainly trying to attract her attention. Then he saw that her eyes were closed.

She threw back her head, exposing more of her neck, and as she turned, he realized with a shock that she was naked.

Dominick hugged the rough brick and began, with horrible stifled sobs, to cry. He ground the flowers into the wall, punching the thorny stems until his knuckles bled. Even with the hot, lonely tears in his eyes, he couldn't look away. He saw the man's hands on her naked shoulders, pulling her downward.

Dominick closed his eyes. Unable to watch, but unable not to, he opened them again. He saw her throw her head back rhythmically, tilting her chin down and then up to the ceiling. He reached toward her image, pleading silently. Then he saw her throat tense and heard her emit a faint cry.

64

Kate felt sweat on her hairline and she heard a pigeon warble tentatively outside her window. Finn's fingers brushed her nipple, but she gently pushed his hand away.

"Hmmmm, enough," she said, leaning on her elbow, her head on the palm of her hand.

Finn opened his eyes quickly and saw that she was smiling, but there was something different about her. Something closed off, cold.

"You sure?" he asked.

"For now," she said, playfully brushing his lips with her fingers.

Finn was studying her hair. Trying to ignore the change in her, he concentrated instead on solving the mystery of her black hair. Close up against her pale skin it looked almost blue.

"The more time we have to practice, the better it'll be," he said.

"Hmmmm," Kate answered, noncommittally, as she rubbed a leg over his thigh.

There was a faint slapping sound as another pigeon landed on the windowsill.

Somewhere a car alarm wailed.

"Will there be time to practice?" he asked.

"I got you thrown off the Severing case," she reminded him.

The pigeon warbled again.

She ran her fingers along his chest but said nothing.

"I need an answer," Finn said, thankful his voice didn't quaver.

Kate jumped out of bed, grabbed Finn's shirt and threw it over her head. The warm dew between her thighs made her shiver as she walked out of the room.

65

Because she was wearing only a shirt, she kept her body behind the oak door when she opened it, so she was momentarily trapped between the door and the wall when Dominick pushed his way in.

His face, red with cold and tears, contorted into a grin when he saw her.

Kate stood before him, open-mouthed and silent.

"I brought you these." He reached into his oversized anorak, and handed her the muddy, torn newspaper still wrapped around the broken stems. A handful of red petals fluttered to the floor.

She stared at him until he shook the stems slightly, sending more petals cascading down. Then she reached out mechanically, her eyes never leaving his vibrating eyeballs.

Dominick's eyes swept over her naked legs, dwelling on the front flap of the shirt, which barely covered her pubic hair. Without telegraphing the move, he batted her across the jaw with an open palm.

"Why did you cheat on me?" he said as she fell. Then his voice became a squeal. "Why did you ruin everything and go out with that cop when you knew I loved you?"

Kate's heartbeat sounded loud in her ears. She tried to think of a way to restore reason and remembered the words of a victim's counselor she'd once interviewed for a story.

"Try not to lose control," the woman had recommended. "Don't plead. You'll only make yourself look weak."

Kate struggled not to wipe the humid print of his hand off her face.

If Dominick had seemed weird and distracted at the Captain's Table, she guessed that now he was hallucinating. His eyes were jumping wildly in his head, and his lips moved involuntarily.

She flinched as he lunged, but instead of hitting her again, he grabbed the flowers. He stared at her, his face leaping with tics, his eyes full of reproach.

"We gotta good thing here. We can't let these little problems . . . destroy us," he said, then he turned on his heel and headed into the kitchen. She heard his shoes on the tile floor as drawers were being opened.

The shrink had said to reason with your assailant. Try to take control.

"What are you doing?" she stuttered at his back.

"A vase. We need a vase for the flowers," he said.

She stepped toward the bedroom, but Dominick had already returned with a kitchen knife. He gestured with the long blade for her to sit down. Kate eased herself onto a copy of the *Daily Herald* spread out on the couch. Dominick settled down beside her. For a moment, he said nothing. His eyes seemed to absorb Kate, then take in the details of the room. He spotted the gray teddy bear under the chair and smiled. Then, tentatively, he placed his free hand, the middle finger wrapped in blood-saturated electrical tape, across her shoulder.

Kate stiffened.

"I love you, I want us to be happy together," he said, tears and drool running down his face. "You can write the story about Gusano. You can write my story. Just don't cheat on me again."

Kate stared at the wound on his forehead.

"Dominick, there's been a mistake," she whispered.

But he interrupted. "I don't want you to cheat on me again," he yelled. Then he reached out and sliced her arm with the knife. It didn't hurt. It felt more like a pinch followed by a burning sensation. Hot sticky blood covered her fingers.

Her chest sank protectively toward her arm.

Dominick was perched next to her on the couch like an attentive date. "Don't cut yourself. That knife is sharp," he said, pointing to the widening stain on her shirt.

Don't look weak, she told herself and tried to stop a whimper. Then she leaned back and forced herself to take a deep breath.

"Dominick, if I've harmed you in some way, I'm sorry. But please—"

Before she could finish, Dominick ran the blade closer to her elbow, cutting her again.

He tsked. "You have to be careful."

"Why are you doing this?" she asked frantically. "What do you want?"

"I want you to take my telephone calls. I want you to listen to me when I talk!" He was screaming, then he reduced his voice to a moan. "I don't want you to cheat on me anymore." Then he placed the knife on the rickety end table next to a picture of Kate's father and pulled the gun out of his anorak.

"Is this your father?" he asked, sounding happy, tapping the photograph with the muzzle. "I'm looking forward to meeting him."

66

Finn tried to stop his hand from shaking as he formed a trajectory line from the bedroom doorway, where he stood, to the living room. He could see the bloodstains spreading on Kate's shirt and he could hear her weepy words as she tried to reason with Dominick.

If he shot now, he would probably hit Kate. They were seated too close together.

If he waited, the guy would kill her. He paused, at first to see if he could get a clearer line of fire. Then he found that he could not shoot.

Frozen, he saw Dominick pull a handgun out of his pocket and he realized that it was too late. He felt as if he were behind a glass wall, except that he could hear Kate's cries and the man's curses growing louder. But he could not break through the barrier. He just watched as Dominick leaned back and placed the gun against Kate's forehead.

He heard her sniffle and the click of the safety coming off the gun.

Suddenly, Finn was back in the empty apartment with Marvin Plank. Time began to slow down. He felt yellow eyes boring into him, the crazy drive, the limitless rage. But something was different. He didn't feel himself die. This time, he was lying on the floor, but he was alive.

"Get away from her," Finn said, and Dominick turned, leering.

"Ah. The other man," Dominick said, mocking.

"Get away from her."

"I'm going to shoot her," said Dominick solemnly as he turned to Finn. "But you're the one who killed her. If you weren't here, I would have let her live."

"Just drop it," Finn said.

"Take a good look, Mr. Po-lice-man," Dominick said, waving the gun wildly.

"I'm looking," said Finn, "and you know what I see?"

Dominick looked up at him, curious.

"Marvin Plank."

Dominick leaned back, confused. Kate, her eyes wild, pushed off his chest and propelled herself backward.

Finn fired.

The bullet passed through the living room and dented the refrigerator like a fist, then tore through the wood butcher-block table on the ricochet.

Dominick jumped as though electrocuted, wheeled around to face Finn and squeezed off two bullets, sending wood, paint, and plaster chips flying.

Kate slid to the floor, cradling her bloody arm.

Dominick, his face dancing with anger and insane laughter, advanced toward the bedroom, pressing off one bullet after another.

Finn aimed directly at his head and fired, missing him by about a foot. But the bullet's high whizzing sound whispered a secret message to Dominick. He changed direction and dashed out the front door.

Finn, dressed only in his trousers, ran after him.

67

By the time Finn reached the stoop, the wide street was clear except for an old man cowering behind an aluminum garbage can. Finn heard an iron gate clang and saw Dominick leave his temporary hiding place under a stoop and run around the corner. Finn followed, his bare feet pounding on the icy pavement.

He was panting, and cold air burned his lungs.

By the time he rounded the corner onto a busy commercial street, Dominick was far ahead of him, running unevenly with the gun at the end of his outstretched arm. Christmas shoppers were rolling back like a carpet.

Finn didn't shoot at him because the street was filled with people. He had to get closer. When he saw that Dominick had rounded the next corner, Finn sagged against a bodega window, suddenly shivering.

The clerk, a birdlike little man, came out from behind his counter. Startled but unafraid, he put his head close to Finn's, whispering, *"Como? Como?"*

"Teléfono. Call nine-one-one. Tell them ten-thirteen. Ten-thirteen," Finn chattered, "I'm a detective. *Policía."*

The old man hopped back to his store, and through the open door Finn could hear him screaming into the telephone.

"Police officer, police officer naked with a gun. He says tell you ten-sixteen."

Far away Finn could hear a siren.

"Ten-*thirteen.*" Finn tried to catch his breath. "Ten-thirteen."

"Ten-thirteen!" the man shouted. And the single siren was joined by a second and then a third.

Someday I have to learn Spanish, he thought.

Finn's face bent into a stupid smile as he remembered a few words.

"Gracias, señor, gracias."

He was still grinning when Dominick charged around the corner, his gun leveled at Finn's belly.

Dominick was laughing.

Roaring like King Kong in wordless surprise and outrage, Finn raised his revolver and squeezed the trigger, again and again, until the chambers were empty and the gun responded with a dull, mechanical click.

Dominick sank to his knees, then pitched forward onto the pavement, blood already soaking through his coat. His open eyes stared at nothing. His breath made a rattling sound.

Finn took a step forward and knelt down. He placed two fingers over the exposed artery in Dominick's neck, but they sank into the wound.

Dominick's lips began to move and Finn thought he was having a convulsion. Then he heard a hiss. Finn put his ear next to Dominick's lips.

"The meat. The meat."

"Don't talk, man. There isn't much holding your throat together," said Finn grimly.

But Dominick made the hissing sound again.

"An ambulance'll be here in a minute," Finn said, wondering why he was consoling the man who had just tried to kill him.

A bubble of blood formed on Dominick's lips and slid to the left corner of his mouth. Then another. And another. Finn saw his lips vibrating and felt something, like the beating wings of a dragonfly, against the hand that held Dominick's throat.

Dominick, fading into a coma, was humming.

Finn leaned over him again. His cheek was getting spattered with Dominick's blood.

"St'night, 'changing glances," wheezed Dominick. Then, slightly stronger: "What were the chances . . . " A large bubble formed and seemed to block Dominick's wind.

The bubble burst.

"We'd make love"—his breath was ragged—" 'fore the night was through . . . "

Then Dominick sighed and was dead.

68

There were so many people in her section of the emergency room that the rewrite man could barely hear Kate's dictation. A doctor, sewing like a garment worker, laced the long black thread into her arm. Investigating detectives posed for the *Daily Herald* photographers. Fat Tony hustled down the hall like an angry hornet, glowering at Kate until he was directed to another wing, where Finn was being treated for trauma. A young assistant district attorney, hoping for a whiff of a police scandal, kept asking, "Where was the detective's clothing?"

The police union representative, Doug Johnson, who showed up in tennis whites, kept interrupting him.

Ridgeway sent over a uniformed guard to prevent other news organizations from sneaking into the hospital to interview his star reporter.

Finally, Kate was pushed in a wheelchair to the admitting desk, but the nurse had disappeared with her file. After waiting for almost half an hour, Kate got up and pulled on her coat.

Before leaving, she limped past Finn's small room, but it was blockaded by a wall of blue uniforms and wrinkled trench coats.

"Where's John Finn?" she asked weakly. "Detective John Finn."

"He doesn't have any comments for the press," said Officer Brian Edwards, and turned his enormous back to Kate.

69

When his eyes were open, Finn could hear the swell of men's voices and the sound of backs being slapped in the corner of his room. With his eyes closed, he could hear his own roar and Dominick's laugh and feel, rather than hear, his own gun, bucking in his hand. As he lay in his hospital bed, he surveyed the variety of police personnel shoved up against the white walls. He wanted to wave them away, but his hands felt weak, as if he had strangled Dominick rather than shot him.

He smelled Fat Tony's rancid breath before he appeared at his bedside.

"My cousin in Internal Affairs says they're treating it as an open-and-shut case of self-defense." Tony leaned over him as if he were paralyzed. "They might even give you a medal for saving a civilian's life."

Finn had to listen carefully, since Fat Tony's voice was coming to him as if he were speaking out of a fast-moving car.

"I don't think they're going to make a big deal out of the fact that the civilian was a reporter for the *Daily Herald*," he continued conspiratorially. "My cousin says it's not going to matter." He paused and gave Finn an appraising look. "Are you all right? You look like shit. You really in shock?" Then he continued his one-sided conversation. " 'A civilian is a civilian,' my cousin said. Even if she is a reporter and a pain in the ass to the department."

Finn turned his head away from Tony when he heard Edwards say something, then, faintly, he heard Kate's voice.

"Tony," Finn said quietly. "Get them out. I want to talk to Kate."

Fat Tony looked at him, then shook his head.

"No way, hombre. No. You're in shock and I'm looking out for your best interests. You've dipped into that well for the last time."

Finn beckoned to Fat Tony, and he leaned his face closer to Finn's pillow.

"Tony, get the girl," he said, "or you'll be riding with someone new tomorrow."

Tony looked surprised, then he shrugged. He threw a fat arm around the union rep and gestured for the rest of the group to follow him out.

For a moment, Finn was alone, listening to the sound of police sirens, trying to figure out if he was remembering them or hearing them for the first time.

He turned his head and saw Kate, dressed in jeans and a fresh shirt, standing by his bed. Her color was bad but her eyes were luminous against her wild frame of hair.

"Do you hear sirens?"

She tilted her head, listening.

"How's your arm?" he asked.

"A lot of blood, then a lot of stitches. Did you get hurt?" Her voice was fading in and out, and Finn strained to hear.

"They're treating me for trauma. Police procedure after a shooting."

"How do you feel?"

"Traumatized," said Finn, and he smiled because it was true.

Just then the union rep, hitching up his tennis shorts, burst through the door.

"The commissioner is stopping by to pay you a get-well visit," he announced, then looked surprised, and not altogether pleased, as Finn waved him out.

Kate smiled cautiously at Finn.

"I guess you were right about Dominick. But I still can't believe he was part of Gusano's operation. He seemed so unstrung about Gusano killing the nurse."

"You can't tell with guys like that," Finn began weakly. "I told you not to get involved with—"

Kate smiled and held up her hand. He didn't want to continue anyway. He just wanted to hold her.

"So tell me something, though, who's Marvin Plank?"

Just then Edwards barreled through the door.

"I've been trying to arrange to get you a phone in your room, in case you want to call a friend or a priest or a sex line." The words died on his lips when he saw Kate. Edwards looked confused.

"It's okay, we're talking," Finn said, and Edwards backed out of the room.

"Who's Marvin Plank?" Kate asked again.

Finn waited for something inside him to crack open, but he felt nothing.

"No one, really. Just a kid I once met. A kid." He wondered if she would kiss him, long and slow, on the lips.

Kate considered his answer.

"I do hear sirens," she said finally. "Must be a fire close by. Or a building collapse."

"Good," Finn grunted, and he let his body go slack. He wanted to feel her fingers on his chest just to remind him that he was alive.

"At least you won't have to cover it for the newspaper," he said, struggling to keep up his end of the conversation. He wanted her so bad he could have wept.

"No, I think I've done enough for the newspaper today."

"What do you mean?" Finn asked her blankly.

"Unless Gorbachev reunites the Soviet Union overnight, they'll probably go page one with my story."

"Your story?" he asked. "When did you . . . "

"Over the phone, to rewrite. Ridgeway and Wilson were both very excited," Kate said.

For the first time, Finn noticed the hard set of her mouth when she spoke.

She noticed the look on his face.

"Don't worry, you're a hero. You saved my life and the lives of the crowd along Seventh Avenue. The story will get you made a lieutenant. Maybe even a deputy inspector."

Staring into her eyes made him believe that they were beckoning, that she wanted him, that she would hold him until the rushing in his head stopped. But then he looked at her again, and he froze. He realized that it was the excitement of a good story that was making her look at him this way.

Grimly, he forced himself to think of the kind of petty information she would want for the newspaper.

"You'll want every detail for your story," he said flatly. "Dominick did something weird before he died. He hummed and tried to sing."

She leaned closer. "What was he humming?"

He felt his heart snap shut.

"You know, 'Wondering in the night, what were the chances.' Da-da-da-de-da," he finished tunelessly.

"Sinatra," they said together.

Kate looked delighted, and Finn felt his stomach turn over.

He pressed his head back into his pillow and closed his eyes, willing himself to feel nothing. He heard the sirens, farther away now, rushing to some unseen disaster. When he opened his eyes, Kate had edged toward the door. He heard Fat Tony laughing and Edwards shouting in the hallway.

"As for me, you can write that Detective John Finn had no comment," he said quietly.

70

The snowflakes settled on Gusano's black fedora as he scurried out of a discount drugstore on Forty-second Street. He had just bought a container of SlimFast for his trip to Florida. Montoya had told him that Brooklyn was getting too hot, so Gusano had grabbed a cab to the Port Authority bus station and purchased a ticket to Orlando. It was a two-day ride, Gusano knew. And sitting in a cramped Greyhound bus seat would make his new wool trousers sag at the knees. But he could always get new clothes.

He stared up at the neon signs around Times Square and tried to imagine palm trees where the street lamps stood. Once he got to Orlando, he would go straight to Sea World. Seeing Shamu the Killer Whale would be worth the trip.

Epilogue

By the time the men from the Emergency Service Unit tear-gassed the sniper into giving up, most of the television reporters were doing live feeds from the scene. It was not every day that a seventy-year-old man went berserk, climbed to the top of a mail-sorting plant with an AK-47, and wounded three holiday shoppers.

"He was suffering from seasonal depression," Division Chief Mark Troutman was explaining expansively to the newspaper reporters who were standing on wet pavement boxed in by blue police barriers.

Kate checked her watch and sighed. Seven o'clock. After a year and two months, this was her last day on the crime beat.

She framed the headline: HOLIDAY RAMPAGE: MAN WOUNDS THREE. It wasn't going to be exclusive. It wouldn't be the front page, more like page five or six. But it didn't matter. She had already won the Publisher's Award and been nominated for a Pulitzer.

She stared up at the sky, which had a sickly yellow urban glow. No question about it. Her luck had changed the day she got stabbed. In the last twelve months, she had been breaking at least a story a week. No reporter in the city could even get close to her.

" 'There was nothing merry about his Christmas,' is what he said," Troutman was explaining, and the reporters scribbled it down.

Kate watched Troutman's lips and smiled, remembering that John Finn always called him Troutmouth.

Behind Troutman, the sniper, whom the *Daily Herald* editors had already dubbed "the Grinch," was being led away in handcuffs, his red eyes streaming from the gas.

The newspeople turned away from Troutman and began to heckle the Grinch into making a comment. Klieg lights threw shadows up and down the block. Flashbulbs went off. Cameramen strained and shoved. In seconds, the Grinch was locked out of sight in the back of a police wagon. It was over.

The lines of police officers relaxed into convivial knots. The reporters and cameramen began to drift away. Kate scanned the crowd of detectives for a familiar face but found none.

The last crime story, she thought, putting one hand on the rough wood of the barrier. Reed, the *Herald* photographer, picked up on her nostalgic mood.

"Nice evening for a shooting," he said, lighting an unfiltered Camel. "Nice place for it, too, beautiful Bushwick."

"Bushwick's not so bad."

"Right," said Reed, pulling a piece of tobacco off his tongue. Then he gestured to a ramshackle building in front of them. "Seven pair of perfectly good hundred-and-ten-dollar sneakers hanging off the electrical wires in the front of a building filled with people on welfare. What a great place."

"It's the kids." Kate turned away from the street to face Reed. "They throw them up there and make a wish."

"Makes me think we should cut back on the welfare rolls," said Reed.

"It makes me think of God." When she looked up again at the street, John Finn was standing next to her. She blinked three times and swallowed hard.

"I was wondering if you'd be here," she said, suddenly nervous. She pulled a hank of hair out of her face.

"I was standing over there," said Finn, gesturing with his thumb at a group of detectives in trench coats.

For a few seconds, neither of them said anything. Kate's arms locked around her midsection.

"It's been over a year," said Finn.

"I tried to call you," Kate blurted at the same time.

Finn nodded.

"I left messages at the station house and tried you at home but you changed your number," she said, talking too fast. Reed, who had started to walk away, leaned back toward them.

Finn nodded again, then scanned the block, like he was ready to move on.

"Wait!" she said, too loud. Finn looked at her, shifting his weight from one foot to the other.

"You know, it's funny you should be here. I was just thinking how much my luck has changed, since the, you know, Dominick and all that. I mean, things are really different now."

Finn shifted his weight again.

"What's different?"

"Well, I got my promotion. As of Monday, I'm covering city hall." It wasn't exactly what she meant to say, but she didn't know how to start.

Finn nodded but said nothing.

A long silence began to dawn.

"And I got the Publisher's Award."

"I always knew that you would."

Kate was touched. "You did?"

Finn shrugged. "Sure."

Just then, the Grinch's wife, dressed in a tattered bathrobe and a disheveled wig, stepped out of a dented blue Cadillac and began pounding on the wagon that held her handcuffed husband. "Herbie. My God. What have you done to my Herbie?"

The reporters, who had drifted away, suddenly rematerialized, crowding around the woman. Reed gripped his cigarette between his teeth and plowed into the throng. "C'mon," he said to Kate.

"It wasn't Christmas, it was that whore from Williamsburg that drove him crazy," the Grinch's wife was screaming. "He lost his house. He lost his car. He lost his self-respect on a twenty-year-old streetwalker named Delight."

Kate was caught between two tides. The Grinch and the Hooker. Page one for sure. She felt a familiar rush of adrenaline, but this time it only made her feel weary. She looked at Finn and gave him a lopsided smile.

"Go on," Finn said, gesturing with his chin. "It's your job."

She took a step to follow Reed. Then stopped and turned.

"Will you call me?"

"Go on," Finn said.

"The story can wait a minute," Kate said uncertainly.

Finn shook his head.

"A common twenty-dollar whore!" the Grinch's wife bellowed.

Kate opened her notebook and fished inside her pocket for a pen. She began to move slowly across the damp pavement, like she was being pulled by a magnet. Over her shoulder, she saw Finn retreating.

"He wanted to give her a decent life, but she brought him into the gutter," the woman shouted.

Kate squinted at the Grinch's wife. Her feet were moving but she wasn't getting any closer. She saw Reed elbow another photographer out of the way. A flashbulb went off, startling her, dotting her eyes with blue light. She turned but Finn was gone. She looked down. Her feet were still moving. Her notebook was out. Her pen was ready. But Kate knew then that even if she ran, she would never get there.